LIFE by COMMITTEE

COREY ANN HAYDU

KATHERINE TEGEN BOOKS
An Imprint of HarperCollinsPublishers

Katherine Tegen Books is an imprint of HarperCollins Publishers.

Life by Committee

www.epicreads.com

Library of Congress Cataloging-in-Publication Data
Haydu, Corey Ann.
Life by Committee / by Corey Ann Haydu. — First edition.
pages cm
Summary: "A girl puts her heart, reputation, and friendships on the line when she spills her deepest secrets to a website that may not be as innocent—or as anonymous—as it seems"— Provided by publisher.
ISBN 978-0-06-229406-7
[1. Love—Fiction. 2. Friendship—Fiction. 3. Secrets—Fiction. 4. Web sites—Fiction.] I. Title.
PZ7.H31389Li 2014 2013043187
[Fic]—dc23 CIP
AC

Typography by Erin Fitzsimmons
15 16 17 18 19 PC/RRDH 10 9 8 7 6 5 4 3 2 1
❖
First paperback edition, 2015

To my cherished friend Honora,
who is brave enough to share her secrets
and kind enough to listen to mine

Secret:

I haven't eaten anything but celery and hard-boiled eggs in three days. I want to be as skinny as my little sister, and I'm pretty sure I can do it.

—Zed

Secret:

I have gone to the doctor seven times this year without telling my parents. Just in case I have cancer.

—Roxie

Secret:

I brought my mother's $100,000 ring to college, and I wear it as a necklace when I am going to parties. Clearly, she has not given me permission. Nor would she.

—Star

One.

Hey, Tabitha? I have a secret, Joe types.

What is it? I type back. We've been chatting for three hours. My fingers hurt, my eyes are watery and strained, I have the light buzz of a headache, and it's well past midnight. Joe and I have been chatting almost every night like this, hours on end, for almost a month. In school we smile closed-mouth smiles at each other, and sometimes he finds an excuse to cup his hand over my shoulder for a moment. But at night I sit wrapped in an old quilt and braid my hair, unbraid it, and braid it again. We tell each other everything we're thinking, and everything we were thinking during the day. Sometimes the pauses in between our words are so long, I have to get out of the computer chair and pace the room, brimming with the restless energy of falling in love.

Tonight I'm so focused on the screen, it seems the whole world has turned bluish and backlit, and I don't think I've even taken a moment to blink. He just finished telling me about the money he's been saving up to take a trip to New York City on his own. I didn't know jocks wanted to leave Vermont. I didn't know they went places by themselves. What's even better is I told him all that and he just said *LOL* and told me that the things I say surprise him.

What I really want, though, is to hear his secret.

You can tell me what you're thinking, I type.

I don't want to say, Joe responds at last. I exhale sharply.

It's okay, I type. My hands grip the sides of my laptop. I know he's going to say it tonight. I know we are about to cross from something fun and bad and flirtatious to that other thing. The real thing.

When I say it, we can't go back, Joe types. *I don't trust myself.*

It is delicious, pulling this out of him. I'm glad it's so late and quiet, and that the world keeps going but Joe and I are both glued to our computers, waiting for something terrifying and real and secret on the screen.

I can't figure out what in the world to say to make him spill his feelings, what possible combination of sentences will make this moment last. So I sort of tap out words and delete them. I settle on: . . . ?

Another long pause. That wasn't right. I need something else. Like, a poem. Or something quick and heart-stopping that will arrest him, trap him right in this moment and make him love me.

We're in it together, I write. Press send. Wait.

Wait.

Wait.

I am falling for you, Joe writes. *I want you. I'm questioning everything.*

* * *

I can't sleep. My mind is buzzing from the conversation with Joe, and by three I've made the executive decision to stop pretending to sleep and grab my newest copy of my favorite book, *A Little Princess*. I head to Cate's office, where I love to curl up with a book, and start doing my active reading.

Active reading is this thing they started making us do at my crunchy private school as soon as we transitioned from picture books to chapter books at the beginning of second grade. Back then, active reading meant starring words we didn't know or drawing smiley faces next to parts of a story that we liked or laughed at. Now we're expected to write notes in the margins, ask questions on the dedication page, and underline, asterisk, and highlight anything that "hits us emotionally or intellectually," according to Headmaster Brownser.

Headmaster Brownser cares about our feelings. He wants us to share them. He tells us so all the time. It doesn't make people at school any nicer, not really, but it means we do a lot of lame trust activities and keep journals and had an entire unit on Feeling Identification in seventh grade. As if by seventh grade a person doesn't know the difference between anger and sadness.

I'm not into trust falls or school-wide bonding picnics or most other things Headmaster Brownser likes, but I am really into active reading. I totally active read for fun. Like a hobby. And I love it when other people active read. So I do what I do best: break the binding on *A Little Princess* and start marking it up. It is the most beautiful book in the world, and as soon as Sara's handsome captain father starts buying her furs and dolls and gifts of every kind, to keep with her when he leaves, I tear up.

I make a note: *This is where I start to cry. It's so damn beautiful I can't stop myself.*

A few pages later, when he tells Sara, "'I know you by heart. You are inside my heart,'" I am wiping my eyes with the sleeves of my snowflake-themed flannel pajamas, and bits of the ridiculous glitter get stuck to my teary face. I make another note: *This is what love should be.*

I don't hold back. It's like having a conversation with the book. It tells me things and I respond with semi-illegible scrawlings, and exclamation points, and wild circles around phrases that hit me really hard. We talk like that all night, *A Little Princess* and I. With only one lamp on and my red-framed glasses in the next room, I have to hold the book so close to my face that I can smell the pages, and it makes it even easier to get lost in this other world. Which is a relief and honestly a testament to how great that book is, because for me to think of anything but Joe is a miracle.

At seven Cate walks in and serves me oatmeal with brown sugar and what she calls a home-latte, which is just French-press coffee and microwaved milk with a heaping tablespoon of sugar. It's been weeks since she's been this motherly, so the morning really feels exceptionally *good*: Joe likes me, I'm in the final chapter of the best book of all time, and I'm eating oatmeal on the superthick carpet of Cate's office. In a few hours I'll be kicking myself for not having slept, but right now things are pretty effing great for a Monday morning.

"Drop this off at Recycled Books?" I say, when I finally leave the office and start packing my backpack in the kitchen. Paul and Cate are putting away their meditation mats, and postmeditation is usually the best time to ask Paul for favors.

"I can do even better. I'm heading down to New York for a meeting right now. Quick in and out—I'll be back this afternoon—but I'll drop it off with one of those street sellers. What is it this time?" he asks. Paul reads exactly like I do: with a flurry of excitement and messiness.

I hold up the book and he grins.

"Want me to pick something up, too?" he says.

"Wanna see if they have another marked-up copy of *A Little Princess*?"

"I like the way you think, buttercup. I'll see what I can do." Paul winks.

This is the greatest thing my father ever taught me: Taking notes in your own book is fun. Reading someone else's notes in the same book is even funner.

Paul starts flipping through *A Little Princess* and raises his eyebrows.

"You sure you want to donate this one?" he asks. I shrug. It's something I started doing this summer. Not just reading other people's notes, but letting them read mine. I guess that's what happens when you're really, really lonely. You start looking for connections *everywhere*. Back when I had friends, I could tell them what I was thinking and feeling. Now I tell hypothetical strangers who don't know I exist. Paul doesn't judge, but he gives me one of his patented frown-smiles and half a hug. "I got a great copy of the first Harry Potter the other day," he says. "Weird, I know, but whoever marked that thing up is deep. You want it?" He's already heading for his bookcase and running his thumb along the spines of the books to find it for me.

"Yeah, I want it," I say, and throw it in my backpack, as if it weren't already heavy enough.

"Weirdos," Cate says. "Aren't you worried some sociopath is going to pick up that book and learn everything about you and then, you know, use it against you?" she says, which is what she always says when I do this. It's also more or less what she says when Paul and I get really intent on someone else's notes, too: *What if those are the notes of a serial killer that you are fawning over?*

"What kind of sociopath buys a used copy of *A Little Princess*?" I say.

"I think you just answered your own question," Cate says, and then she and Paul are giggling like little kids and I'm rolling my eyes, and even if Joe hadn't told me last night he was falling for me, this would be a great day.

"Our Tabitha's a romantic," Paul says. "Just like her old man." I can't hide the blush and the smile, and I'm sure they both know me well enough to see I'm thinking even more than usual about love. If my outsides match my insides, I must be glowing. I'm not great at hiding actual feelings.

"Pleeeeease tell us who it is," Cate says, while I try to will the flush off my cheeks. Pregnancy may be making her read less, but it makes her no less nosy. I shake my head like she's crazy and bite the insides of my cheeks to at least temper the big-ass smile threatening to spread all over my face.

"I gotta get to school," I say, matching her singsong voice. And I really, really do. Because I'm afraid if I don't see Joe immediately, last night's conversation will somehow disappear, the way things sometimes do.

Two.

Life totally sucks, so I do not see Joe all day.

Or rather: I do see Joe, but only with his girlfriend, Sasha Cotton, wrapped around him. She sits on his lap in the cafeteria, eating cheese-and-lettuce sandwiches, taking bites so small, I wonder if she is even human. During assembly she crosses her legs over his and puts one arm around his neck and another around his stomach. Sasha Cotton grabs him from behind in between classes and kisses the place where his hair meets his neck while he smiles and rubs his thumbs against her wrists. When we play cards during free periods, Sasha Cotton doesn't actually play, but she rests her head in Joe's lap and reaches up to touch his chest from time to time.

It is torture.

He walks her to math class, which she and I are in together, and he squeezes her ass before leaving her at the door. If it were me, I'd giggle and push him away. I think that's how most girls flirt. But Sasha leans into his touch. She doesn't smile. Locks her green eyes on his. Puffs out her lips, a slight opening in between the top and bottom lip. That small space is the difference between Sasha Cotton and every other girl in the world.

The annoying thing about Sasha is that she's not cheerleader sexy. She's more like fortune-telling Gypsy sexy.

I white-knuckle it through math class, do homework in an empty classroom for a while after school to regroup, then walk to my family's coffeehouse, Tea Cozy. I have earned coffee. And a cookie. Or, like, three cookies and a brownie. Joe and I haven't so much as made eye contact since he said he was falling for me. You'd think this would be impossible at a tiny school in a tiny town, but he makes it happen. There is a corset around my heart, and every time I calculate how long it's been since we've shared a secret wave or smile or breathy *hey there*, the corset tightens. I attempt one of Cate and Paul's meditation techniques: looking out the Tea Cozy windows and focusing on the mountains, losing myself in the way the fog collides with the snowy peaks, and thinking of nothing else.

It does not work. Meditation is bullshit. That's my official opinion.

"Long day?" Paul says, bringing me a coffee, no milk, tons of sugar. Cate hates the way I drink my coffee and tries to make me drink milk-heavy lattes like the ones she makes at home, or, ideally, green tea.

"Longest day," I say, and take a few long gulps of the strong, sugary stuff.

"The mommy-and-me class that meets here just left, so I hear you, Tab. These women had guitars and tambourines and—what's the little silver thing called? The one that dings when you hit it? The one shaped like a triangle?"

"Um, a triangle?" I have already finished half a cup of coffee.

"That's hilarious. Yeah. A triangle. Oh man. Hilarious."

Paul is high. I know because his voice goes all squeaky when he smokes up, and his chattering is mostly of the *hehehe* variety. Cate's making drinks, manning the register, and looking all pissed at Paul and me, since she's stuck doing everything while we're in the corner hiding from my former best friends, who have paraded through the door like they've forgotten my family owns this place and they are not welcome.

Cate and Paul may be my parents, but I use that term loosely, since they had me when they were sixteen like me. Paul's a stoner and Cate's a flake but they're mine, and if nothing else, at least they care about stuff like that my former best friend, Jemma, and the girl who was our third wheel, Alison, are taking over the couch we used to all sit on together, and drinking my mother's famous hot chocolate like everything's fine.

"They don't even look, you know, *sheepish*," Paul says. "Shouldn't they be embarrassed? They know we hate them, right?" He's a bigger kid than me, my handsome, scruffy father. He's also not talking quietly enough. Alison and Jemma crane their necks to look from the paisley couch to our collage-top table. Paul must be immune to things like the stink eye, or maybe all adults are, so he's rambling on. "You were basically doing them a *favor*, hanging out with them. Who are they to ditch *you*? They'll last about five seconds in college. You know that, right? Queens of the world right now, but in college being awesome actually counts for something, you know?"

Paul never went to college. He was too busy staying home with me and playing with blocks and teaching me the alphabet.

"I remember when they started getting all judge-y. I'll never forget the way they looked at you when you said you wanted to put in highlights. Like you'd said you wanted to start doing crack or something." Paul keeps shaking his head. He can't get his mind around what happened with my friends, and I can't either. They stopped liking me. I guess it's simple, except for how surprising it was. Cate says sometimes change makes people very angry.

I can't stop looking at Jemma and Alison and the way they still feel 100 percent comfortable in my parents' café.

Cate used her parents' money to open Tea Cozy, and since there's pretty much nothing else to do in Vermont, it was super popular right away. Plus, like I said, there's Cate's hot chocolate, and that stuff's for real.

Jemma laughs, and it punctures the quiet. "She's playing some part. She, like, thinks she's in some movie that we're all here to watch," Jemma says. The whole place seems to be listening, and although it is absolutely possible she isn't talking about me, my heart drops and my limbs ice over with fear and shame.

She's smirking as she sips her hot chocolate. She was totally talking about me.

"I could use a hand, guys," Cate calls out. She's got two mugs in one hand, a wad of cash in the other, and tortoiseshell glasses balanced on her head like a headband. She has hair like mine: fine and golden blond, easily tangled. She's knotted it at the base of her skull with a pencil, but damp, renegade pieces cling to her forehead and her ears, threatening to move into her eyes. She's the vision of the word *overworked*. Plus there's a growing line of after-school customers who are trying to be polite and calm but are jiggling their legs and sighing.

Paul doesn't even uncross his legs, and I want to stand up and help but get momentarily distracted by Alison's deep frown and new glasses. She's reading *The Fountainhead*. I am fascinated by *The Fountainhead*. I miss having friends who do things like wear uncool glasses and read *The Fountainhead*. I miss having more than one friend, period.

"Paul? Babe? Backup?" Cate calls out again.

Paul and I are even bigger assholes, because Cate's pregnant and it shows. She touches her stomach every few seconds and even puts a hand to her lower back from time to time, as if she is eight months in and not five.

"I'll go," Paul says. "You stay right here. Show 'em who's boss."

"You okay to work?" I ask. My dad's smoking up is no secret. Not to me, not to Cate, and not to the other town stoners. But a lot of people wouldn't like knowing he is high on the job. Around their kids. Making their soy lattes.

"Yeah, yeah," he says. "You okay by yourself? Those girls aren't gonna start anything with you, right?"

"Paul," I say, loving him even now, with his T-shirt fading and old and his hair a hot mess of bed head. "They're not, like, a gang. Their weapons are basically silence and backstabbing." He nods. Alison and Jemma snort. They probably heard that, too.

I don't mind being at the table alone. The café is my home, and I collaged this table myself when I was ten and too small to know that Peter, Paul, and Mary are not actually cool, even though they are from the sixties or whatever. Pictures and lyrics from them are glued in overlapping enthusiasm, and then laminated. The table is one of my many masterful contributions to the decor, which is all homemade craftiness and ironic kitsch. Heaven. And pretty much the same basic design choices as our actual home, a little house a few miles down the street in the shadow of a mountain.

Anyway, now that I'm at the table alone, I can turn on my computer and hope to see Joe already online.

No such luck. Maybe I imagined the whole ecstatic conversation last night. Maybe I've imagined every late-night conversation with Joe. I look up old chats, and there they are. Pages and pages of Joe calling me adorable and asking me what I love about used books, and telling me how out of place he feels around the other hockey players sometimes.

The chats are all there, but in real life, nothing has happened. I get headaches from thinking too hard about what it would be like to kiss him, but it can't happen while he has a girlfriend. Once in a while our fingers will touch in the middle of a card game, and that accidental touch is so electric, I wonder if I could survive an actual kiss.

My one and only friend, Elise, is online, and I throw out a *hey lady*, but she doesn't respond, so she's probably actually doing homework.

Or she knows I'd be using her as a distraction. Even though we have only been friends since the summer, she sees right through me.

I don't love her with the decade-long devotion that I had for Jemma, but she's kind and effortlessly cool and as smart as my old friends. But we don't share that special history of hot chocolate stands, snowball fights, pig Latin conversations, chocolate chip cookie baking competitions.

That said, she has also never told me I am going in the wrong direction as a person, so she wins.

I keep accidentally looking up and over at Jemma. If Joe were online, I'd be 100 percent distracted and wouldn't have to wonder what Jemma thinks of my clothes and my hair and the tightness of my black pants today.

Note: they are tight. But everyone is wearing tight black pants lately. And my ass has grown into a shape that makes every pair of pants look kind of tight. Not a bad shape. But a new shape.

I am a new shape. And they hate that shape.

My foot starts twitching of its own accord, and I'm dizzy with the anticipation and the knowledge that it could be hours *(hours!)* before Joe logs on and we can enter back into banter and whatever that other thing is: daring each other to push it further? Anticipating what could be? Gambling? I'm not sure, but it feels good and buzzing and warm, and it makes me ill with anxiety. I can't decide what makes me more nervous: the idea that it might happen in real life, or the worry that it might end before it begins.

I'm not a person who would kiss someone else's boyfriend. Except that I am someone who is desperate to kiss Joe. I've never been two people at once before, and I don't like it.

I send Elise a few more chats, begging her to stop being a good student and gossip with me instead. When that fails, I get up and sneak myself another mug of coffee from behind the counter. Paul winks at me. I head back to my table and stir in the requisite three and a half packets of sugar.

"Tabitha?"

Alison doesn't speak to me ever anymore. But Jemma butts in from time to time. I don't even hate it. It still feels good to have her close by, even though it then feels totally terrible if I actually listen to the words she's saying.

I look up and for a split second forget she's not my friend anymore. She has on the same style hoodie she wears almost every day, today in red, and she crosses her arms awkwardly over her chest. She's not pretty, not hot, not popular or talented in any particular way. She's smart, which is why I liked her so much. She's ambitious and listens to NPR and has a really fascinating opinion on almost everything. Including, lately, *me*.

"I mean this as, like, friendly advice," Jemma starts. Alison looks on with interest. Hugs *The Fountainhead* to her chest like a raft. "But one of the seniors told me I should mention to you that the black eyeliner is, like, a little out of control this week."

Oh right. This. This is why we aren't friends. *Now* I remember.

My skirts. My makeup. The looks I give boys. Maybe even the looks they sometimes give me.

The looks her brother, Devon, gave me.

And okay fine, the fact that I started touching my hair a lot around him, and wearing extra makeup and my smallest skirts when I went over to her house. I started flirting. I guess that was sort of bad.

But not *that* bad.

"And today . . . are you wearing some kind of crazy padded pushup bra?" Jemma continues. "Because, um . . . that is a lot of cleavage. And my mom said some of the teachers are mentioning it as being a problem too. . . ." Jemma keeps the same look of bullshit-concern on her face for all of this, even cringing with mock humility at the word *bra*. We're sixteen, not seven. The girl has seen my nipples, for chrissakes. We compared nipple size in the seventh grade. I lent her one of my training bras when her mother wouldn't get her one. We Googled "blow job," like, two years ago when we heard everyone was giving them.

"I'm wearing a normal bra," I say, as if that's somehow the only pertinent part of the conversation so far. Jemma gives me a look like she doesn't buy it, and I wish this was a problem a change of bra could solve. "What did you need, Jem?" I immediately wish that I'd stopped myself from using a nickname. It hurts, the remembered intimacy hanging in the air between us.

"You've just changed so much."

"I haven't changed at all," I say. And this I actually mean. Because a sudden jump in cup size isn't the same thing as changing who I am.

Can't you be bookish and chill and also sort of a little bit hot? I'd still rather spend my Saturday nights curled on the paisley couch with a book and a chocolate croissant. I just want to do it with makeup on.

"It makes me sad, seeing you like this, hearing people talk about you the way they are, asking me what's going on with you," Jemma says, gesturing vaguely at my face and maybe my low-cut peasant top, which is hardly stripper wear or anything. "We said we'd never dress like those girls, remember? We said we'd never prioritize guys over everything else. We weren't going to be like this."

Maybe I shouldn't have let Paul go behind the counter. I'm obviously not capable of being on my own right now. Paul would have chimed in with something snarky and cool, something that shows Jemma's a bitch *and* that I don't care.

I open and close my mouth like a fish because I can't think of actual words to say in response.

"You're becoming this Other Person," Jemma says very, very slowly. "And hanging out with Elise . . ."

Elise wears baggy pants and a Don't Mess with Me look on her face. That's what Jemma's trying to get at, but she's choosing her words carefully so as not to sound judgmental. In Vermont we are not judgmental. We are *concerned*.

"Elise isn't exactly trouble," I say. Also true. Elise doesn't party or wear low-cut shirts or anything. Just has short hair and pushes the dress code by wearing obnoxious T-shirts underneath her chunky cardigan sweater collection.

Scandalous.

Elise wants to go to Harvard. She volunteers at the hospital and plays with sick kids. She's practically a saint. A lesbian saint.

Jemma has glassy eyes like she might cry.

It didn't only make her angry, when I started liking boys more than sci-fi movie marathons and when I started getting catcalls in the halls. It also made her sad.

I think I hate her sadness even more.

Which makes no sense, because I'm the one who got ditched and is still getting assaulted by random insults and slut implications, even if I'm in the supposedly safe haven of Tea Cozy. If anyone should be crying, it's definitely me.

"I hate everything about this conversation," I say, because at a certain point you have to say exactly what you're thinking.

"It's a small school," Jemma concludes. "People notice. That's all I'm saying."

I feel myself blush even though I want to stay tough. I feel a little sinking in my stomach, and my hands go to my collarbone, protecting the naked parts of me. I wish I had a turtleneck sweater and a big knit scarf to cover up whatever they're seeing. I wonder which customers are listening in on our conversation. I know if the situation were reversed, I would be eavesdropping the hell out of this moment. I love little more than watching other people's lives happen to them.

Jemma sees the blush spreading on my face and pats my shoulder. *Pats. It.* Like I'm a child and she's a teacher and I have sooooo much to learn. I shrug her off and turn my attention to my computer, where Joe has finally logged on, and the machine is pinging at me urgently.

I see Jemma see his name.

I don't cover the screen, even though I should.

She nods at it, and I know she's taking note and that I will hear a rumor about me and Joe in the next week. Except by this time next week, maybe it won't really be a rumor so much as the truth. I'm a terrible, terrible person for how good that feels, buzzing inside me. The thought of there being an *us*.

I grab hold of my huge mug and let it cover my face (and my smile) as I take a long sip.

Jemma wrinkles her nose and is going to say more, I think, but Paul reappears, hands on hips as he stands too close to her for it to be comfortable.

"Are you and Alison getting something else? Because I really can't let you take that table for very long if you're not purchasing food or another beverage," Paul says. Sometimes I think my father is a high school girl too.

"I'll get a cookie," Jemma says. Jemma and Paul used to be friends in their own right. She would tease him about his spaciness, and he would fight back with jokes about her crazy knack for organizing everything, including our own refrigerator when its messiness started really bugging her.

Then they would talk books for, like, hours. Because the only people in the world who read more than me are Jemma and Paul.

"I think we're out of cookies," Paul says. An entire glass display case filled with cookies of every variety is a few feet behind him. He looks over to it and shrugs at the trays and trays of cookies.

I have no idea if I am proud to have Paul as my dad right now, humiliated, or a little scared he's going to get in trouble for harassing a teenager. He leans on the spare chair at my table and makes a kind of clucking sound with his tongue against his teeth. I'm sure Jemma can sniff out the stale, hay-like, almost-sweet smell of just-smoked weed coming off him.

Jemma knows too many of my secrets.

She looks back at my computer one more time. Joe has not stopped chatting me. I doubt she can read the words from where she is, but she can definitely see his name, in bold, popping up a half dozen times in a row on my screen. She opens her mouth to comment but changes her mind.

"Right" is all she says. It seems to be a commentary on everything she has disdain for at this moment: my cleavage, Paul's childish meanness, my flirtation with Joe, the rules of being a normal human being.

I am left in the wake of the things she said, and I don't drown in them, exactly, but I'm having some trouble catching my breath. She and Alison stay in their corner, after Alison purchases a tea that Cate doesn't know better than to give her, and they share a set of headphones and lean over an iPhone together. I picture the bespectacled or maxidress-wearing angry rocker chick they are probably listening to and Googling right now. She is probably singing a song that somehow tells them how right they are to hate me.

I'm not really listening to much music lately. I don't know who to listen to, or what it would mean about me if I started liking them.

I'm determined not to become someone else. So I've given up music altogether basically.

"Ridiculous," Paul says. He is still gripping the top of the chair and rocking back and forth a little with the music Cate's playing over the sound system. "And also, ballsy." He grins. Almost everything terrible in life kind of amuses Paul. I'm hoping I'm moments away from growing into that trait, and that I will be a little more like him someday soon.

Except without the yoga mat.

"You can't be weird about them, okay?" I say. "Like, give them cookies. It's fine. They can eat cookies if they want." I want to chat with Joe and watch the rest of the day float away.

Especially the part when Joe grabbed Sasha's ass.

"I'll find something else to be weird about, I guess," Paul says, and he nudges his foot against the bottom of my chair so that it shakes a little.

"Can't wait."

"I have the perfect Forgive Your Ridiculous Father present," he says, and reaches into his back pocket. Pulls out a beat-up copy of *The Secret Garden*. It's not *A Little Princess*, but it's the author's other beautiful effing book, and I'm dead-on impressed. Not to mention, books from New York City are the best, because anyone could have written in them, and they have this infinite sense of possibility that books from the town bookstores don't have. People in New York, or other cities, are probably like that too. Full of all kinds of hope, while I'm stuck here being small and limited.

"Seriously?" I say, and grab it from his hands, flip through the yellowed pages, and see them covered, absolutely slathered, with margin notes. Dark-red pen. Curly, swirly, beautiful handwriting.

"You haven't had the easiest time, and I figured my favorite daughter needed something good," Paul says. His dimples deepen, if that's even possible, and there are one hundred things wrong with my life right now, and a few of them are in Tea Cozy with us, but man, I lucked out in the dad department. "Plus I found a marked-up copy of the terrible live-in-the-moment, self-help, we-are-all-small-specks-in-the-universe book I hate, *The Power of Now*." Paul hates positive-thinking books. *Hates* them. They don't jibe with his yoga and meditation. Seems like all the same thing to me, but whatever. "So it was worth walking around the East Village for an extra hour before driving back today. Hate those quick trips. Turn around the second I get there, basically."

I'm not even really listening anymore, because this book is amazing and whoever wrote these notes is amazing, and I want to dive right in. I wave him away, and he chuckles as he walks back to the counter. I have described the plot of *The Secret Garden* to him many times. He knows all about sullen Mary and her trip to her uncle's kind-of-creepy mansion and her discovery of a beautiful, secret garden that leads her to be a better person and to live a brand-new, unexpected life. Paul's never been super interested, but he likes when I'm excited about things, even if he doesn't share the excitement.

On the front page, the Red Script Note Taker has drawn a picture of a garden and written a haiku about rose petals and loneliness.

I'm all in.

I blast through five chapters of *The Secret Garden* and linger on every margin note like it's a message from the universe directly to me. The note taker writes, *Mary is real. Confused by life. Pissed at circumstance. Forgotten. Ready to explore the world, regardless. Brave.* That place between my jaw and my eyes swells, and I am teary. I'm a sucker for a character who other people hate. And Mary has long been a favorite of mine. Not only after she finds her garden and makes friends and changes. I love her from page one. She may be cranky, but she's also honest. She explores that terrifying house and its grounds with a delicious anticipation and openness, in spite of the fact that her life so far has sucked.

When I finally remember to look up, my computer's still pinging, Joe all desperate and wanting me to be there. *Tabby?? You there? Tabitha? I'm missing you!!*

I kind of can't believe I forgot about him for as long as I did. I have a distracting kind of liking for him. Sometimes I stare at my math homework for hours but can't do a single problem, I'm so busy suffocating from feelings. But whoever wrote these margin notes in *The Secret Garden* captivates a different part of me.

I turn back to the computer, and Joe and I swim in our special brand of awkward ecstasy for the next hour. We recall, for maybe the twentieth time this month, how we fell for each other. It's one of our favorite conversations to have, the way mothers tell their children the stories of their births. I recount his smile and the zap of interest on the first day of school this year, how good he looked after a summer of football drills and beach days.

You told me I looked good, I type. *You asked me why I wasn't with my friends.* I remember how his face fell when I struggled to explain that my friends weren't my friends anymore.

You did look good, he types, his signature winking face punctuating the sentence. *And kind of sad but also kind of like . . . you weren't going to let them win. You looked determined. I liked that.*

I smile at that, because it reminds me of Mary. Sad and determined.

You liked that my hair was longer and blonder, I type, winky-faceing right back at him.

Hey, that didn't hurt. But it was electric, right? Like, immediately I just . . . I had these feelings for you that I hadn't had before.

I guess it doesn't qualify as love (or lust, or whatever) at first sight, because we'd known each other for years. But what do you call it when you see each other for the thousandth time but everything has changed all at once? Our liking each other wasn't gradual or earned. It was sudden, immediate, and overnight. Love at thousandth sight.

Invite me over, he says. No ellipses. No question mark. Certain.

"Tab, I need a latte assist here," Cate calls out across the café, and the customers who aren't too lost in books and laptops and overly intimate conversations giggle. Cate is good at making strangers giggle with her funny turns of phrase.

I can't today, I write back. But I don't say no. I don't say never. I don't say, *Not until you break up with Sasha Cotton*. I know I should say all of that, but I can't. My fingers won't do it.

A gaggle of young moms has all ordered skim lattes, so I tell Joe I'll be back, and head behind the counter to help. I burn a whole bunch of milk, so stuck I am in the wonder of what Joe and I will do or say next. I try to imagine the exact texture of his thick black hair and wish myself pressed against those red, red lips.

I decide not to care about anything else.

Tomorrow, Joe has typed by the time I'm back at my computer. He's signed off, but the word remains and I keep it on my screen, staring me down, for the rest of my time at Tea Cozy. I sort of capture the word inside me and let it stir things up and get me excited and anxious and terrified and blissed out. *Tomorrow,* my brain says on repeat. *Tomorrow.*

Three.

Tomorrow does eventually actually occur, thank God.

Tomorrow is today, I text when we're playing hearts together during a free period. I get to watch him check his phone, register that it is me texting, arrange his face into something casual after reading the words. He types a response immediately, and my phone buzzes. I inspect my cards instead of checking the message. Let him sweat it out for a minute.

He grins. He likes the anticipation, too.

Your place after school to do homework? his text reads when I finally look in my lap. I try not to blush. I rearrange my cards so that the hearts are all together on the far right side. I can't look at him, for fear of breaking into a ridiculous grin.

It's not a decision so much as a reflex when I type back *Yes.*

A few hours later, we're on my carpet, I've got a Top 40 playlist shuffling, and we're singing along to every stupid song that's come out in the last few months. We are also "doing homework," and Joe keeps giving me this look like he has to have me. He moves about a half inch closer to me every five minutes.

"You have a good voice," he says.

I do not have a good voice.

"You're in my room," I say, and giggle like it's the world's greatest secret.

"I'm definitely in your room," he says with a grin. "I like your room."

"I like you in my room," I say. My mouth feels funny. My limbs feel funny. I can't stop swallowing. And we are having the world's stupidest conversation.

"I like that you like me in your room," Joe says. He puts a hand on my knee and sort of taps along with the music. I can feel myself shaking but I don't want him to feel me shaking, so I try tensing every muscle in my body to see if that works.

I give what I hope resembles a smile, but my mouth feels so strange that I can't tell.

Then Joe's mouth is on mine and it tastes exactly the way I thought it would: sweet and red from the berry-scented ChapStick he uses. His body is wide, and he has a thick, scratchy stubble, so he can do things like use girls' lip balm and not seem any less the tough guy he is.

My chest is tight with desire and joy and that other thing too. Guilt? Fear? Worry? I try to push it down, so I can enjoy the way his hands rub my back and the insistent pressure of his lips and tongue. It doesn't exactly work—I'm positive I can feel my heart shrinking and expanding with terrifying speed—but the physical confirmation of how much I adore Joe wins out for a few minutes at least.

"What are we doing?" I say in between kisses, but I know the answer. What I want is for him to say it's over with Sasha Cotton and that we are marking the start of our new, committed, totally legitimate and morally palatable relationship. This is not going to happen, but asking makes it feel like I am doing my moral duty.

Joe pulls back, and we have the sort of extended eye contact that could make me do something terrible, which is exactly what I'm doing.

"You're so beautiful," Joe says, and tucks my hair behind my ear. He kisses my neck, and I let him, because we've been chatting almost every night until two or three in the morning for the last month and I'm not friends with his girlfriend, Sasha Cotton, anyway, and being against him is better than any other single feeling I think I've ever had.

"Thanks," I say, and blush hard. I push Sasha Cotton out of my head and focus on the certainty in Joe's eyes.

"I really want to just be here with you," he says, moving his face so close to mine that our noses touch. Then my hand is on the back of his neck and my lips are locked on his and I'm basically saying, with my mouth and my hips and the swing in toward his body, *I trust you*.

When we finally break apart, Joe holds my face in his hands and I grin so hard it hurts.

"What are we gonna do?" he says.

I think he should leave Sasha Cotton and become my boyfriend, but short of that I think we should keep kissing. Of course, I can't say that. I'd sound like some old corny movie, and I'm simply not willing to be that person around him. So we sit and stare at each other for the longest five seconds in the history of the world. I think of when Joe and I first started talking in the parking lot, after school or practice every afternoon. He teased me about the way I braid my hair when I'm nervous or spacing out, and he laughed hard when I made fun of him and his hockey friends, imitating the loud grunts and hypermasculine energy they have on the ice. I told him he was the only stoner-hockey player I'd ever met and that my dad would love it.

He joked about smoking up with my father.

"Stoner Jock Joe! The least useful but hungriest of all the jocks!" I said, and he laughed along with me and told me he'd never met a girl as funny and hot as me.

I'm thinking about that right now. About the fact that he basically said he likes me more than Sasha Cotton.

I kiss him again, pressing as much of my body against him as I can. I put a hand on his face, and he makes a happy noise into my mouth.

"You have to decide what we're gonna do," I say when he moves his lips from my mouth to my neck. He takes another break to look me in the eyes, and I can't hold back a ridiculous smile.

"You're so freaking pretty," he says. He is a little high and I am a little drunk on the way it feels to be around him.

When his phone rings, I know it's Sasha. He could ignore it, but he doesn't, and his voice goes soft on his "Hello?" which hurts since I've still got a leg over his leg and a slight breathing problem from how deep and ceaseless the kissing was. If she strained, I bet Sasha could hear the unmistakable shakiness and rhythm of my breathing even over the phone.

All of a sudden, I want to throw up.

"I'll be over soon," Joe says. "Are you okay? Can you stay where you are for ten minutes? Don't move. Don't do anything until I get there. Hug the bear I gave you, turn on the TV, and I'll be there before you know it."

He hangs up and we have to untangle our limbs. He clears his throat and I wipe my mouth. The kisses were good, but not neat, not expertly delivered. They were messy, which is exactly what Joe is. A huge mess. He stands up fast so I stand up too, but he sort of shakes his head at me like I shouldn't have gotten up, like he's not gonna even hug me good-bye. Which is crap, 'cause I know, I *know* he'll be online in a few hours telling me how badly he wanted to stay.

"I have to go," he says without looking at me.

"Sasha," I say. There are implicit quotation marks around her name.

"Don't say it like that. She's really . . . fragile. I told you, she has, sort of, problems. Like, depression and stuff. It's bad." I hate when guys say the word *fragile* like it means hot or lovable.

"But what about what happened today?" I say. I am fighting the urge to hold him down and physically make it impossible to leave.

"She's having a panic attack. A really intense one. She was hyperventilating, Tabby. And she's, you know, I do love her. She needs me." He pauses, and there's expectation in the wordless gap. Like I'm supposed to give him permission. Like I'm supposed to tell him it's okay and I understand and to go, go, go. But my jaw drops and my eyes well up and it hurts, not only in my heart but also in my blood, in my muscles. "Look, I don't have time to talk about this," he says, not really looking at me or my teariness. "My girlfriend's sitting on a couch breathing into a paper bag, and she just has me and some weirdo online friends to help her out, so you know . . ."

I can still taste the berry from his lips. But I cannot compete with an anxiety attack and a year-and-a-half-long relationship and mile-long legs and hair that looks like sparrow's feathers. So I allow myself one more grimace and don't make him hug me good-bye.

If I did, I wouldn't let go. My arms would lock around his neck and refuse to loosen up. Everything in my stomach twists and turns, which I guess I deserve. It's not like I didn't know what I was getting myself into. This is basically exactly what someone like me deserves.

"If everything were different—" Joe says. He hasn't stepped out the door yet. If he really loved her, if he really thought she was in *peril*, he would be sprinting to his car and running red lights. I take note of this and store it as a reason to sign on later and let him chat with me.

"Everything could be different," I say, and make my eyes go as wide as they can, which isn't very. They have a tendency to squint when I'm smiling or nervous. So, always. My shirt's slipping off one shoulder, and *God* I hope that looks sexy. I may be a terrible person, and Joe may be complicated and confused, but I am vowing to make this work. Him and me.

"I need you to try to understand—" Joe says. I will not, under any circumstances, tell Elise that he said this. In fact, I may not tell Elise anything about tonight at all. She won't understand. I'm not sure I understand. I swallow and shrug and shake my head all at once. Anything, *anything* to keep from howling with sobs.

Joe adjusts the gold chain around his neck. Plays with the little gold cross. I asked him about it once—the cross sort of freaked me out, and I wondered if it meant he was really into Jesus or something. I knew he was Italian Catholic, but wearing a cross seemed more serious than that. He said it was his grandfather's, given to him from his deathbed. Is it weird that that made me fall even harder? Stoner-Jock, Grandfather-Loving, Kinda-Catholic Guy. His phone's ringing again, and then he does actually leave, runs out of my house, and I listen to his car turn on, his ridiculous rap music blast and then fade out as he drives away from my house.

I touch my own shoulder, the way he might have, and try not to think about the sweetness he uses when he touches her, versus the desperation when he grabbed at me. I give myself a moment to let the tears spill out, and then I spend an hour closing my eyes and breathing deeply to deal with the reality that Joe and I finally kissed.

He doesn't come online the way I predicted he would. I sit in the computer room and stare at the screen, willing the computer to flash with his name and a flirtatious message about the taste of my lips or his hands on my back or how doing the wrong thing felt so right. I occasionally look away and text Elise because a watched pot never boils, so I delusionally believe maybe if I talk to Elise about something else

I'll forget he exists, and then he'll chat me, and the gray, damp feeling in my chest will turn golden and sparkling and alive.

It doesn't appear to be working.

"Tea?" Cate says around ten, when my eyes are burning from the light of the screen.

"I'm not thirsty," I say with a small smile. She knows better than to leave me alone, though.

"I meant to say it not as a question. We're reading. We want you there. I brought cookies from the Cozy. We can't risk you becoming some weird tech-obsessed video game kid or, like, chat room lurker, you know? You have a sister on the way."

"Saving me from myself, huh?" I say, and I can't imagine what it would be like to have normal parents of normal ages, instead of Cate and Paul. Cate shrugs, and I laugh and shut down the computer the way you are supposed to pull off a Band-Aid: too quickly to notice how much it hurts. There's a hiccup of pain that comes with leaving the computer and the possibility that Joe will say something awesome to me tonight. But Cate's right. Every minute that passes with Joe not signing on is more depressing than the moment before.

"I'm not a techie weirdo, by the way. I'm a book weirdo," I say, because joking with Cate and Paul makes the actual world hurt a tiny bit less.

"Good. Let's keep it that way," Cate says.

Paul has started up a fire and is bundled up in hiking socks and Cate's purple Snuggie, which he has taken to using way more than she ever did. Cate's got an old quilt and one half of the couch, so I take up the other corner and sneak my feet under the same quilt. Our toes touch, and she wiggles hers against mine and I don't stop wanting Joe to text me *right this second*, but something small in my heart releases from being near them.

I open up my copy of *The Secret Garden*, but I'm barely reading the actual story. I'm mostly going margin note to margin note and spending extra time on any underlined passage. Luckily, the person who owned this book before me took a lot of notes and underlined a lot of moments. They made an excited squiggly line under one of my favorite passages: "She had never felt sorry for herself; she had only felt tired and cross, because she disliked people and things so much. But now the world seemed to be changing and getting nicer."

Sometimes it just takes one tiny thing to make the world seem right again, the note taker writes. *Mary's garden and the way new perspective and experience bring hope. The way a few roses are the difference between ecstasy and depression. Which is great. Because how easy is it to find a few roses, right?*

I effing love this girl. I have decided it's a girl. Mostly because guys don't really read *The Secret Garden*. But also because I am falling for Joe, and I don't have room to be madly in love with a red-pen-using, children's-literature-reading dude, too.

"Not too many more nights like this," Paul sighs out. "Once the baby comes, I mean." I don't know what he read in his book or tasted in his mug of tea that made him say it, but it breaks the perfect comfort in the room, and my stomach drops.

More things changing.

What if change were the greatest comfort? the Red Pen Note Writer writes in the margin, and my shoulders jump from the creepy relevance. This is why I love books. They so often address exactly what I'm going through at that precise moment.

I close my eyes and try to decide if I agree, that change could be comforting. Maybe I could. I'd like to.

"Bedtime for me," Cate says, and tucks me into the quilt alone.

"Me too," Paul says. He gets up and kisses my forehead. He smells like chocolate and honey and aftershave.

"Stay with me," I say. I almost never ask either Cate or Paul for anything. I've never really had to. "I'm having a—I'm feeling sort of—" I feel my voice shaking, and the threat of tears rushing from my throat to my nose and probably inevitably to my eyes. But if I really lose it, I'll have to explain myself to them, and I'll let it slip that I am hooking up with a guy in a long-term relationship, and I'll lose two of my last three allies. I can't afford any more people thinking I've *changed* and I'm *boy crazy* and I'm *making bad decisions*.

So I won't tell anyone. I'll let Elise and Cate and Paul keep seeing me as good, even though I know I'm also a little bad.

I shake back the desire to open up with a nod of my head and a few painful swallows, and tell Paul I'm actually probably going to go to bed soon anyway. He looks relieved to not have the burden of sitting with me and talking about my problems. He looks relieved to get to go to his bedroom with his wife and their unborn kid, and I think: *This is how it's going to be.*

I'm nearing the end of *The Secret Garden*. I savor the last few pages and last few amazing observations in the margins. I'm a little heart-broken to not know this stranger. I want her to be someone I can call up and talk through my problems with. I want more books filled with her thoughts. I'm not ready to let go of another friend. Not right now.

I flip through the book, hoping there's something I've missed and trying to memorize the best notes, the ones that make me feel like I could actually be okay. The notes that make me feel like I'm not alone and like maybe I'll get some of the things I want: love and the one million other things I'm missing. Maybe it's tiredness, but I feel a little giddy.

On the last page, there's a website link. Written in her pretty red script, all numbers and random letters, and below it the following words: *My own garden of secrets*.

Secret:

I wish I were hotter.

—Agnes

Secret:

I drive drunk. Often. There have been some seriously close calls.

—@sshole

Four.

Morning Assembly.

It's the kind of crap Circle Community Day School comes up with: most days we have a twenty-minute Morning Assembly, where we get school announcements in the auditorium. Every Thursday morning the headmaster hires a speaker for an hour (sometimes academic, sometimes inspirational, always boring), and the tiny student body, all three hundred of us, settles into our squeaky, itchy seats and tries to not get caught napping. So basically, thank God it's Wednesday.

I'm procrastinating outside the auditorium and hoping Elise will come by, until I remember I can't tell her anything about last night and Joe and the things I've done that feel great but make me terrible. Even without reassurance from him online last night, I smile thinking his name. I replay the kisses in my head, the moments before the kisses too, and I worry the spaces between my ribs are being literally crushed with feelings.

I do some imitation of Cate and Paul's yoga breathing, but it only makes me more hyped up, more ready to explode. I was certain it was best not to let Elise in on the secret that I am a bad person who makes out with other people's boyfriends, but the more I breathe, the more convinced I am that the words will spill out from physical necessity.

Sun's streaming in the floor-to-ceiling windows, and grumpy kids in fleece and corduroy are all squinting against the light. Joe walks by with Sasha. I reach for my hair on autopilot, push it behind my shoulders, and try to look normal.

"Please, no," Elise says, coming up behind me and squeezing my sides so that I jump in surprise. She gives me a good, hard stare, like I'm in trouble. Which, given Elise's distrust of hockey-playing cheaters, is probably exactly what she thinks I am. "Aren't we done with the Joe Donavetti crap yet?"

"I know, I know. I'm the worst. The League of Great Feminists from Throughout History will come down and haunt me." I wrap an arm across my body so that my hand rests around my ribs and tell the words and feelings to stay there and chill out.

"I'm not kidding, Tab. He's gross. And everyone loves his girlfriend. So get that look off your face."

The unspoken end of that thought: *You've lost enough friends already. Don't make it worse*. She notices my wince and shakes her head, like she's forgotten herself.

"You can do so much better, is all I mean. You're fucking gorgeous. And hilarious. Basically I'm obsessed with you, and your future boyfriend will be too." Elise bumps my hip with hers, and I get a lift from her words because she says them with such total sincerity that I think they might be true.

Except Joe's the one I want.

We follow Joe and Sasha into the assembly hall, and I don't even try to stop looking at them. I want a glimpse of his lips. It will feed the total bliss I feel at having kissed them.

Elise and I sit a few rows behind them, and I watch the hair on the back of Joe's head, looking for meaning. I know he wants to get out from under her thumb. He tells me he does every night. But his arm is around her, and I think from the way her body sort of shudders against his that she's crying.

Sasha Cotton is always crying.

"All right, lady, you obviously need to talk, so talk," Elise says with a huge sigh. Her lip is curled in disgust at having to listen to this, but she's a good friend, so she leans in, elbow on my armrest, chin on her fist, and gets ready for my gushing. "What's the update?" Assembly must be running late. The headmaster hasn't made his way onto the stage yet, and the din of voices isn't dying down.

The thing about Elise is, she comes around. She hasn't been the greatest listener lately, but she certainly *tries*. I don't tell her about the kissing or his running away; I just tell her about a conversation Joe and I had a few days ago online. I am desperate for her to approve of me and Joe, so that someday I can tell her the whole story.

"Well, so Joe did tell me that Sasha's on some new antidepressant medication. So as soon as she adjusts, he'll break up with her and—"

"Are they sleeping together?" Elise interrupts. It's the question we ask about every couple lately, but I haven't tried to find out about Joe and Sasha yet. I don't think I want to know the answer.

I shake my head and shrug and sigh all at once, and Elise adjusts her black T-shirt. She buttons and unbuttons the snaps on the brown leather cuff she wears on her right wrist. She musses up her own pixie cut and leans back in her seat.

"I guess I'm asking because they're passing out the lit journal today, and I hear she's got a poem in it," Elise says, choosing her words so carefully, I don't even recognize the rhythm of her voice as her own. Sasha has cupped her hand around the back of Joe's neck. It's the kind of gesture I've seen Cate and Paul do, and I shudder at the thought of Joe and Sasha as some kind of old married couple: comfortable, impenetrable, and in love.

"Hm?" I say.

"Heather said something. About Sasha's poem," Elise goes on. I'm so sick of hearing about her new friend Heather and their amazing connection that I don't immediately ask a follow-up question, even though the words she's saying and their vaguely ominous meaning make my stomach twist. Not to mention I owe her a good listen after she listened to me talk about Joe without gagging.

"What, did Sasha write about, like, dark thoughts and unicorns and Sylvia Plath or something?" I just can't stand the weepy pseudo-deepness that is Sasha Cotton. But she's fooling everyone else, I guess. Even the lit journal. Even Joe. He's whispering something into her ear, and I swear the feeling travels right to the skin of *my* ear. I shudder from the abrupt desire. I want his lips to be on my ear so badly, I could scream. I force myself to swallow instead.

"I know she's lame," Elise says, "but she's smart, too. And sort of . . . weirdly sexy. So, I don't know. Just be prepared. I heard her poem is kinda . . ." Elise can't seem to come up with the right word, so she makes her eyes go wide and shimmies her shoulders a little. I want to ask for more, but the announcements are starting and the teachers are on high alert, so we both shut up. There's that rumble of nerves in my stomach, and I grab Elise's arm for support. She pats my hand quickly and then slides her arm out from under my grip.

After twenty minutes of reminders to buy baked goods at Friday's sale, and to not park in faculty spots, we're dismissed for first period. On our way out of the hall, as promised, Heather and the other literary magazine evangelists hand out *Libretto*, the journal they produce every other month that is chock-full of tortured poetry, SAT-word-heavy short stories, and black-and-white self-portraits. Everyone is obsessed with *Libretto*. It's like a barometer for the gossip in the school: who is in love, who is breaking up, who is losing it, who's fighting, who's got family issues, who's talented and artsy versus who is just annoying.

I've submitted some writing, and it never gets in. That's the embarrassing truth that makes me hate them even more.

Elise has a self-portrait on page three: spiky hair, duct-tape-covered mouth, sleepy-sad look in her eyes. She told me the photograph's title is "Out," but in *Libretto* they're calling it "Just Me." Elise may be a lot of things, but she's not *out*. People suspect. People make fun. People ask me about it. But the simple declarative "I'm gay" has only ever passed through her lips when she's talking to me.

I'm proud of her, though. The photograph is a step.

I flip through more of the magazine: sketches of the mountains, photographs of inanimate objects, someone's poem about their dead uncle.

Then there's Sasha's poem. It's not long. It's extra deep because she uses slashes instead of line breaks, like a real Artist.

When you said not to be scared/ I believed you/ because when I can't trust myself/ I can trust you/ to know what my body wants./ Underwater your body looks/ like something I could love/ Naked/ and these are things no one else will see/ and we are keeping secrets in the cold and the dark and the way you hold me/underneath/ if you touch me again/ I will drown/ but maybe I wouldn't mind/ if it's your hands (mouth? skin?) stopping me from breathing.

It's titled "Underwater Joe."

I make myself throw up in the bathroom just to see if it will clear the feelings out of my chest.

It doesn't. I'm so not cut out for bulimia.

Secret:

I hate my best friend's boyfriend. Really, really, really hate.

—Roxie

Five.

I hide in the bathroom for, like, twenty minutes and miss part of Women's History because I cannot possibly face the day. I do a Downward Dog in the handicapped stall, but it does nothing to make me feel calmer. And since I also can't throw up my feelings, and I can't scream without attracting some serious attention, I reopen *The Secret Garden* and consider a few of my favorite notes before lingering on the last page and the website written there.

The link is circled in silver ink, which I hadn't noticed in the crappy lighting of our living room. Which I guess means my school's bathroom has better lighting than my family's living room, but that's a different issue. The silver ink gives it a magical quality. I lean against the locked stall door, take out my phone, and type in the address. I'm not sure exactly what I'm expecting. Maybe the note taker's blog or a *Secret Garden* fan page or something.

But the link doesn't take me straight to a website. A little gold box appears on the screen first. **Are you sure?** it says. I press yes, but I am suddenly not.

Can you keep a secret? another gold box asks. I laugh. A tight laugh, the uncomfortable kind that comes from my throat and not my stomach. I look around the stall, like someone might be in there with me. I look in the book again, too, in case there's some clue that this website is sort of crazytown.

I press the silver-script yes. It reminds me of this princess-themed video game I used to play when I was little. Except when I press yes this third time, the actual website pops up. Dark with gold and silver writing. **Life by Committee** it reads on the top.

A silver spiral spins in the top right corner. Hypnotic.

I can't process what I'm looking at, but I also can't look away. Like a car crash or an eclipse or Joe's face. I could get lost in it, but it scares me.

There's a squeak as the bathroom door opens and a group of girls enter.

"She doesn't even know it's hot, which is what makes it so freaking hot," one of them says. "You, like, can't even hate her, you know?"

"She's not, like, traditionally pretty. Not out-there pretty. She's, like, mysterious pretty. Which, I mean, is the best kind of pretty, you know?" her nasal-voiced friend agrees.

I close the website. Put my phone away.

I'm dizzy from this day, but I refuse to hide in a stall and listen to everyone talk about how amazing Sasha Cotton is. I push the door open and try to see if they know who I am, if they know about me and Joe, if anything registers on their faces.

One of them clears her throat, and I try to interpret the tone behind the cough.

Definitely judgmental. If they don't know about me and Joe, they've at least heard from Jemma and Alison that I'm the wrong kind of girl.

Everyone's talking about Sasha's poem. The artsy kids are saying it's totally beautiful, and the young teachers are stopping her in the hallway to tell her she should be applying to colleges with great English programs. Everyone else is acting like she wrote soft-core porn, and even the jocks are looking at awkward wispy-haired Sasha in a whole new light.

I'm spending my free period drowning my sorrows in shitty on-campus coffee at a little table near the alcove where the hot athletes hang out. Joe isn't quite one of them, maybe because he's not very tall and fails to buy the Right Sweater every fall, but his big-toothed smile and varsity-athlete status make him something of a sidekick. He can go to the parties, but they don't think to invite him. They talk to him when they are bored, but they wouldn't list him as a friend.

Athletes aren't supposed to have special status at Circle Community Day School, but these guys are gorgeous and their parents let them throw ragers after their games, so they end up popular despite the best efforts of the vegan potters who run our school to keep them down.

"Joe, my friend," Luke, the tallest and hunkiest of the guys, calls out. Joe beams, knowing what's coming, because I'm sure he's been hearing it from every guy since assembly let out. "What's up with your girl? She a freak? Your girl like it a little crazy?" Luke talks like he's from Detroit or something, but his parents make homemade jam and run the tourism office, so they're real Vermonters.

"I don't know, man," Joe says. He's grinning, though, a huge, shit-eating grin.

"Come on. She seems like a secret freak. She's one of those girls . . . kinda nuts, writes in a journal or some shit, reads a bunch of books with naked people on the cover. . . . Am I on the right track?"

My stomach turns. I blush, even though no one is looking at me or talking about me. I blush so hard, my own face is warm to the touch. I blush so hard, I'm pretty sure it is distracting to everyone around me. A bright red glow must be flooding the hallways.

"She's a little like that, sure," Joe says. He seriously cannot stop smiling. He's standing up straight, his feet wider than his shoulders, like he suddenly requires more room than your average person.

I am going to vomit. I am going to vomit right here, in front of everyone. Which will make my lack of Sasha-style sexiness even more obvious to the whole school and to Joe.

"That's what I thought. I know what those chicks are like. You're a lucky man, brother. Lucky, lucky man." Luke sticks out his hand and Joe shakes it; both of them flex their ridiculous muscles as they grip hands.

"You're gonna get me in trouble, dude," Joe says, his chest all puffed up. I'm full-on watching them now, no longer trying to hide my interest in a book or my coffee or anything. I'm just slack-jawed *staring* at Joe and Luke and the now-applauding football team. They are giving Joe a standing ovation.

I want to die.

And then, of course, Joe sees me and there's no way for me to quickly shift my gaze or anything, I'm just stuck with my mouth open and my eyes pinned to him. His face tries to rearrange itself into something mildly apologetic or friendly or gentle or something, but it really just looks scrambled and still glowing from stupid pride.

He gives a half wave, not big enough for anyone but me to notice, and I wonder if we'll talk online tonight, or if this is how it ends.

Then Elise is at my side, and I have to turn off that line of thinking for a second.

"Don't kill me," she says, which means she's done something ridiculous that doesn't affect me at all. This is exactly how she told me about stealing a hundred dollars from her mom to buy a fake ID from some sketchy dude in Burlington.

Not to buy beer, but to get into gay bars. Elise has no interest in drinking; she just wants to be around other lesbians, which I totally respect. Elise is both fearless and straight edge, which is a killer combination. I can only miss Jemma and Alison so much with Elise around.

"I'm not gonna kill you," I say. She's wringing her hands, though.

"I kinda like the poem."

"Elise!"

"I *kinda* think it's hot," Elise says. "I want to be honest. I'll probably tell her I liked it."

"But it's weird. I mean it's . . . everyone in the whole school knows who her boyfriend is. And everyone in the whole school knows that she lives near the lake. And now everyone knows what she and Joe *do* in the lake," I say. I drop my voice to a whisper so that the crowds of people picking up books and making jokes and texting and holding hands don't overhear us.

"But isn't that hot? That she just doesn't care? Like—that she's so into sex or Joe or whatever that she *has* to publicize it? That she can't keep it in, and doesn't care, and all the societal proscriptions fall the fuck away?" Elise is getting all worked up and forgetting to look at my face, which I'm almost certain is turning shades of pink and gray from humiliation and disgust.

"I mean, you're obviously in the majority. Sasha Cotton just became the hottest girl in school," I say.

"It's also kinda genius," Elise goes on, this time actually looking me in the face while she talks to me. This time, she's really considering the words.

"Genius?"

"She must have known. About you liking Joe. And Joe thinking you're cute or whatever it is he thinks. Or maybe she could tell he was thinking about breaking up with her or something. She must have felt it coming, and what better way to stake her claim, right?"

"We're talking about my life here, Lise," I say. I'm still waiting for my best friend to pull me into a hug and tell me it's going to be okay, or to help me hate on Sasha, but Elise is in a whole other realm with all this.

"Right," Elise says, and grabs my hands in her own. "Sorry. I know you like him and stuff. And he's a dick for leading you on. But she's upping her game, and I think you need to step out of this one. That's what I really wanted to say. Don't get in some weird girl-fight over stupid *Joe*, right?"

"Yep," I say. But now it hurts even more, the fact that Joe and Sasha are probably-definitely sleeping together, and that she is so confident in their love for each other that she would put it all out there like that. Turns out Sasha is some mystical nude-swimming sea nymph who needs both saving and screwing, and I'm just Tabitha: freckled and sad (but not depressed). No one is mistaking me for a damaged, alluring daughter of a philosopher like Sasha. The girl wears silk scarves like headbands. She knits her own sweaters. She laughs out of context and is probably right now sculpting a purposely lopsided vase with organic clay. You know, if clay can actually *be* organic. She has deep feelings that the rest of us cannot possibly understand. And though she has friends and a boyfriend and the basic respect of everyone in school, she's somehow the special, depressed one, and I'm just mopey.

"I can't have a crush on her, right?" Elise says, watching as Sasha walks by, too in the clouds and distracted by her own fragility to overhear the boys catcalling her. She just walks right by, long legs, wide hips, silvery silk scarf tied to her head and trailing a few inches behind her like fairy dust.

Basically: Sasha is a strange, sad mer-creature, and I'm just some virgin-girl who is not even as interesting as her own parents.

Secret:

I listen in on my mother's phone conversations. Especially the ones that are all about me.

—Agnes

Six.

Everything is wrong. I can't get the smudge off the glass counter at Tea Cozy, and most unfair of all, I've seen Alison and Jemma eating cheese sandwiches with Sasha Cotton at lunch, and as far as I can tell, no one's telling her to be careful about giving the wrong impression, even though she just published a porn poem in the school journal. I guess it has something to do with her scrubbed-clean face and feathery hair and the fact that she has hips but no boobs. Since she doesn't *look* like trouble, she can have all the sex she wants and still have friends.

She can even, apparently, publish erotic poetry about it and still be a teacher's pet and Alison and Jemma's new best friend.

I couldn't be more of a virgin, but somehow I'm the one who's changed.

These are the kinds of conundrums that slow down my shift at Tea Cozy the Sunday after Sasha's poem hit the school. I'm trying to wipe down tables and refill cups of water, but I keep managing to do the same ones over and over. Plus, Cate is playing kids' music on the café's iPod, and the way it jingles out from the speakers is completely distracting.

Everyone around me is struggling to understand the tinny chipmunk tunes, so the only upside of work today is watching all their confused adult faces wrinkle and wonder at the lullaby-chipmunk-princess song playlist while they try to enjoy their hot teas.

I bring my laptop to the counter and log back on to the website from the Red Pen Note Taker. I don't want to click on the links with Cate and Paul watching me so closely, but I can't stop staring at the spinning spiral or the name Life by Committee or the logline underneath the title: *We can do a little alone. We can do a lot together. Be more.*

It sounds like a commercial for the army or for Nike, but it also hits the saddest parts of me. I would like to be more. Especially since right now I am boring Tabby who sits and waits for Joe to pay attention to me and who lets Jemma say horrible things to my face with zero repercussions, aside from my father depriving her of cookies.

Be more. I turn the phrase over in my head. I can almost see a better version of myself. She has longer legs and a cute smirk and sends racy text messages and doesn't give a crap what anyone thinks.

She is out of reach right now, but maybe I could, somehow, be more. Be her.

Aside from the title and text and the dizzying spiral, the only other thing on the page is a picture of skinny freckled legs connected to tiny feet wearing shiny red shoes. Patent leather. Thick heels.

T-strap. Vaguely reminiscent of a hipster Dorothy in an alternative *Wizard of Oz* situation.

It makes me smile.

In the middle of a rousing rendition of "The Teddy Bears' Picnic," I notice Joe hiding behind his Spanish textbook. He's in one of the overstuffed armchairs that Cate keeps by the constantly blazing fireplace. He looks sheepish, which means Sasha suggested meeting here and he couldn't come up with a valid reason why not to. It also means Sasha doesn't know about me yet, which is either an enormous relief or a sobering reality. I can't seem to decide.

I inch away from him, doing my best to hide my face from his line of sight so he won't notice that I'm barely keeping it together. *WHY HAVEN'T YOU BEEN ONLINE IN A MILLION DAYS?* I want to yell. But knowing that would be a huge mistake, I say nothing at all. I'm an all-or-nothing kind of girl today.

"Your friend Joe's visiting you!" Cate says. She saw us chatting outside school one day and has decided he's my hope for friendship. "We're not too busy. You can hang out for a sec." She gives me an encouraging smile and waves to him. If I hadn't been ditched by all my friends two months ago, she wouldn't be so brimming with joy at the sight of brutish Joe, who she knows is crazy Sasha's boyfriend, but with things the way they are, she's practically panting, golden retriever style, at the prospect of me having someone to talk to.

"That's okay," I say.

Cate looks at me funny. "Please tell me he's not giving you trouble, too," she says. "He seems like such a nice boy. And I know you don't *like* him like him, but having male friends can be really—"

I sigh, loudly, before she can finish her thought.

"Cate," I whine out, and her hand goes to her stomach and her eyes go as deep-down far as they can into my gaze and I have to tell her everything's fine and then bring Joe a peanut butter cookie like the total asshole I am.

"Can we pretend to talk for a minute? My mom's driving me insane," I say when I get to his chair. Sasha's coming any minute, and there's no way he wants me to sit down at his table or anything. He nods, though, and maybe a little bit of the way he looked at me Tuesday night in my bedroom is still in his eyes, because I can't seem to stop the flutter in my throat from going batshit crazy.

The better version of Tabitha would take him by the hand and lead him to the backyard of Tea Cozy and grab his face and kiss him like crazy. The better version of Tabitha would tell him he can't even look at me until he ends things with her. The better version of Tabitha probably wouldn't even be at Tea Cozy, actually. She would be doing something fabulous in New York City and not caring at all about anything in Vermont.

"We don't have to pretend to talk," he says after an awkward pause. "We can be friends, right? We can be . . . something." It's the pause before the word "something" that causes the big burst of simultaneous hurt and hope. He's not actually letting me go, and I'm not wrong about the intense way he's staring at my lips. I wonder if he's remembering all the things we told each other or thinking about his hands in my hair.

Both of us think mountains are overrated. Does he remember that?

The fire's hitting my back, which is always at first cozy and then turns into a sting that you have to step away from. I slide over a bit, but the second that sting is gone, I miss the warmth. I slide back into place. Screw it. I'll just get burned.

"We can be something?" I say, and hate myself for repeating his words and for being this girl right now. Belle and Sebastian whistles through the speakers, the sound of sweet indie love, and I could kill Cate for obviously changing the playlist to suit my mood.

"Something," he says, and now we're caught in a loop of longing and regret and an unidentifiable third thing . . . is that deceit? Danger? I don't know, but it makes Sasha's stupid poem run through my head again. I flush, which Joe must take as a good sign, because he reaches out and brushes my fingers with his. It is the smallest and best gesture imaginable.

"Hey," he says, and it's so quiet I take a step closer in. The heat from the fire singes the backs of my legs. I'm uncomfortable, but I just can't step away. "Please don't hate me. I couldn't take that. You know I feel—"

But the door opens and I recognize the sound of Sasha entering, because she sighs when she enters a room. She sighs so much, I think it might be her way of breathing, but Tea Cozy is tiny and I don't have to look to know that the pretty, half-vocalized exhale expelled right in time with the chimes on the door belongs to her.

The leap in my chest makes me grab at Joe's fingers, but that of course makes him pull his hand away, and the result is an awkward moment when I lose my balance a little and my hand grips into a fist and the cookie I never set down on the table falls from the plate to the floor.

"You really couldn't meet somewhere else?" I hiss, choosing *now* to get pissed at him, even though Sasha can probably hear the tail end of what I've said.

"Oh my gosh! You dropped something!" Sasha says in her breathy, always-surprised voice. "Joe, were you buying me a cookie?" She leans over to kiss him on the mouth before he has a chance to answer.

I can't look away.

"Joe knows I love cookies," Sasha says. Then she giggles, as if what she's said is dangerous or quirky or adorable or in any way even remotely unique.

Doesn't everyone like cookies? Isn't that more or less the actual definition of the word *cookie*?

"Oh," I eke out. "That's sweet of him." Sasha bats her eyes like a cartoon-character version of herself and smushes into the armchair with Joe, so that the two of them are piled on top of each other.

Joe's not correcting her, not telling her I brought the cookie over myself, or that it was some other table's cookie or anything. He's actually going to sit there while she rubs his thigh and take the credit. Still looking sheepish at least, but mute, too. He keeps pressing his lips together and opening them again, like a fish who gets less attractive by the minute.

What's the word for being red-hot-angry and kind of shamefully in love at the same time? That. That is what I am feeling right now, while Belle and Sebastian sing what should be my anthem, "Get Me Away from Here, I'm Dying."

"Can you bring a replacement cookie?" Sasha says. I hadn't even realized I was still standing here.

"Oh, sure," I say. Sasha giggles again and blushes. There is no reasonable explanation for the sudden modest flush on her cheeks, but Joe likes it, that much is obvious. He brushes some hair out of her face. He smiles like she is a child and he must take good care of her. All that *and* she's a fragile, emotionally disturbed sex addict, apparently. I am rocked with the understanding that I can never compete, no matter how low my shirt is or how silky and straight I get my hair or how dark and screw-you my eyeliner is. I have the cleavage and the make-up, but Sasha has the little-girl voice and the mystical-creature look and has actual sex. She doesn't need cleavage, I guess. My toes turn in toward each other, and I cannot think of a single word to say or a single move to make.

I clear my throat and hate the fact that I am weirdly shy in any situation that actually matters.

"I'll help you pick one out," Joe says, unwrapping himself from Sasha's legs just as I have taken one half step away from Sasha and her watery eyes. It's only a few steps to the counter where we keep the extensive cookie selection, but it feels marathon long. After my seriously heated stare, Cate gets the hint to move to the other end of the counter. Her eyes flit to Sasha Cotton, to Joe, to me, to the cookies, and then to Paul. I stare harder, until she turns away and busies herself with unsticking a bottle of honey.

"I'm sorry," Joe whispers as we gaze at the oversize cookies and superthick brownies in the display case. "You hate me."

"I don't hate you," I say, and roll my eyes at myself. I take a huge inhale and let the exhale out in a perfect slow stream of breath.

"I know this all sucks," he says. If Sasha strained, she could hear us, I'm sure. "Let me get you a cookie. I'll buy you whatever you want."

"It's my family's café. You remember that, right?" I pull out our worst cookie for Sasha: it's vegan and overstuffed with dried cranberries. I call it a pregnancy creation, since Cate came up with it to satisfy a craving and is the only person who actually enjoys it.

"Right. Of course," Joe says. He's squirming, and I like it. Yes, his gaze keeps traveling back to Sasha and the armchair and the fire, but he stalls next to me. Shuffles in a little closer. Cups a hand over mine and squeezes. "Well, I'll buy you a cookie somewhere else sometime soon, okay?"

His hand is warm and his voice is so low and close, I can feel the breath and vibration of it on my neck.

"Please don't hate me," he says. His eyes meet mine, and they are coffee brown and watery with feeling. His long lashes look both beautiful and absurd on his stubbly, thick-jawed face.

"I wish I could," I say at last. Joe's hand leaves mine, and he gives me a half smile before finding his way back to Sasha with the crappy vegan cookie and another smile that I guess is made just for her. What was so full a moment ago is immediately empty when he's not locked on me anymore, and I have to close my eyes for a breath at the counter before returning to the chaos of the café and the rest of my life. I consider logging back onto that website, with the silver font and the freckled knees and the cryptic deep thoughts. I could use some escape.

Sasha squeals like Joe is tickling her, and the sound travels from the base of my spine all the way to my mess of hair.

I'm boiling with how much I hate Joe. Also: how much I love him. And hate myself. And love how he makes me feel. So there's a lot going on inside, and it's starting to show in the way my fingers and arms are starting to shake.

"I need a break," I say when Cate slides back behind the counter a moment later. Not that I've been working hard anyway, but she softens her mouth and opens her eyes up wide and nods like I'm the saddest girl in the world and can have whatever I want if it will just maybe make me smile.

And maybe I am the saddest girl in the world. Maybe, right now, I'm even sadder than sad, sad Sasha Cotton.

We have a breakfast bar set up in front of the registers—a few tall, wobbly stools in a line so people can sit at the counter like at an old-time diner. I take a stool and reread conversations Joe and I had over the last month. It's torture and I know better, but I can't stop clicking through them, searching for clues to I don't know what.

At the end of September, a little over one month ago, Joe told me he liked my new haircut and he'd never noticed how blue my eyes were until that very day. He told me Sasha wasn't as much fun as me. He told me he'd had a dream about me.

I glance behind me when I reread that chat conversation, to see if

Joe and Sasha are maybe somehow looking this way. But they're not. They're locked in some kind of extensive eye contact, and then Sasha starts breaking pieces of cookie off and feeding them to Joe. He does the same to her, and she giggles every time in total surprise. This *cannot* be the same guy who told me I'm "incredible."

This cannot be the same guy who I sort of considered showing my life-changing copy of *The Secret Garden* to.

Anyway, Joe can probably only stomach that shitty cookie because he's high. I have a nose for that particular smell, and it was rubbed into his fingers, wafting off his neck. I don't know what Sasha Cotton's excuse is, but she licks her finger after every bite, like it's chocolate chip and not pregnant-lady vegan-creation. The woman sitting next to me, a regular who seems nice, with thick bangs and a dozen strands of turquoise beads hanging from her neck, smirks. She's noticed how annoying Sasha is too.

In my ideal world, the Red Margin Note Taker looks exactly like Bangs 'n' Beads here.

I email Elise: *Sudden realization. Sasha Cotton has man hands.* Elise probably won't respond, because she doesn't really like when I get bitchy about other girls. Girl power or something, I don't know. She'll probably just send back a smiley face or ask me if I'm okay. I love Elise, but when I need to say terrible things about Sasha Cotton, it's Jemma I really miss. She was jealous and angry and bitter and judgmental too.

I flip back to an old chat with Joe and try to remember what it felt like to have him telling me I was special.

"Okay, no more computer," Cate says, swooping in and pressing her face close to mine. "You're getting all worked up. We're losing business." She's smiling, but I know she's serious too, and I can feel my heart going crazy underneath my bulky wool sweater (I still rock the cozy winter wear even if I like a deep V-neck. I mean Vermont in November is no joke). Adrenaline. Serious, heart-pumping, hand-shaking adrenaline. I'm on it. Plus the coffee I keep refilling. I take a deep breath and Cate rubs my shoulders.

"Sorry," I say. "Got caught up in stuff."

"They're gone," Cate says, and I give in to a rush of relief that Joe and Sasha are no longer right behind me, living out some deep and tragic love story. My whole body relaxes.

"Oh, no, I mean, I don't care about—" I try. It's awkward. Cate's face is stuck in that gentle-pity mode.

"Jemma and Alison should really stop coming here," she continues. "Paul said it the other day and I thought he was just being . . . Paul. But he's right. It's not fair to you. It's mean." I stare at her blankly for a moment before realizing she actually *isn't* psychic after all. I hadn't even known Jemma had come back today. But Cate's looking at me all proud and expectant, like she is Mother of the Year for figuring out what's gotten me all worked up.

I give a smile that takes approximately as much energy to muster as running a marathon would. Give a quick glance to see that Joe and Sasha are still here, of course.

"You gotta get over those bitches," Cate says. I love her for it. For the words she chooses and the secret way she whispers them into my ear. But she's looking at me like she *gets* me, and there's nothing lonelier than the fact that she doesn't.

"Thanks," I say, and Cate closes my computer screen for me and heads back to the counter and I'm alone.

I reach into my bag and make sure *The Secret Garden* is still in there. That there is actual evidence of someone in the world totally getting me.

"I love you," I hear Joe say behind me. If I closed my eyes, I could pretend he was saying it to me. But then there's Sasha's ridiculous giggle, and the whole fantasy vanishes so fast, I lose my breath.

That night I hole up in Cate's office as usual.

Elise and I chat about the meeting she had Friday with our impressively ignorant school counselor, Mrs. Drake, who passive-aggressively asked her about her dating life before launching into a speech about Elise's chances of getting into an Ivy League school.

I ask Elise if she'd stand up to Mrs. Drake if she had a whole group behind her. If she thinks maybe people can do more if they act together.

There's a long pause, a smiley face emoticon, and a vague *uh sure?* But I was hoping for more.

Elise logs off, and I stare at the screen waiting for Joe for another few, full, heavy minutes. He's never missed this much time, and I feel an inside itch at the thought of him not coming on at all.

I know what to do. I know because I want Elise to approve of me, and I want Cate and Paul to be right about their idea that I am special and good. I know what to do mostly because it hurts too much to sit here waiting for Joe.

I write him an email.

Hey. This is wrong. So we can't. It's not who I am.

It feels good, writing it out. It's the Right Thing to Do. I'm relieved, thinking I can sit back and cry in the bathroom every time Joe and Sasha kiss or make googly eyes at each other in Tea Cozy. I can be sad and lonely and not have to worry about anyone being angry at me.

I won't be a bad girl anymore. I won't be a cheating immoral person. I'll be regular, comfortable Tabby. The one Jemma and Alison and everyone else want me to be.

The inside itch doesn't go away after I send the email, though. I'm relieved that I have stopped something terrible and amazing from slowly destroying me, but now the mountains seem even larger, Cate's office is even smaller, and I am even further away from liking my life.

It's that itch that makes me type in the website from the book again. The site comes to life in blue and gold and silver. The freckled knees and Dorothy shoes make me smile even harder than they did the first time.

This is the first time I've seen the site on my computer and have had a moment to really look at it. I click on the "Members" link and hold my breath. There's a list of nicknames, and a picture of each one from the knees down. About a dozen members, apparently.

The spiral logo twists and turns, animated, and the whole site is practically breathing.

I make a profile. Call myself by the nickname my parents have been using since I was small: Bitty. Take a picture of myself from the knees down: worn jeans and gold ballet flats. **No names**, it says. **No locations. We are from everywhere. We are everyone.**

I vaguely remember a Morning Assembly we had about how Google can track all our searches and privacy doesn't really exist online. But with a fake name and only, like, a dozen people belonging to the site, it doesn't fit any of the "red flags" that lecturer talked about (credit cards, identifying pictures, meeting up with people you've never met in real life, webcams).

And then it tells me I have to share a secret. One secret, big or small, to join the group.

Secret:

I kissed someone else's boyfriend.

—Bitty

Seven.

It's past midnight. Joe hasn't logged on all night, and Sasha's poem is still streaming on an endless loop in my mind. But I'm blocking it out by sifting through random secrets posted on the site, while reading and rereading the list of rules that are firmly stated on every page.

> **RULE ONE:** Post at least one secret a week to keep your membership active.
> **RULE TWO:** Assignments will be given for every secret. Assignments must be completed within twenty-four hours to keep membership active.
> **RULE THREE:** An active membership is the only way to protect your secrets.

The rules didn't appear until after my secret was posted, which is sort of not the best. It's also too late to ponder them, and besides, according to everything I'm skimming, these Assignments are intended to better people's lives, and I'm nothing if not in need of some betterment. So I swallow down the little instant of worry, remember they don't have any of my identifying information, and decide that it's fine. And anonymous. So I can stay calm. All Zen-like. Paul and Cate would be so proud.

Also, Joe often talks about taking risks. He wants to go skydiving for his eighteenth birthday and likes snowboarding and meeting new people and really spicy foods. And, of course, weed. He typed fast when he was telling me about all of these passions, and I just reread that conversation earlier today. I think Joe would like Life by Committee, and that makes me less scared of it.

Sort of.

Agnes is one of the more active members, so I zero in on her profile and her secrets. One of her knee-down pictures has her in black leggings that stop with a ribbon of lace just past her knees, no socks, and beat-up, possibly ironic penny loafers. Judging from her collection of faceless photos, she's from somewhere sunny and silly. Everything in the background is usually too green or too blue or too yellow. Never snow. Never the shadows of mountains. I wonder what living in a mountainless world would be like.

Nice, I think.

I'm so happy to be transported out of my head, I actually smile, which is a ridiculous thing to do when you're all by yourself. I can't help it: Cate says it's the mountains that make me feel trapped. Sometimes it's cozy, like the perfect nook in the expanse of the world, but right now, when everyone hates me, it's more like a crawl space I can't properly stretch in.

Poking around LBC makes me feel like I found a trapdoor, Tabitha-sized, to let me out of here.

I click through a bunch of the secrets the Agnes girl shared, then Roxie and someone going by Elfboy, and the leader, Zed, who always gives the official assignments. It's like reading someone's diary, except other members can comment on each secret.

Agnes has this strange, lonely, squirrely life that I pity so much, it's almost uncomfortable to keep reading.

Secret: I like my father more than my mother.

Secret: My mother keeps calling her doctor's office and leaving messages. I listen in as often as I can.

Secret: I know my mother is snooping in my room and taking things, so I'm snooping in hers.

Secret: My mother told me to go on a diet.

Secret: I lie to my boyfriend. Often.

Secret: I picked up a pamphlet on depression and another on birth control and a third on anorexia when the school nurse stepped out of the room.

After every one of the secrets, there's a discussion with all the other members, a list of comments ranging from the brief (smiley face) to the lengthy (an in-depth retelling of Roxie lying to her boyfriend about her age when she was fifteen and he was twenty). After the comments, there's always a silver-fonted post from Zed titled

ASSIGNMENT. He seems to take the conversation of the members into consideration, then construct an Assignment that addresses the secret and the members' feelings about the secret.

Zed posts secrets too, but he lets the community discuss his options and come up with an Assignment. If a majority of members agree, he'll do what they've come up with.

I guess that's what Life by Committee is. And with a mother like Agnes's, who steals her books and her journals and anything she decides is "too troubling" or "informative about her emotional state" and takes them to Agnes's doctor, it's obvious LBC is a serious safe haven.

> **SECRET:** I don't want to go to college.
>
> **ASSIGNMENT:** Apply to do a year of volunteering before college in Africa or Honduras or Romania. There's more to life than the path everyone is told to take. Do it differently.

I wonder if Agnes will do it. If she'll work in an orphanage in Romania and become a bigger, better person before college. I wonder how seriously they take these Assignments.

It must be pretty serious. She posts a link to a service program and says she's filling it out immediately. I am watching someone change her life, just like that.

Sometimes there are only written descriptions of how Assignments went, but often Zed seems to require "proof." Without faces and with so much anonymity, "proof" only really goes so far, but it looks like everyone takes it seriously.

This chick I am totally girl-crushing on, Star, posts pictures of her Assignments, filtered with some kind of vintage-y green look, and they all look vaguely magical and strange. There's one of her feet, and each toe is wearing an expensive-looking ring. Diamond. Emerald. Sapphire. Ruby. I guess she's sort of this major klepto. I like that she has her own style of picture taking. Agnes's pictures are more straightforward. Roxie uses audio files. Elfboy obviously has some crappy old-school camera and an even crappier scanner, because his photos are all blurry and pixelated. @sshole draws pictures, which isn't proof exactly, but he's been a member for years, so no one is questioning it, I guess.

A girl named Brenda (seriously? Brenda is your magical nickname?) has amazing photos. Like every photograph on the site, they are faceless. Usually knees-down, sometimes neck-down, expertly anonymous. Hers are black and white, classically beautiful, and obviously taken on a real camera, not a phone. One Assignment Zed gave her was to crash her estranged father's wedding, and she did it in an actual wedding gown. Her *mother's* old wedding gown. She managed a photograph of the cumbersome gown and its long train as she stepped off a horse-drawn carriage she hired for the event.

I'm dying to see her face. I'm dying to see all their faces. It's strange, entering into their faceless universe. Unsettling. Cool.

In the best photo she's lifting the gown, so we can see her sneakers underneath.

It's in black and white, except for the purple sneakers. I mean, it's basically the best photograph I've ever seen. Her description of completing the Assignment is great too. I can't stop cringing, reading it. She says she could see every realization on her father's face: the fact that his daughter was there, the fact that she was wearing a wedding gown, the fact that it was the wedding gown of the woman he last married.

It was bad for a while. Her dad was obviously pissed. Like, shaking-with-anger, wouldn't-return-her-phone-calls-for-months pissed. But he ended up not marrying the obviously evil would-be stepmother, because she flipped out when Brenda made a scene. And from what I can gather, when the anger faded, he realized that he'd been ignoring Brenda and started making an effort to see more of her.

BRENDA: I did something. An unfixable problem got solved. My dad's making steak tonight. For me and him. He's making pancakes for dessert, since he knows those are my favorite foods. Steak and pancake dinner with my father. WTF life is crazy.

A few days later, Brenda posted a picture of steak and pancakes on a huge ceramic plate. I laugh out loud. My eyes go a little watery.

BITTY: YES!

It's like dipping a pinkie toe in the waters. The picture is from a week ago, and I'm not exactly adding to the conversation, but it's something. It's saying, I don't know, maybe I'm ready. Maybe I'm one of you.

I click over to Star's profile, to see if she's as ridiculously cool as what little I've seen of her so far suggests. She's in college, which about half the members seem to be. She uses a lot of caps locks and comments on other people's posts pretty often. Her picture is barefoot and barelegged. Freckled knees and red toenails stretched out in the sand. Her most recent secret (posted just an hour ago) intrigues me:

> **Secret:** I'm obsessed with someone who lives across the country and probably forgets my name.

When my eyes start to hurt, I turn away from the computer for just a moment and notice my hands are clenched and my toes are cramping from the way I am scrunching them up in my slippers. It feels like my whole body is one huge fist with nothing to punch.

My screen reloads, and I see that a few people commented on Star's secret, and that Zed has already decided on an Assignment based on just an enthusiastic *Go for it* or two.

ASSIGNMENT, silvery bold font screams across the screen. **Go get him. Book a flight. Find him. Tell him you can't stop thinking about him.**

I smile.

Not because I think it's a great idea; I don't. But it is something someone in a movie would do, and it's scary and delightful and hopeful and sweet. And I guess everyone needs something hopeful. It may be a crazy-person thing to do, but at least it's powerful and optimistic.

I tear up, the way I do watching the end of *Pretty Woman*, when Richard Gere climbs up the fire escape and Julia Roberts lets him meet her up there, and her smile is so big and toothy and absurd that life seems like it might actually be mostly good instead of mostly annoying.

STAR: Ticket bought.

I look around the room like maybe she's hiding somewhere in here. The words popped up and the whole story is unfolding in front of me, but it's *not* a movie, and Star is *not* Julia Roberts, although Zed is basically Cupid, apparently. A laugh rises from my belly straight to my mouth, but I hold it in and let it hum on my lips. Between the buzz of the unsurrendered giggle and the head-swirling tears, I'm temporarily just a snow globe of feelings and not a person at all. And that feels *good*. Because it's hope, mostly, that's coursing through me.

It's weird that I care at all. For all I know, Star's not even telling the truth. She can pretend to be on some romantic transcontinental journey and really be sitting in some sad bedroom in some sad city far away.

There's a shiver inside me.

I'm surprised at how badly I want Star and her Assignment to be real. I need it to be happening. I need there to be a whole mess of craziness and loveliness and unexpected steak and pancakes and red Mary Janes and plane tickets and secrets beyond the snowy mountains.

My screen scrambles again. Life by Committee is telling me I have new comments on the secret I posted.

Underneath my confession about kissing someone's boyfriend, a few people have asked how I feel about the guy, and some others have expressed concern for the poor, wronged girlfriend.

And underneath all that, Zed has infiltrated with his thick, silvery font. **ASSIGNMENT**, it reads. I rev into heartbeat overdrive. Which is silly—it's a game. If I don't like what he has to say, I just won't do it. I guess I'd pictured my secret dropping into the void, but something is happening and I'm too tired to stop it. I read what comes next: **Kiss Him Again**.

Secret:

I eat alone most nights. If I eat at all.

—Zed

Eight.

I'm not going to do it.

I've totally decided.

I can explain to the group that I've ended things with Joe, and that maybe losing me will bring him back to me eventually, and that I'm okay with that.

I can explain to them how I won't get to really appreciate the kissing until Joe has left Sasha. I'm a new member—they'll understand. They'll come up with a way for me to get Joe and Sasha to break up, and then I will happily, joyfully, ecstatically kiss him again.

I can explain that I can't kiss him again now and still be Bitty.

I fall asleep dreaming of the post I'll write to let them know I'll need a new Assignment, and I wake up at four in the morning and open the computer, to see if Joe responded to my email.

He didn't.

I log on to Life by Committee, but before I ask for a new

Assignment, I find myself back on Star's page, and even though it's only a few hours later, she's updated.

> **STAR:** I'm at the airport. It's the most romantic thing I've ever done, so I tied a silver scarf around my neck for the occasion and probably drenched myself in too much perfume, but I wanted to smell and look exactly the way I feel. I have on red high heels even though it's November, and I snuck my roommate's fur coat out of her closet.
> I've never seen *Casablanca*, but I'm pretty sure it's just like this. I feel like *Casablanca*. I feel unstoppable. And in love.
> So. Effing. In. Love.

There's a picture attached, neck down this time. A delicate silver necklace hangs far past her collarbone. Some kind of butterfly. Pretty and innocuous. Maybe Tiffany's. The airport in the background is a blur of bodies. There's a plaid suitcase in the bottom left corner. It could belong to anyone. She could be anywhere. Airports all look the same. But she's glamorous and messy and absurd, and I can tell, without seeing her face, with only really focusing on her stockinged knees, that she is happy. Reckless, but happy.

The other members post *X*s and *O*s and smiley faces and quotes from old romantic movies, which I only recognize because Cate has those movies on in the background when she's ironing.

I realize I'm licking my lips over and over in anticipation. They're dry now, and stinging a little. It's not like Star can show up on the other side of the country instantaneously. As of now she's just hours early for a morning flight, and reporting on every flutter of her heart as she waits for her life to change.

> **STAR:** Thank you, Zed. Thank you, LBC-ers. This is life—live it, right? Be more.

I try to decide what to type. I want to be part of whatever this moment is about to become. I want to be front and center, cheering her on. I tap words out but erase them. One step forward, two steps back, I guess.

Also, it occurs to me that maybe Star is my red-penned stranger. And it occurs to me that I want her to be.

> **BITTY:** This is the most romantic thing ever. And awesome shoes. You should bring a book of sonnets or something. Poems. Neruda. You read him? I guess he won't be at the airport, but you could go to a bookstore when you land. . . .

I press send on the message, even though these strangers will now be the first people to ever know what a romantic I am, aside from Cate and Paul. No one really knows what a good poem can do to me. I got into poetry the way I get into everything else I read, by looking at the margins. I have a book from a guy named Henry to a girl named Alice. He inscribed it. For their anniversary. Then, on the last blank page of the book, he wrote the lyrics to "Rainbow Connection." You know, the one Kermit the Frog sings. He said that was the most romantic thing he'd ever heard, and that every poem in there *plus* "Rainbow Connection" couldn't accurately describe how much he loved her.

I listened to "Rainbow Connection" on repeat for hours after I found that. And even now, I consider texting Joe to tell him to listen to the song or read a Neruda poem that reminds me of the way I feel about him, but I know better. No one's ready to see that side of me.

Except, apparently, a bunch of strangers from around the country who are taking over my computer.

Because before I know it, I've typed the story of Henry and Alice and Kermit the Frog and the things I never say to anyone into the comment box on Star's LBC page. I guess it's safe, to show this tiny part of myself here. Star has no idea who I even am. As far as I can tell, everyone stumbled into Life by Committee with equal degrees of randomness. **We don't pursue members,** Zed wrote on the Rules page. **We trust they will find us.** I want to ask if anyone else found the website in the back of a book, but I think it would give something away that I have to keep hidden.

Anyway, if I let them know who I am, they'll understand why I need a different Assignment.

"Tab?" Cate says, a disembodied voice from who knows where. She comes in to find me pajamaed and cross-legged and typing so fast and hard, it's basically a workout.

"Did I wake you?" I say. I want to click away from Star's page, but I don't want Cate to notice any flicker of fear, so I keep it up and hope she hasn't put in her contacts yet.

"No. The baby did." She touches her belly. "You need to get off that thing, babycakes." Cate hates computers and cell phones and anything remotely useful or modern.

"I know, I know."

"Want to go for a walk?"

"Now? It's fucking late."

"You're going to have to watch the language when the baby comes, Tab. We've been terrible influences." Like I'm some starter child they can mess up, but now that the baby's coming, they'll be doing things right.

"Yeah, okay. Let's walk," I say, instead of agreeing to watch my language or anything else she wants to change about me. It occurs to me that this is another secret. That I'm jealous of this unborn baby. That I don't feel all happy about the upcoming arrival. But that's a way worse secret to share than the thing about kissing Joe, and I don't need a bunch of strangers commenting on it.

I leave the Assignment be and vow to deal with it after I've gotten some air. Maybe a walk with Cate is exactly what I need. I log off and give a little half prayer to the gods of love that everything goes amazingly with Star and her mysterious long-distance guy. One of those smiles sneaks onto my face: the kind that happens without thinking. So rare, it makes me jump with surprise when I realize it's found its way to my mouth.

And we walk. Cate brings a flashlight, and neither of us changes out of our pajamas. We wear sneakers and winter jackets and can only see a foot ahead of us at a time. I like the way our legs end up striding in sync, and the unquestioning silence we fall into even though it's way too late on a school night for me to be up without being interrogated.

I stop paying attention to the direction we're walking in and trust Cate to take the lead.

"You okay, sweetness?" Cate says every three minutes or so, and I mm-hmm, and that, too, becomes part of the rhythm of our walking. That, too, becomes a reason to stop being afraid of what will happen when the baby is born.

Then, after all that dark, there's a pool of light. It's not too strong, just someone who's left their porch lights on, so the lawn and the house are partially lit.

"You have a destination in mind? Do we know anyone on Village Hill Road?" I ask, taking a look around and realizing what street we're on.

"Just wanted to get you away from that thing. Don't want you missing out on life because you're in front of that computer worrying." She turns off the flashlight, like we don't want to be seen, which maybe we don't. Anyone in town who runs into us now will be chatting and questioning and friendly, and that's not why we went on a late-night walk.

"I'm fine," I say, stiffening. She keeps on about me making new friends and getting out of the house and spending more time at Tea Cozy instead of on the computer, and it's not terrible, having her care, seeing her worry about me. It is that special mix of super annoying and totally heartwarming. Cate's gotten some burst of mothering energy, and I'm not used to it. Pregnancy has made her unpredictable—sometimes distant and spacey, sometimes full of energy and interest and sentiment.

"You have to push yourself," Cate says. I'm getting so uncomfortable with her pestering that I almost tell her about the website and the Assignments.

"I actually think I am going to try to push myself; it's sort of funny you brought it up—" I start, but something stops the words.

Because that's when I see it, a long ways down the road.

Not it. Her.

I know it's a her because when we are just that one step closer, the whole scene comes into focus. The dark is like that. One minute it's all shadows, the next minute your eyes adjust and the darkness shifts and you can see the world almost as well as you could in the light of day.

At first the shape is simply a person on a porch. But then it's something more. Not just a girl sitting under the porch lights in the middle of the night, but something actually much, much stranger. An almost naked girl, sitting on the front porch: so milky white and so curvy and so undeniably there. No top, but a long, ballerina-like skirt covering her legs. I must see her only a half moment before Cate does, because I hear Cate's gasp right after mine. Then, of course, Cate's quiet giggles.

The houses are close together and similarly shaped on Village Hill Road, so I can't immediately decipher whose house this is and who might therefore be on the porch.

Either that or I'm in denial.

"Oh my God," Cate says as quietly as she can with all the laughter pouring out of her. "Oh my *Christ*, what is happening?" She's even snorting a little. Cate's a big laugher and finds almost everything funny: little kids wearing designer clothes, old ladies in high-waisted pants, poorly translated Chinese food menus, the times when I have awkwardly caught her and Paul getting it on in unseemly locations like the kitchen or the shed. So of course she's laughing now.

I blush first and then join her laughter. It feels good, to laugh like that. I hope the wind and rustling of leaves and scurrying of animals cover our voices.

I have noticed something else: the mostly naked girl has costume fairy wings on. It adds a mystical, magical element to the whole scene, and I feel a familiar jealousy at how strange and special and sexy this person seems. The feeling grows when the girl gets up and starts dancing and twirling and swinging her hips.

I look around at the surrounding homes and get over the shock of a naked fairy dancing in the light of the porch. The image was so alarming, it distracted me from what is obvious about the house and the girl, what I already know. Because it makes perfect sense. There is only one family in our tiny town who would have a ridiculous purple door with gold moldings and a naked fairy-girl on the porch. And an available set of fairy wings. One more look, and yes, it's there. A camera set up on a tripod. And the now-unmistakable, soft shape of the winged girl in the distance.

I try to catch my breath, which has dropped from my lungs to my toes, where I can't access it. I wrap one arm around my belly. Some part of me is scared my guts will fall out if I don't hold them in with a skinny forearm.

It takes a little too long for my laughter to stop, so I'm laughing even after I've realized who it is, even though it stopped being funny.

It's Sasha Cotton's house. And that is Sasha holding her own breasts in her hands like a Playboy model but *not*. She has a sunflower behind her ear, and I would do anything to see the look on her face: Is it sexy or sad? Is it playful or serious? Maybe if I could see through the shadows to her facial expression, I'd know how to be that tragic sex kitten, instead of whatever I am now: cute and safe. I want to be loved and dangerous.

I flush with jealousy. My heart twists with it; I could never do what she's doing. I couldn't write the poem, I couldn't flit around topless late at night. I can't make Joe leap every time I call. This is so, so Sasha Cotton.

About a year ago, her mother had a yard sale, and Jemma and Alison and I went by. This was back when Jemma and I didn't like Sasha Cotton together. A different universe of time.

Everything at the yard sale was very Cotton family. Unicorn figurines. Pink wigs. Rare books. Fancy pens. Leg warmers. Piles of sheer scarves, patterns on top of patterns making new patterns. Old perfume bottles.

So seeing Sasha with wings and a ballet skirt and even no top is not surprising, exactly. But it's painful. It twists me up inside. It's the very representation of what makes Sasha fascinating and complicated, and me just kinda slutty.

I force my hand to find its way to my mother's mouth, since she won't stop laughing. We're close enough to be heard, if we're not careful. I want one more moment to look at Sasha; then we need to get the hell out of here so she doesn't see me seeing her. I'm also feeling a certainty that I need to cry. Not really cry: wail. The threat of it burns on my cheeks, my nose, my sleep-tasting mouth. The tears are right there: salty and on the surface. One or two even latch onto my eyelashes. But they don't spill; I can't do any of that right now. Cate lets her breathing regulate under the pressure of my palm on her lips, and I put my other hand to my chest, where all the feelings are whirring around.

Sasha moves her body into new shapes, and the camera must be set on some kind of autotimer, because it keeps flashing. The girl doesn't giggle at herself or move quickly or glance around, looking for Peeping Toms. She's wholly focused on one singular task: recording her body on film in whatever way she can; in every way she can, I guess. For Joe. It must be for Joe.

Cate ends up being the one who has to pull me away. I keep looking back, but I'm happy to be leaving. The image of naked, dancing Sasha is seared into my head, and it's already taking up so much room and telling me so many things to feel insecure about that it's just full-on lucky that Cate's getting me out of there before it can do any more damage.

"I always knew something was wrong with that girl," Cate whispers when we are a few blocks away. "And isn't she freezing? At least she could have worn, you know, earmuffs!" It's meant to be a joke. I imitate a laugh. We're walking at a much brisker pace, the sky lightening in tiny pre-sunrise increments. "Not okay," she says. My parents may be young and hip and disturbingly attractive, but they are not all "sex is a beautiful thing" the way Sasha's parents are. I get the feeling the reason Sasha wasn't looking around nervously isn't because she is so cool and confident, but because her parents actually wouldn't mind her doing a creepy sexy-angel photo shoot on the front lawn.

"Yeah" is the only word I can push out of my mouth.

"What the fuck?" Cate says, breaking her own rule about swearing. "Who does that girl think she is? We're in Vermont, not . . . Vegas."

"Typical Sasha Cotton," I say.

"Stay away from that one," Cate says, shaking her head and crossing her arms over her chest like she needs protecting from what she just saw. We both give an awkward laugh: I don't have to stay away from anyone; they're all staying away from me.

"Uh-huh," I say. My mouth is mostly closed over the sound. I'm feeling weak and tired and so, so tiny. Those pictures, I'm sure of it, are for Joe. I sigh loudly, like that will help expel all the terrible feelings sparking up in my chest and in my brain and all over my body.

But the feeling is too heavy to be quelled with a single deep sigh. It hangs on me.

The whole walk home, Cate keeps talking about "that naked Sasha girl" and I nod, and try to laugh or groan at the right moments, but really I'm shaking and spinning, knowing how far, far, far away I am from being that magical or free or enchanting. I am in a different universe from Sasha Cotton, who apparently can't feel the cold or the shame or the fear the rest of us do.

When we finally get back home, there's only one thing I absolutely must do: I need to get on Life by Committee and have something to think about aside from my own relative lameness. I need to believe in Star's romance and the power of a group, and someone else telling me how to fix the mess that is my life.

And then, before the day is up, I need to do my Assignment and kiss Joe again. Not because I have to. Not because I'm scared of the Rules. But because I want to, and now I have permission.

Sasha Cotton can be as weird and artsy and naked as she wants. But I have something better. I will be part of something bigger. I will do things and be more.

Secret:

I got my history paper off the internet.

—@sshole

Secret:

He wasn't my first. I told him he was.

—Agnes

Nine.

BITTY: Okay. I'll do it. I'll kiss the guy again. Assignment accepted, or something?

Cate and I alternate showers and hair drying and head out to Tea Cozy to open the café and fill up on tea and baked goods for cranky Monday-morning customers before I have to force myself to school.

By the time we drive into the Tea Cozy parking lot, Cate and I are wiping tears away. That's how hard we are still laughing about Sasha Cotton. It is one of the things I will miss most when this baby arrives. Coming early to the Cozy and making a batch of scones just for me, Cate, and Paul, before the customers get here. Bitching about my math teacher. Dissecting the latest thing Jemma did or said to me. Quoting our favorite lines from *The Princess Bride* over and over again. We open to customers at six thirty, so with Cate and me being early risers and morning lovers, we get to do this every week or two. Family tradition, I guess.

I know when the baby is born, the early mornings will be reserved for catching up on sleep or breast-feeding or cooing.

This morning I use batter we made yesterday to bake some chocolate chip scones, and while we wait for them to come out, Cate makes a pot of vanilla-rose tea. We keep the lights dim and set ourselves up in the blue paisley armchairs by the fire.

"Cute dress, by the way," she says when she gets up to grab the scones. She smiles, and it's weird to hear a real live compliment and not some passive-aggressive backstabby comment.

"I don't look like a slut?" I say.

"Uh, no?" Cate says, stopping midwalk to look at me again. "A slut? It's from the Gap. It's beige. You're in flats. And the thickest tights I've ever seen. Am I missing something? Is it backless?" She pretends to try to get a glimpse of my back, but I just shrug. It's short and I feel good in it, which I've decided must be wrong.

"Never mind," I say. I don't want Cate getting all riled up on a feminist tirade, but I also can't stop turning Jemma's comments over and over in my head.

"Hey," Cate says, emerging from the kitchen with scones and a fretting face. "You know, in my day the pretty girls with perky breasts were the popular ones, so I'm just trying to—" I cover my chest with my arms. The relative jauntiness of my breasts is not up for discussion.

I send an emergency text to Elise telling her to get her ass over here and that I'm saving her a scone and a cup of tea. She lives literally next door to Tea Cozy, and she is basically the best friend ever, so she's walking in the door minutes later. Cate's no dummy—she knows I've called in backup.

"Oh, Elise, good," she says. "Right on time." She winks at me and I sigh, but deep down I know she knows she's as close to a perfect mom as anyone's going to get.

"Thank God," I say to Elise when Cate's in the back getting ready to open. "She was talking about my boobs. Like, she's probably eager for customers to come in so she can ask them their opinions about them."

"No prob," Elise says, pulling at her pixie cut so that more little strands of auburn hair poke up. "I was actually gonna come by anyway." She doesn't laugh about Cate's ridiculousness, and I hate the air that follows. The last thing I want is something awkward and empty between us.

"You knew we had the chocolate chip scones today?" I ask, grinning. Dishes clink and clatter from behind the counter, and Cate's singing along with her rockabilly playlist, so we're safe to talk. Paul doesn't appear to be showing up anytime soon; maybe he didn't see our note yet.

"Well, sure, that," she says, before taking a big breath. "Also. Okay. Did you ever actually . . . follow through . . . on your feelings for Joe?" Elise is blushing, which I've never seen before, and I choke on my tea and feel the back of my neck go instantly damp and hot. I pull my hair into a ponytail. It's gotten really long and even blonder—probably another sign of my sluttiness.

"Act on my feelings?" I say, trying to buy a little time before having to answer. I'm not the best liar, and more importantly, I *hate* lying.

"Some people are saying—"

"Which people?"

"Sasha's friends mostly. People who like her. I dunno." I can't figure out the look on Elise's face. Maybe it's the unfamiliar flush washing over her that's making her suddenly unreadable, but for someone I know so well, she's definitely not knowable right now. I take a sip of tea and try to unblock my mind. It's all swimming and out of focus in there—I can't make it work for me.

"Jemma, I assume? I mean, let's not sugarcoat."

"I mean, I guess Jemma, yeah."

"I don't know why she's all worried about what me and my slutty non-A-cups are up to." I know I didn't answer Elise's question. But I'm thinking about my Assignment and the fact that she should be worried. It's a terrible thing to feel good about.

"So the answer is no? To you and Joe hooking up?" she says. They are careful words.

"Right," I say. I will myself not to blush. But it feels lonely, to lie to her.

"Okay," she says. "Just thought I'd check."

"Okay," I say, and we don't make eye contact for a while.

"Hey, if you did do anything . . . You know I'd still effing love you, right?" she says when the scone is mostly a pile of crumbs.

I didn't really know that, and it's so like Elise to tell me what I need to hear, the second I need to hear it, and surprise the hell out of me.

"I effing love you too," I say. But I still can't tell her the truth.

I excuse myself to go get one more scone, and check LBC while I'm alone in the back kitchen area. I am not all alone with my secrets. There are people in towns with cactuses and lighthouses and palm trees and wheat fields who know something important about me. And are watching me, from afar.

It sounds weird, but I think this is how people feel about God. Like he's watching and is in everything and is everywhere, giving purpose to the parts of your life that have started to feel stale or strange or too sad.

There's an encouraging comment from Agnes and another from @sshole, reminding me that sometimes doing the wrong thing is actually the right thing.

ROXIE: We aren't here to judge. We're here to get you to the next level.

I picture a video game where your bikini-wearing avatar moves from a dungeon scene to a poisonous flower scene, where the move to the next level brings a new soundtrack, new dangers, bigger prizes, surprising terrains.

I guess I am a little tired of my current scenery. I guess I am ready to take a flying leap to the next level.

BRENDA: We'll be right there with you.

Right before eight Elise drives us to school from Tea Cozy, and I try to remember to breathe and talk like a normal person. Of course we run into Sasha and Joe right after assembly. Sasha's sitting in Joe's lap on the bench outside the auditorium, and she's whispering into his ear and he's blushing. No teachers are around, or the cuddling would have to stop. The teachers manage to ignore the sexual harassment, but not the cuddling. Vermont values, at their best.

I try not to look. The combination of jealousy and white-hot pain is basically unbearable.

Joe isn't looking either. He never responded to my email, and he's looking everywhere but my direction.

Instead of obsessively watching them, I check LBC once again. There's that little red exclamation point that means something is *happening*. There's a countdown on my page. A countdown from Zed.

Twenty-four hours from the time the Assignment is given, the message reads. **You're on hour seven.**

My heart's going batshit crazy in my chest. I think of Joe's lips and the conversation I just had with Elise and wonder how both things can exist in one world.

"What if you dated, like, Greg Granger?" Elise says while she hangs her coat up in her locker. "I've seen him check you out. And he's smart. He's in my English class."

"His name is Greg Granger," I say. I'd laugh, but there's too much tightness in my chest to get out even a grunt. "Are you matchmaking now?"

"Oh! Adam Furlan!" Elise says. I glance up from my phone and raise my eyebrows.

"I'm not, like, desperate for a boyfriend," I say. Elise looks disappointed and tries to sneak a glance at my phone. I'm sure she thinks it's Joe. I'm sure she doesn't believe me.

"I guess I'm trying to say there are seriously a million guys you could go for, you know? And I want school to suck less for you. And I want everyone to lay off your shit. . . ."

Jemma walks by with Alison, and Elise cringes. Jumps in front of me, like she needs to shield them from my sluttiness. Alison's got on some outfit her mother picked out for her, and Jemma's in her purple hoodie today and jeans that go all the way up to her waist instead of hanging on her hips. It's not the height of fashion or anything, but she looks good to me. Safe. Familiar. Expected. But they look at my beige dress and hot-pink scarf with masterful, practiced hatred. I guess there's no hiding my C cups anymore. But *come on*, I want to say.

"How bad is this rumor, seriously?" I whisper in Elise's ear. She's acting like I'm about to get scarlet-lettered or something.

"I mean, people trust Jemma. She's not exactly a rampant rumor spreader. So. When she says something's shady . . ." Elise looks at her feet.

"Has Sasha heard anything?" I don't know what I want the answer to be. Both answers suck. And are great.

"No. It's Sasha. She's, you know, too busy being Sasha Cotton." We never clarify what this means, but obviously we all agree that Sasha

Cotton exists in some realm above the rest of us, where she doesn't bother herself with normal human facts like how long it takes for water to boil, or who the vice president is, or which reality show star we are all in love with, or what people at school are saying about her.

Elise pats my back before heading down the hallway, but I think I can see a flicker of not-believing in the way she looks at me. The particular stiffness of her hand tapping my shoulder. She's not going to stick by me no matter what. I can tell. She'll judge me. At the end of the day, she thinks Sasha Cotton is sweeter and purer than me, too.

I watch the school counselor, Mrs. Drake, walk down the hallway.

Mrs. Drake is my parents' age, and I've seen her high before. She hates this about me. When you have young parents who like to "socialize," you see a lot of things you probably shouldn't. Our town is tiny, after all, and there are only so many people my parents' age. So there's a postal worker and a yoga teacher and the gallery owner and, one time, Mrs. Drake, who all come to the house for wine and cheese, but that has on occasion turned into weed in the backyard.

"Let's chat at the end of the day," Mrs. Drake says when she reaches me. I know from the way she looks at the shortness of my dress exactly what our chat will be about.

"About what?" I ask anyway.

"Nothing scary, I promise," Mrs. Drake says with a firm hand on my shoulder. I shrug, which I guess is a tacit agreement, because Mrs. Drake walks away. Jemma and Alison kept their distance during the conversation, but they're not exactly hidden from view. I meet Jemma's gaze.

We hold eye contact, but her face is softer than I would have thought. It's not a challenge, the weird extended staring. It's something else. Like wistfulness. I take a step toward them. I have no intention of saying anything at all, but the words come out anyway.

"What's the endgame here? What are you hoping to accomplish?" I ask. Jemma is still a few yards away, and I say it quietly, so I'm not sure if she even hears. Alison busies herself with textbooks and her laptop and her shoelaces to avoid eye contact.

"I don't— I'm not—" Jemma is not usually one to stutter or stumble over her words.

"I already feel like I suck, so, you know, mission accomplished. Is there anything else you'd like to do to me?" I regret admitting to that self-hatred. My friend Jemma would have comforted me, but my nemesis Jemma will totally use it against me.

"That's not— I'm not even sure— You're turning it all around." Jemma keeps shaking her head as she turns a corner into a classroom.

It's been so long since I've seen the part of Jemma that is unsure and vulnerable that I'd forgotten what it looks like on her. The moment she's out of view, I miss her. We used to stay up really late and talk about what in the world made us saddest, what embarrassed us most, what we hated about ourselves. For me it was the way I couldn't help being jealous when other people were happy. For Jemma it was the fact that she sometimes cared what other people thought, even though she knew she was too smart to care.

I wonder if she remembers all that.

After math and before bio, I log back on to LBC. I have another countdown announcement from Zed, who informs me of every passing hour.

Thirteen hours to go. Will you make it?

There is a sloppy mixture of fear and thrill inside me. I am going to kiss Joe again. I am going to feel his hands in my hair. I am going to change the course of my life and go for what I really want.

My toes scrunch with anticipation, so I distract myself by reading Star's latest post from the road.

STAR: Love.
When I showed up at his apartment, he was in pajamas and smiling hard. Hugged me harder. Kissed me hardest. Thank you isn't enough. California Love. xoxoxoxox.

Attached to the post is a picture of Star's feet, sans red heels, tucked under some guy's thighs. There's something beautiful about trying to capture a moment without a face, and Star is an expert. Again, her knees are in the shot, and I know from the way they lean against each other, askew, that she is sleepy-eyed and blissful. When Joe and I kissed, our knees touched, and the shock went from that joint to my head, where it made me dizzy and exhausted. I know what knees can do.

And now, I guess, I know the best of what Life by Committee can do. What Zed can do. I pray again that somehow Star is the one who wrote in *The Secret Garden*, and that her words are the ones that brought me to Life by Committee. That would shrink my loneliness even further. It could become almost manageable if that were the case.

So I'm in. I have to be in. What else do I have?

Joe and I have a free period together in the afternoon. We could do homework, but Circle Community doesn't enforce any activity on a free period, as long as you are on school grounds. You get them because you've earned them, and sometimes I'll read or catch up on math homework. But usually I play hearts. Hearts has taken over the junior and senior classes, and I'm addicted. So is Joe. I guess it's maybe when I started falling for him. That competitive sort of sparring that turns into flirtation and then morphs into desperation when you realize how badly you want him and how taken he is.

Yep. That pretty much sums it up. Hearts. The card game that changed it all.

It's two p.m. and the last period of the day, so I've got eleven hours left to make something happen, and Joe is dealing cards out. Four people are already gathered around a little table, so I pull up a chair and sidle up next to him.

"Need help?" I say, smiling.

"Not really a team game, Tab," Joe says, keeping his gaze squarely on the cards and not letting his eyes dart even for an instant in my direction. I guess he didn't like my email. And maybe the avoiding eye contact is supposed to let me know that he's not interested, but it does the exact opposite. All I gather from that lack of eye contact is how scared he is. And how sad at the prospect of losing me.

"Then I'll watch," I say. I don't say it sexy or move any closer to him. I don't think I have to. I can just sit here and watch him and trust in the slow simmer between us leaping into a boil.

Joe doesn't respond except to bite his lip.

I watch. He keeps not looking my way. I lean in from time to time like I want to get a better look at his cards. I steel myself against the girls who look at me funny when they walk by. If I were Sasha I'd seduce him, or write him a sexy poem, or, if last night is any indication, slip him a naked picture of myself. But I can't do any of that. So I sit, and wait, and watch the game unfold play-by-play.

Until: The school day officially ends, and everyone puts their cards down, gets up to leave. Joe has to pack his cards back up, and while he does, I take his chin and press on it so that his face has to finally shift toward mine. It does not feel the way it looks when women in movies with hair extensions and diamond earrings do it, I can tell you that much. It's a lot more awkward, for one thing. He looks at me like I'm going to knock him out.

"Can we talk?" I say. There's a shake in my voice. It's not smooth. It's not pretty or breathy or low or intimate. And even as the words come out, I can feel that head-swell of feeling and the possibility of crying. I am becoming one of those crying girls, but only in theory, because I never actually let the tears out in public. Which is maybe a mistake, since it's apparently so becoming on Sasha Cotton, but I won't sink to her level.

He nods in agreement. I wasn't expecting it to be that easy. I was amped up for more convincing, so I let out a funny laugh. It's contextually awkward, but probably better than the crying or vomiting that my body is threatening to do, so I'll take it.

"Car?" I say. I need to get this done quickly so I don't miss my meeting with Mrs. Drake.

"No. That will look weird."

"Okay. Where?"

"Gym," he says. Which seems much weirder to me. Plus, it's a hike from here, a good seven-minute walk, since our campus is sprawled out over acres and acres of Vermont's finest land.

"Fine," I say anyway. I can do this anywhere.

And we start the walk down to the gym.

We don't talk. We keep a safe distance between us, like maybe we're walking together but maybe we aren't. Halfway there, Joe doesn't shift his gaze to meet mine, but he finally speaks up. His voice is a beacon in the cold November air. It interrupts the white-noise whooshing of wind.

"Okay," he says. "Talk."

I shake my head. "You said at the gym. We can have our talk at the gym." This is an unformed plan. I have never done something like this without a mapped-out strategy, a script in my head about how things will go. I breathe deeply while the silence between us stays put.

Once we're at the gym, Joe looks at me like he's expecting a beating, and for a minute that's all I want to do. I want to bitch him out, tell him how much I feel for him, how messed up what he's doing to me is, how ridiculous a human being Sasha Cotton is.

I want to beg him to be with me.

And I almost do it. I almost give in to the dizzy about-to-cry feeling and the shakiness of my limbs and the tough handsomeness of his face, and the way the very fact of him makes me feel: unhinged and furious and in the worst kind of love.

Almost. But I don't. Instead, I grab his face, feel the stubble on the palms of my hands, and thrill at the way he pulls back a little as I keep pulling his face to mine. His mouth to mine.

And then there it is. The lips, the berry taste, the heat inside, and even his rough cheeks burning up under my hands. He kisses back. Like he can't help it, and only with his mouth, at first. His hands don't reach under my shirt or through my hair. He doesn't slam himself against me. Until he does. Until the kiss takes over for both of us and we are lost in something warm and crazed and close.

BITTY: Assignment completed.

Secret:

I ran into the woman who almost married my father. I followed her through the mall for forty-five minutes. She bought a really ugly black dress. She called someone on the phone "baby." She dropped a receipt on the ground and I kept it.

—Brenda

Ten.

I walk back from the gym alone and keep rubbing my index finger back and forth over my lips. They're swollen from the last twenty minutes in the gym, and the boat-neck top of my dress is stretched out from where Joe tried to pull it down over my shoulders to get at the skinny, freckled blades.

I'm dizzy and my face hurts from where his stubble rubbed too hard against my chin. I thought I could only feel this way about someone who was actually *mine*.

I feel closer to Star, to her supersize romance and bravery. It's almost like she's watching me and smiling on. It's like we did it together, me and her and the rest of LBC and the worn and well-loved copy of *The Secret Garden* with all the answers to everything inside.

I start planning the epic poem I will write about the way his lips felt on mine and the beautiful danger of doing the wrong thing that may turn out to be right.

* * *

I get back to the main schoolhouse not too late for my meeting with Mrs. Drake. She lets me into her office and motions for me to sit down on the corduroy love seat while she crosses her legs and makes herself comfortable in her pleather armchair.

"I'm so glad you made it by, Tabitha," she starts. She's Cate's age, early thirties, and was definitely a gawky teenager in her day. She's got a long floral skirt and wire-framed glasses and curly brown hair. She looks like a preschool teacher. She looks exactly the way Jemma and Alison will look fifteen years from now.

"I can't stay for long—"

"I'm sure you have a little time to chat." She cocks her head and smiles, like I'm supposed to already know what we're going to talk about. "So," she says at last, "I want to start by saying I think you're very lucky to have so many people who care about you."

"Oh yes?" I say. Paul and I share a disdain for authority, and Cate says when I'm talking to teachers or policemen or librarians, I take on his subtly dismissive attitude. I guess I'm proving her right.

"Some of the girls are concerned about your reputation. Now I know you are a great kid who makes her parents very proud." She says this to remind me that she's cool. It's crap. She sniffs like her nose is stuffed up or something, but I don't buy that either. "But that said, your current . . . exploration . . . of your . . . adulthood . . . is making some students uncomfortable. And more importantly, worried about you." Mrs. Drake looks proud of herself. She is convinced that she has found a way to call me a slut without actually saying anything substantial.

"Exploration of my adulthood?" I tuck my hair behind my ears. I'm not even pretending not to understand or anything. But I want her to hear how insanely vague and strange that phrase is. "Like . . . I'm growing up too fast?"

"The way you're dressing, Tabitha," Mrs. Drake says, uncrossing her legs and leaning in closer to me. "The way you're carrying yourself. Now, we're not stodgy old fuddy-duddies here. We're not *conservatives*, of course. And you have the freedom to dress how you want."

"But?" I say.

"But I'm concerned about your relationships with other girls and maybe that you are being . . . naive."

"Naive," I say. No question mark. No need for her to answer. My legs itch all of a sudden, and I try to scratch with just one finger, but it's not enough. I start scratching my thigh kinda vigorously.

"Do *you* feel comfortable with the way you've been dressing?" Mrs. Drake says. Her eyes go to my thighs. It doesn't seem to matter that they are covered in tights.

"It's from the Gap," I say, echoing Cate.

"What kind of message do you think your clothes are projecting? I know things at your home can sometimes be rather . . . adult . . . and I want to encourage you to stay in childhood as long as you can."

My mouth goes dry and our eyes meet. She is daring me to counter this statement, to remind her that *she's* one of the people who've been known to keep things "adult" at my home. She raises her eyebrows so high they meet her widow's peak.

Usually Mrs. Drake deals with hot, popular girls bullying nice, smart ones. As a guidance counselor, that's, like, her primary role.

This is something different. She knows it and I know it.

Alison and Jemma are not the hot, popular, bullying girls. And I'm not a loser or a druggie or a slut or a cheerleader at the top of the social pyramid. This is two nice, boring, borderline nerdy girls feeling pissed that their former friend got a little bit cuter last summer.

And this is Mrs. Drake taking their side.

Jemma says she's sad about how quickly things changed, and maybe that's true, but being sad doesn't give you permission to, you know, be a bitch.

Except Mrs. Drake thinks it maybe does.

Never mind that I'm the humiliated one on the corduroy love seat in the cramped cubby-office.

"It seems like maybe you're choosing boys over your girl friends," Mrs. Drake says after a bit of a pause. I'm about to scream. "All this flirting and carrying on and wearing those tiny skirts and all that makeup . . . it's alienating your friends, and it's making your classmates see you in a very particular light. I'm worried about you. You've changed so much, and whenever I see that kind of drastic shift, I wonder what else is going on."

And with that last bit, she's also managed to maybe-sort-of accuse my parents of being bad parents, on top of everything else.

You know what I'm really starting to hate? How superfast my feelings change. How impossible it is to hang on to the okay feeling. Like some bouncy puppy, I have it in my hands and it's totally *great* and then all of a sudden it wriggles right out and runs around and I can't catch it again.

"Well," I say. But I can't think of a snappy retort. The high from kissing Joe on Assignment has stopped banging around in my body. And I'm left on this stupid couch, blushing. "Well . . . ," I say, much more quietly this time. I'm hyperaware of the length of my dress and my huge boobs and my ridiculous mascara.

It's a nearly intolerable amount of discomfort. There are floor-length floral curtains in Mrs. Drake's office, and I would do anything to hide behind them right now. For a good long while.

"So do you understand?" Mrs. Drake asks. She doesn't look concerned, even though I know I'm sweating a little and my eyes are going watery to match my shaky, quiet voice.

"Um, I guess," I say, hating myself for the slump in my shoulders, my rounding back.

"Those are sweet girls who have expressed concern. Those are lovely girls looking out for you, and you should be very grateful."

Implied but not said: Tabitha, you are not a nice girl anymore.

"I just wanna say," I start in a small voice, "this isn't right."

"Mm-hmm?"

"I don't know why they're telling you that stuff? But the bigger problem is basically that they stopped liking me."

"Sometimes things seems very simple, but they're actually very complicated," Mrs. Drake says, taking her time with the words.

"No, but in this case I think it was more sort of simple. They were sort of terrible and I was totally surprised and that's basically it."

“Ah,” Mrs. Drake says. “And what about changes you’ve made? What about your role?” This is not a real question. There is a right answer, and a wrong one.

“I don’t exactly need to, like, have therapy about this or anything,” I start. I move some of the pillows around on the love seat. I’m sure she will find some way to use that against me too. “But they were my best friends and then we went to a dance and they literally said they were disappointed in me. As a person. And that I wasn’t who they thought I was. And that they weren’t sure we should be friends anymore. I mean, it’d been building a little. They’d made some comments for a few months, I guess. But they basically decided to give up on me one day. So, like, I don’t know why they’re feeling all sad and angsty about it. Because they obviously chose to do it.” I don’t know why I’m telling her this, because she’s on their side. Maybe it’s the calm vanilla candle flickering on the windowsill or the vague watercolor paintings hanging up on the wall or the simple fact that I am in the guidance counselor’s office and I am giving in to the implied rules of being here.

“It seems like it’s still upsetting to you. And I’m here to tell you that it’s still upsetting to them, too,” Mrs. Drake says. In her eyes the whole world is a balanced, even thing, with my upset on one side and Jemma and Alison’s equally valid, very important feelings on the other.

And that’s all lovely and Vermont-y and yoga-y. But it’s not the reality.

“You think I did something to them?” I almost yell. “I kissed a lacrosse dude from another school. I wore a V-neck and some eyeliner. I talked about boys a few times. That's not normally grounds for dismissal! But fine. We're different. They don't like me. Okay. But now they're bringing you into it? Now we're going to all pretend I'm some troublemaker?" Mrs. Drake is nodding along with my words like she is a neutral party, but her jaw is tight and her eyes are not looking directly at mine.

"So it sounds like you see what I'm saying, about your reputation and the impression you're putting out there. I'm worried about your decisions. Sometimes when people are lonely, they do things that are out of character. It seems like maybe you have lost a little track of who you are. Does that sound right?"

My jaw literally drops. I wonder if maybe she has gone deaf and heard nothing that I said. I clear my throat really loudly to check, and she responds with an eyebrow raise, so that's not the problem.

I remember Jemma's face the night of the dance. And I guess she wasn't lying. She was actually worried about me. She did want to keep me as a friend. But she wanted to keep some version of Tabitha that didn't exist anymore.

I even know that it's Mrs. Drake, not Jemma, who is the worst right now. Jemma legitimately thinks I needed a talking-to with the school guidance counselor, I bet. Jemma probably thinks V-necks and eyeliner are cries for help.

It's Mrs. Drake who is making me feel like dirt.

"I mean, everyone changes?" I say, as if my ears are not screaming and my eyes are not bulging in disbelief at her response. Mrs. Drake nods, like I've just admitted to doing meth or something. I meant to say Mrs. Drake was *wrong*, not accidentally agree with her.

Mrs. Drake uncrosses her legs and leans forward like she's ready to get out of her seat and let me out the door.

Which she does.

I spend the next half hour crying in the bathroom. And hating myself for crying. Wiping my face and blowing my nose with toilet paper. Vowing never to speak to Mrs. Drake ever, ever again.

Wishing that, like some of the LBC-ers, I'd thought to press record on my iPhone so I could post the conversation online and watch my new friends tear her apart.

Also, there are a million little details that I couldn't tell Mrs. Drake, and I am pulsing with the desire to spill them all now. The tiny injustices. The barely visible omens telling me they were starting to hate me. The cracks in the friendship that became a crumble and then an avalanche until there was nothing left.

I log on to LBC when I get home that night, not sure what to write. I don't want to put down an actual secret, but I want them to know something more about me, something real. I want them to send smiley faces and philosophy quotes and their own anecdotes to make me feel better.

BITTY: My best friend's brother called me pretty once. She stopped being my friend, like, a month later. All that time I wanted someone to think I was pretty so, so badly. Then it happened, and it ruined everything.

Still. I wouldn't change it.

That's probably terrible.

I get goose bumps from the truth of it. The complicated, torn, two-sided truth of how it feels. It's weird, to write something you didn't know was true until the words are on the screen and you have pressed send.

Secret:

I hate someone for the first time.

—Roxie

Hey Tabby,

So, that was weird. Today.

Weird good.

Weird hot.

You're hot.

Crap. What are we doing?

—Joe

Eleven.

I read the email a dozen times, hiding out in Cate's office. I let the feelings that come with it boil inside me a bit.

He said he wants me. He wrote it down. He pressed send.

I mean, he didn't say much *else*, but he said that.

I open up a reply window and watch the cursor blink. It's like hypnotism or meditation: a half hour passes, and I've done nothing but watch the little line on the top of the email pulse, but at least it's calmed me down a little. I am breathing normally, and the heat in my chest from the phrase "You're hot" has cooled off a bit.

I type in a few words: *Hey You*, *Hey There*, *Hi Joe*, *What ARE we doing?* But none of them sound right, so I keep hitting delete. Hitting that stupid button so hard, the pad of my forefinger starts to sting a little.

I think eating might help, so I make cinnamon toast and try to read Cate's trashy celebrity magazines in the kitchen and avoid the cold stare of the computer. I'm worried what they'll say about my completed Assignment with Joe, or my little revelation about Jemma's brother and the fact that I kind of like people thinking I'm pretty, even if my best friends think I'm evil.

Maybe Life by Committee will start hating me too.

For a moment, I focus only on the sound of the heat clicking on and the way silence sounds even lonelier when the sounds of the heater are cutting through it.

No sign of the parents.

I text Elise, to see if she wants to come over and watch TV or something, and she writes back *WITH HEATHER OMG*.

Distracting myself from LBC isn't working, so I go through their profiles, instead of waiting anxiously for them to say something about my post. I click on Star first, but she doesn't have any new updates, presumably because she's caught in a haze of love and sex and long, meaningful looks. She'll have to fly back home eventually, so she must be savoring every last breath of being with this guy.

I get a fuzzy feeling of *yes* in my chest. I think about kissing Joe again. I keep returning to the scene of the crime, because the way it makes my organs flip-flop is addictive. I bet that's how Star feels about her guy. Maybe more than that, even.

Then there's Agnes. I've been following her with almost the same intensity with which I've been following Star, but with less gleeful results.

I picture her with stringy hair dyed black and alien-sized eyes. I picture her skinny, with elbows like arrows and a not-ugly but not-sexy mole on one cheek. She half frightens me and half intrigues me.

She's smart and strange.

She's the best LBC-er, I think, doing every single Assignment without questioning, and pushing everyone else to do the same.

I like her, because she likes me and Joe, or what she knows about me and Joe.

> **AGNES:** DETAILS!
>
> **ELFBOY:** Do you feel bad? Like a bad person? Do you believe in karma?
>
> **ZED:** We expect you to share so we can all learn.
>
> **ROXIE:** ????
>
> **@SSHOLE:** Don't hold back. This shit's good.

I still feel a sting on my lips from where Joe's teeth bit into me a little. When the kiss turned from beautiful to violent. It hadn't really hurt at the time, but it's bothering me now, the way a too-hot cup of coffee burns the roof of your mouth, even though you don't really realize it until at least an hour later. I get the feeling the way he kisses Sasha Cotton is gentle and warm. Careful.

> **BITTY:** There's not much to tell. I dragged him to the gym and kissed him. He kissed back. We stopped when we heard someone coming. He emailed me. Like, two lines. Nothing life-changing. Mostly that I'm hot.
>
> **BRENDA:** Seems like a lot of people think that about you, lately, huh? =)

AGNES: He emailed! That's a great sign! He's still IN IT, you know?

ZED: What you did was brave. And what you posted—that was brave too.

@SSHOLE: Wish we could see you.

ROXIE: Dude. Not cool.

ZED: Not the point, @sshole. Remember, we want people to be safe in here . . .

@SSHOLE: and dangerous out there. I know. I got it. Sorry.

AGNES: I bet you're beautiful, Bitty.

BITTY: I want you guys to know me.

ZED: You're doing an awesome job. We're so glad you found us.

I'm about to reply with something deep and meaningful to tell them how grateful I'm feeling, and how there's fear there too, but I like it. I love that they are interested in the tiny movements in my feelings, the little details. I have so many nuances that I've been hiding, since Elise isn't that into feelings and Cate and Paul mostly deal with Cate's pregnant feelings and Joe mostly deals with Sasha's feelings. I have a lot to tell them, and it's about to rush out of me, but Cate and Paul come in the front door without saying hello, and their voices are louder than usual, and it makes me stop.

I cross my legs so I'm tiny in the big swivel chair and lean back to listen in on them.

"Soon there will be a baby here," Cate says, more shrill than I've ever heard her. Pregnancy has given her a whole new range of vocal expression.

"The baby's not here *now*," Paul says.

"We have a child already! What, Tabby doesn't count?"

"Tabby loves it! What teenager doesn't want a dad who smokes some weed?"

"I'm not saying you have to stop completely, but you know, maybe not at work. Maybe not in front of the whole town."

"It's Vermont, babe," Paul says. "No one cares. Everyone's doing it."

"Not everyone's doing it!" Cate says. I pretty rarely take her side in fights, but she's right. Paul is practically becoming the town mascot for stoner-dom. He's on his own level. "It's not cute anymore. It hurts business. Move to Brattleboro if you want to join all the stoners. It's not like that in this town. You know that."

Paul laughs. It is a huge, huge mistake. Cate storms away, upstairs I assume, and Paul heads outside. The back door slams.

I hover my hands above the keyboard and consider sharing the details of their fight but decide against it for the moment. I pick up my phone to text Elise about it, like maybe I can keep one foot in the real world and one foot in LBC.

I don't do either. I pour all my attention into listening to the aftereffects of the fight.

The walls are thin, and Paul's favorite place to smoke is on the hammock right outside the office window. I know all the sounds and smells of smoking up, just not the accompanying feeling, not whatever the thing is that Paul just can't get enough of. I have no interest in it. I hear the *click-click-click* of his lighter and then a little hum of pleasure as he inhales.

I mean. I love him, but he's an idiot sometimes.

My screen lights up with more replies to my posts.

ROXIE: I think you should tell his girlfriend what he's doing. Make him eat shit. Leave him with no one.

My focus shifts back to the computer, and I try not to hear Cate doing her little weeping bit upstairs. *She's just pregnant,* I say in my head, but it doesn't really help. Hearing Cate or Paul cry is an even worse feeling than what I felt in Mrs. Drake's office today. Unsettling.

I squint, like that will help me focus more on LBC and less on my parents.

AGNES: No! Bitty has a real connection with this guy. Shouldn't she go for it? I mean, if it's real?

ELFBOY: Right.

ZED: Interesting, Ag. So you think she should keep pursuing this?

AGNES: Keep upping the ante, right?

@SSHOLE: Always.

I open the window a crack, and now the smell of pot is floating in and I can hear each and every one of Paul's sighs. He must know the window's open, but he's not breaking the non-wall between us. We have to do this in our tiny house sometimes. Pretend there is privacy where there is not. Act like we're alone when we're feet away from each other.

I imagine this will get even harder to accomplish when there is a screaming baby in the little nursery upstairs. I remind myself what the note taker said in *The Secret Garden*, that change could be a comfort. I want to ask Zed if he thinks that could be true.

I slide my seat in closer to the desk. Let my face drift closer to the screen. I turn some music on, hike up the volume to drown out tears and weed and the memory of my parents fighting.

BITTY: I love him.

I wonder if I mean what I typed. If this thing with Joe is love. I guess if I say it is, then it is, right?

I turn up the volume another notch. The room is shaking a little from the noise, and I sing along.

BITTY: Maybe not love, yet. Something. I don't just like kissing him. I don't just think he's cute. I don't just hate his girlfriend.

ZED: But if we decided you had to tell the GF?

BITTY: I don't get a say?

ZED: You're here to do something better than what you do alone.

Again, a collective pause. The group seems to work like this. Somehow we all are keeping the same call-and-response rhythm, and we all pick the same moments to pause and collect our thoughts. It reminds me a little of Cate's yoga classes, where everyone is somehow breathing as one unit. That's the only part of yoga I ever liked. But this time I guess the responsibility is on me. My mouth is dry from the clarity of Zed's words.

In the stretch of the pause, another post from Star goes live.

> **STAR:** What if I stayed here? What if I just stayed? I'm eighteen. I'm scared to post a secret, because the only Assignment I want is one that keeps me in his arms forever.

I can't move. I didn't know it, but this is exactly what I wanted for her. This feels Right in the deepest, craziest, most exciting way. I have a surge of *YES* that runs through me. She's a crusader. A romantic. She's the girl I want to be. The girl I didn't know I wanted to be until I saw her red heels and her happy knees.

> **STAR:** Don't worry, Bitty, no Assignment until you tell another secret anyway. And I won't let them make you tell the GF.

Her words cling to the screen, promise and threat both. And a reminder that I have to dig deep for another secret and steel myself for another Assignment next week. That this whole thing is ongoing. My stomach turns, knowing I'll have an Assignment bigger than the one before. And that I'll want to complete it. There was a mini high from typing the words *Assignment completed* today, and I want that again.

An hour has passed by the time I hear Paul slip back inside. I'm scanning LBC and alternately clicking back to chat and waiting for Joe to sign on, which he hasn't, again.

"Hey, chickadee," Paul says, peeking his head in. I click out of LBC so fast, you'd think a gun went off.

"Hey, Paul."

"Sorry you had to hear that."

"Wasn't listening," I say. I keep my eyes on the screen. I don't really want to enter into a father-daughter conversation right now.

"Having a baby's a big adjustment, huh?" he says. Out of the corner of my eye I see him lean against the doorframe and cross one foot over the other. He's settling in.

"Yeah . . ."

"Been a big year for all of us."

"Yeah, I guess so," I sigh out. It's funny how much I said to Mrs. Drake this afternoon and how little I want to say to Paul right now. "You really should cut back," I say.

"*Et tu*, Tabby?" I hear him grinning. I don't like it.

"Or whatever you want. I don't know." It seems like anything I say is going to turn into some long talk with him, and I really can't right now. There's a pause, and I almost wonder if he's left his place on the doorframe, so I turn at last, taking my eyes fully off the computer for the first time. But he's still there, and when my eyes are finally on his bloodshot ones, I see just how crazy-sad he looks.

"You really seem so different lately, kitty cat," he says, his mouth turning down into a frown. "You've really changed."

It sounds so much like what Jemma said to me at the dance in the spring, so much like what Mrs. Drake said this afternoon, that it turns me cold. My arms, inside my stomach, the space between my shoulder blades—all icy.

"That's what I've heard," I say, giving him one pinched look before turning all the way back to my computer screen.

Paul sighs, the way other fathers do, then he's gone from the doorframe.

ZED: We need another secret from our newbie. You're having fun with us, right?

I think of the way Joe looked at me after we kissed—like I was brave and bold and sexy—and know I wouldn't have gone for it without the extra push. I wouldn't have been able to be that girl. I think of Brenda's wedding dress photo, and Agnes's story about interrupting a phone call between her mother and her therapist and admitting she'd been listening in on them for months while they spilled her secrets to each other. I think of the perfect shapes the red script in the margins of *The Secret Garden* makes. I think of Star's knees.

I can't quite bring myself to post another official secret. I have a week.

BITTY: Soon.

ELFBOY: The tattoo hurt.

I mean, damn, it's needles and ink drilling right into your skin, you know? Of course that shit's gonna hurt.

Got it on my shoulder. Not the blade, in the back, but the rounded part in front, the place where you get sunburned. Figured that part of my body would be hearty enough to take it.

Not to mention I'll be able to cover it up with a T-shirt anytime, but it isn't so hidden that it'd be pointless. So you know, a lot of thought went into it.

The biker dude with the leather dog collar around his neck knew I was a kid and too young, but when I told him what I wanted, the word PRIDE in rainbow colors on my shoulder, he took pity.

"I hear you, dude," he said. "I got a brother who, you know."

"Is gay?" I said. Not to be obnoxious, but cuz I didn't want him to feel like he couldn't say the word around me.

He nodded, kinda like a Buddha, all wise and slow and contemplative. Don't know how I found my way to a gay-friendly, totally Zen biker tattoo artist, but there you go. These things happen and you just gotta go with it and say thank you to the universe or whatever.

Yeah, that's something the biker dude said, actually. We had a good long talk while he was drilling needles into my body. I didn't exactly come out to my parents, but I did as much as I could. I hope that's okay, Zed. I'm doing the best I can here. I told them I got a tattoo. Sat them down and said, you know, don't be mad, blah blah blah, but I got a tattoo.

My dad kept shaking his head. My mother covered her mouth with her hand and started to tear up.

"Oh, honey," she kept saying, over and over, just like that. "Oh, honey." I'll hear that in my head on repeat for a while, I think.

They asked me what it was. What the tattoo was.

And I showed them.

Up in my room now.

So, there you go.

Assignment completed?

Twelve.

I open the café alone the next morning.

It's not something I do often, but Paul slept on the couch in the den, and Cate's not feeling well, and I'm in need of a coffee after staying up so late last night that I can feel the space behind my eyes. And that space *hurts*.

This morning, Tea Cozy is drenched in that early-morning sunshine, the kind that seeps in all soft and eventually goes hard and overbright, surprising you in the way only violent natural light can.

I have a constant stream of nerves now. They haven't subsided really since Joe and I kissed at the gym. Maybe even before that, when I got the Assignment. Nervousness is becoming part of my blood, and I could probably lift a car from all the adrenaline.

My stomach grumbles. I think my body knows I'm at Tea Cozy, and it wants a muffin and a coffee and a moment to actually wake up. So I pump up the tunes over the shitty speaker system. The Beach Boys. Not even the really respected stuff. I go for "Kokomo," knowing nothing else will even make a dent in my foul mood.

Soon there's the jingle of bells and the first onslaught of early-morning customers, and like Cate, I get lost in the business and familiarity of that.

"Good morning!" I call out. The regulars like when I'm on my own in the mornings. They smile too big like I'm some six-year-old they need to humor. They crack jokes and offer to come behind the bar and help. Usually harried and tapping their fingers at breakneck speeds on the counter, they are suddenly monk-like in their patience. They pick up the paper from the wire racks we keep next to the counter, or make awkward, frog-voiced small talk with the person ahead of them in line. They leave five-dollar bills as tips, and smile so wide and so close to my face, I can tell whether they remembered to brush their teeth this morning.

"Lady Tabitha's in charge," I hear when my back is turned to steam a bunch of skim milk for the dieting new mothers. There is only one person who calls me Lady Tabitha, and I smile before I remember I have to hate him for being related to Jemma.

"Devon." He doesn't go to our school, so we haven't even caught sight of each other since Jemma dumped me. Which means when I do turn around and he is there in his fitted flannel shirt and his shaggy dirty-blond hair and his cowboy boots, I almost drop the boiling milk on my toes.

Just another reason not to wear wedge sandals in November, I guess.

"We miss you, Tabs," he says. I push stray bangs back and blush.

Not because Devon wasn't cute before. He was. He's always been. But right now he isn't throwing water balloons at me or getting into a screaming match with Jemma. He's digging his elbows into the countertop and leaning over enough so that we are eye to eye. He used to be part brother, part crush, but with Jemma no longer my best friend, does that mean he's . . . all crush? "You know, miss having you around all the time."

His smile isn't unlike Jemma's. His eyes drift down my body, and it doesn't feel all lecherous like when some guys at school do it, but I cross my feet and my arms anyway. Neither of us moves or speaks for five seconds, which is forever when no one is moving or speaking.

I turn away to get some napkins and busy myself with the milk I already poured and the coffee I already brewed. If I look away for long enough, I think I can get mad instead of wistful. I think of Jemma's raised eyebrows and too-straight hair and I decide I am totally over the nostalgia. I will not miss that bitch or the life I thought we had together. I refuse.

"Jemma says you've been too busy with a new boyfriend to come by lately," Devon continues. "I think it's been hard for her, you moving on and dating guys and stuff. She's not ready for that yet. Or not confident about it, you know?" I would do a spit take if life were a movie, but instead I swallow hard and smile even harder. I'm sure it looks like one of those scary-angry smiles, but that's all I've got right now.

"That's what she told you, huh?" I say. I am on the precipice, and I know the right thing to do is to shrug and lie and agree with whatever slightly damning lie Jemma has come up with to explain my sudden absence, but I can practically hear Zed and Agnes and everyone else in my head if I were to type it up and tell them about it. So I shift gears and plow ahead into something honest and risky and bad. Something Normal Tabitha would never do.

"Gosh, that is so weird," I say. "Because, you know, I don't have a boyfriend at all. Haven't in over a year." I cock my head and gauge Devon's response. Decide I have not said enough. "But maybe that's why she hasn't talked to me in three months. Maybe Jemma thinks I have a boyfriend?" I keep the edge out of my voice. Try to steer clear of sarcasm. Sound as close to earnest as I can possibly manage. "This is so great," I say. "I can totally clear this up! Dude, I'm *so* glad you came in today. This is, like, a total weight lifted off. Jemma thinks I have a boyfriend! Well. I'm sure I will be seeing you at your house ASAP now that we've figured out this whole miscommunication."

Devon gulps. I hold his gaze and keep my mouth a steely-straight line; I think he gets it. I *know* he gets it, because he blushes.

People in line behind him cough and close in on him, shuffle closer to the register. They've had enough of our small talk, and I have too. I hand him the coffee he didn't order but I know he wants. He clears his throat and starts to move on. I don't want to take back what I've said or anything. I don't exactly regret calling Jemma on her crap and telling it like it is. It's sort of a new rush, and I don't mind it. But I want him to like me. I want him to tease me for my somewhat nasal voice and call me Freckle Face and buy Boardwalk and build three hotels on it and watch me go broke while we sit cross-legged on the plush carpet in the TV room and play four-hour Monopoly marathons.

"Hey, Devon," I say when he's almost too far away to hear me. He turns back sheepishly, but I'm impressed he turns back at all. "I really miss you guys too."

When the morning rush ends, Paul comes in. He's rumpled and definitely didn't shower after his stay on the couch. Not exactly the kind of guy you want serving you scones, but I guess everyone's used to his ratty stoner garb, and it's not the first time he's worked in what I have to assume is a T-shirt from high school and hospital scrubs.

"Dude," I say. "That is a serious fashion choice there."

"Get yourself to school, Tab," he says. Not mean, but not exactly gentle either. I hate when Cate and Paul fight.

"Still too early," I say, and Paul sighs like it's my fault my school starts at eight.

"Homework, then," he says. "Or check this out." He grabs a copy of *Letters to a Young Poet* from the back pocket of his jeans and tosses it my way. It bounces off my chest, and he snickers. Not exactly Paul at his best.

"I'll be on the couch."

"Maybe you should just get to school early," he says in a mumble. Other people's parents don't ever nail that combination of whine and grumble. When Paul's cranky, he wants to be alone, and that means he doesn't even want me visible. I get the feeling that he smoked up this morning, even though it's something he usually saves for later in the day. The shift in his routine, however slight, scares me.

"Nope."

Paul's eyebrows shoot up. He's awake at long last.

"Nope?" he parrots back.

"I'll stay here, thanks," I say. And then right away my mind pokes in and says, *Who are you?* I don't talk to my parents like this; I don't need to. "Keep an eye on you." I mean it as a joke, to lighten the conversation, but it definitely doesn't work.

Paul rolls his eyes.

"You spying for your mother?" he says. I can't imagine what that means. He and Cate don't need me spying. They are practically attached at the hip. They tell each other what they eat for midmorning snack and how many times per day they pee. They hardly rely on me for reports.

"Spying?"

"You ladies are relentless," he says, rolling his eyes.

I don't even know, really, why I'm fighting to stay here, except that I'm pretty proud of how I was with Devon, and I don't want to be at school without Elise, and at Tea Cozy things *happen*.

"I thought you *wanted* to stop smoking so much. So what are you all pissed at Cate for?"

"I really hate this new attitude," Paul says. It's a continuation of our conversation last night, except gone sour, gone mean with his early-morning hangover. "I thought we agreed you wouldn't get all teenager-y on us. I don't even know who you are right now."

"I don't think I'm the one being all teenager-y," I say. Our voices are low enough that the customers probably can't hear us, but it's still so far outside our normal interaction that we're both a little stunned at the way we're speaking to each other.

"I've got enough on my plate, Tabitha," he says. And I get why he and Cate are fighting. I get why she wants him to get it together. I'm terrified of the new baby, but I also want the best for it. I'm not a sociopath. I want that kid to have the best version of Cate and Paul. And me. "We're both trying to be nice to you, given what's happened, but we have limits, you know?"

I look right in his bloodshot, squinty eyes. I am not his charity case. I am his daughter. I don't care how much he's had to smoke today. I don't care how many awesome scuffed-up books he gets me. I don't need to take it from him. Not anymore.

"I didn't ask you to take care of me. I don't need your fake niceness. I'm all set. Trust me," I say. And maybe leaving Tea Cozy would make more of a point, but he *wants* me to leave. So I stay.

I stomp away from Paul and grab my laptop and my coffee. I sit in one of the armchairs near the fire. I want to write about what happened with Devon, and maybe post a secret about Mrs. Drake, that I've seen her get wasted. Maybe I'll get a crazy Assignment to take down Mrs. D in some sizzling, scandalous way. I'm ready for whatever Zed and the rest of the group throw my way. Look at me: I'm on fire.

Then I see a post from Roxie.

> **ROXIE:** I told my boyfriend I'm on birth control. I'm not. It's not like I want a baby, exactly. But I want to have a family. A real family.

I wait for an onslaught of judgment, but instead there is support. Love. Understanding. She's done a terrible thing, but we aren't here to make her feel worse about it. We're here to get her on some new, exciting, better path.

That's what Zed says, anyway.

And I think I agree.

AGNES: Maybe there's a way to get a family without deceiving him, you know?

STAR: Do you love your boyfriend?

ELFBOY: Just because someone says something is wrong doesn't mean it's wrong.

ROXIE: Honestly, just telling you guys made it feel more manageable. It's like Agnes says. You have to really commit to the group if you want it to WORK.

STAR: TRUTH. Gotta go big. Gotta do it for real. Remember that girl, Lucky15? Said she did Assignments, but we found out she didn't. Told bullshit, unimportant secrets. You just knew there was more underneath the surface. And if she'd really told us, it might have worked out, you know? For her? But she didn't really DO it.

ZED: I'm proud of you, Roxie.

AGNES: What happened to that Lucky15 anyway?

STAR: I mean, nothing. That's the point, right? You can have SOMETHING happen, or you can have NOTHING happen. I vote for something, every time.

ROXIE: Staying is an active choice.

ZED: Staying is THE active choice.

STAR: Lucky15 had to leave the group. She tried to reenter a few months later. Everything was a disaster. Like, her life. But rules are rules.

I discard all the little, unimportant secrets I thought I might tell. I decide to write out a real secret instead. The kind of secret that is bigger than me and Joe and ridiculous Sasha. Bigger than Mrs. Drake. Bigger than anything Lucky15 might have said before she failed and left the group. I won't get kicked out. I won't let my secrets float around on the internet, without any point. I won't risk these brave, exciting, boundaryless people turning on me. I won't become some girl who does nothing and is nothing and lives a nothing life.

I tilt the screen down in case anyone's peeking. Paul changes the music to Metallica, and the Tea Cozy vibe shifts dramatically away from morning sleepiness and the calming sound of people turning the oversize pages of the *New York Times*. People sigh and tense up and jiggle their feet. Couples who were just sitting there splitting the paper start arguing. And Paul's king of it all, frowning even as he serves his favorite regulars. He sings along with the chorus. He keeps looking over at me like he's expecting me to be gone. Like he's *wanting* me to be gone. Like Metallica is enough to get me to do whatever he wants.

Like I'm weak and predictable. Except I'm not. Not anymore.

I wait until he looks at me for the tenth time, and I slam my coffee mug down and raise my eyebrows, like *if you have something to say, come over and say it.* He waves his hands, like I'm a mosquito and not his daughter, and I make the *come over here* look even bigger, more obvious on my face.

He does finally come over.

"Seriously. What's the point of your guidance counselor if she's only going to make it worse?" he says. "I thought you liked her."

I can't quite process what he's saying. "Mrs. Drake? No one likes Mrs. Drake."

"You can't hate everyone, Tabby," he says. "I thought she could help."

"That was you? Telling her to talk to me?" I say. I know Jemma and Alison said something too, but Paul must have made it way worse.

"I made her coffee. She had some concerns. I told her she should chat with you. You've become some teenager who hates everything and can't talk to anyone." Paul rubs his eyes and then his hair and then his scraggly beard. And I know he's not doing so hot. But I also don't care.

Maybe I am the angry teenager. But maybe I have a reason to be angry. I give him a dagger-stare and a sigh so loud, it makes people turn to look at us.

"That. Is. So. Messed. Up," I say. I think I growl a little. Paul takes a step back, then another. He throws his hands up in the air and stomps away. I'm pretty sure I hear him dropping a mug and yelping from burning his hand on something, but I don't care.

I. Don't. Care.

* * *

I bang on my keyboard.

I can't say this to anyone I actually know—I'd never want the town buzzing about Cate and Paul. I almost don't want to say it to myself. But in the anonymous world of LBC, I can say anything.

I can get solutions to problems I'm scared to admit I have. I can change the bullshit things I've accepted lately.

I can do something about Paul.

> **Secret:** My dad's a stoner. Okay: An addict, really. It's getting bad. And if he doesn't stop before my mom has a baby, she's gonna make him move out.

I almost don't know it's true until it's written there, until I've made it public to Agnes and Brenda and Zed and the rest of them. Whoever they are. They're mine.

Thirteen.

After the secret is out there, I decide I can leave Tea Cozy and go to school and forget about Paul for the rest of the day. It's out of my hands.

My heart's a little fluttery, but I'm getting used to that. I'm maybe even starting to like it.

I have my afternoon free period, and the student council is selling baked goods in the large foyer where we all hang out, off the main hallway, so there's a crowd at the table where we usually play hearts. Alison is on student council—as one of the peons, not one of the elected officials, of course. But I want a brownie so that I'll have something to do while I wait for my Assignment to come through.

"Will you get me a brownie?" I say to Elise as she's flying by to make it to math class. She gives me an in-motion hug.

"You're not scared of that girl. She's scared of you," she says in my ear, and it helps, but it's a drive-by bit of encouragement, and I need the kind that comes from a sit-down and a mug of Cate's hot chocolate and extended eye contact. But it's enough of a boost to get me to the table.

"Brownie," I say to Alison. Her face shifts from smile to scowl before I get to the second syllable of the word.

"Three," she says, because I guess we are now speaking in only one-word sentences.

I'm scrounging through my pockets for the last dollar and Alison sighs and shifts in her seat.

"I've got it," Joe says, appearing next to me. The tips of his fingers sort of grab my elbow, which isn't the height of affectionate gestures exactly, but it feels good. More than good, it's like a kiss between two other body parts, a nonlips kiss, and I think he feels it too.

"Hey there," I say. It doesn't sound like me—not the words, and not the tone of voice I'm using to say them.

"I owe you, remember?"

"I do seem to recall that." We are both grinning, stupidly, and in a way that Alison definitely doesn't miss.

"You want to get something for Sasha?" she interrupts, her words jumping up between us.

"She's out today, actually." Joe gives a huge smile that looks like it takes a lot of effort.

"I'm sure she'd love you to bring a brownie by her place after school," Alison says. She's getting desperate.

"Oh," Joe says, and his fingers jump away from my elbow. "Yeah. Sure. Two brownies, I guess."

I hate that he is getting us the same thing.

"Tabby, yours is on the house," Alison says. "Years of you hooking us up at Tea Cozy, right?" She's smiling, with her mouth only, and I'd forgotten how goddamn smart she is. The three of us could all hold our own with good grades and devouring books and witty comments, but Alison has a quiet cleverness that used to impress me.

"Right. Thanks," I say. I try to make eye contact with Joe, but he won't turn his head in my direction, and I kind of can't believe Alison defeated us so easily. "And thanks anyway, Joe," I try. If I say his name, he has to look up at me, right?

And he does. I think it's a reflex, rather than a decision, but his eyes find mine while Alison gets his change, and there's that spark between us again. He shrugs, and his fingers reach for my hip bone, feathering against it so that I can feel the tiny gesture no one can see.

Then I'm all full from the sensation, and I don't care what my Assignment is, because I can do *anything*.

I go to the stall in the bathroom that is becoming my LBC stall. It has an inoffensive air freshener and less graffiti than the other stalls. It's been only a few days, but checking the site is already becoming a habit—like checking email or eating.

There's no Assignment, just Elfboy saying he wishes he had a dad who smokes weed, and Star talking about rehab programs. I guess Zed hasn't gathered enough information yet.

Roxie says: **Gutsy.**

I'm not sure if she means Paul for smoking up all the time, or me for telling everyone about it.

There are updates on my conversation about Joe, since Star and Agnes both seem to love a good romance.

STAR: Tell us about him.

AGNES: OMG yes. I want all the gooey, sticky, pretty details. When I was first falling for my BF, I talked about him All. The. Time. So karmically, I owe a good listen.

STAR: Same here. I mean, I'm still falling. But you know.

AGNES: What's he like?

Someone comes in and washes her hands. I think she peers under the stall doors to see if she's sharing the bathroom with anyone, and I make a throat-clearing sound so she doesn't think she's alone and therefore smoke or have some kind of illicit phone conversation or anything. I sort of can't handle any more secrets.

Agnes's question is the kind that requires actual honest-to-goodness thought. Because with Joe I'm acting on deeply instinctual feelings, and I've never had to explain them to anyone before. Or, really, I've known not to. There's all kinds of things Joe says to me that he'd never say to anyone else. With his friends he talks about hooking up and drinking beer and maybe on occasion whether a particular class or teacher sucks. I don't think he gets a chance to say much of anything when he's with Sasha.

The hockey guys don't participate too much in Headmaster Brownser's bonding and intimacy and trust activities. They don't meditate on the lawn outside the gym or read the assigned reading or keep up with the Gratefulness Journals that we have been forced to keep since we could write.

But Joe isn't a normal hockey guy. He has secrets. Secrets he's told me. Secrets I can tell them, to make them understand.

BITTY: He likes ridiculous books about road trips and angry graffiti and men with beards.

I picture his face. His hands and his mouth. The *ding* on my computer when he comes online. The searching way he looks into my eyes. That shining feeling that comes from really loving someone spreads in my chest, and I'm ready to speak a tiny bit of truth.

BITTY: We talk, you know? About everything. He talks to me like I'm his best friend. He calls me kiddo, which I would hate with anyone else, but it makes me feel like I'm cute and he's gonna watch out for me. He reads and plays sports. He's, like, all these contradictions. He wants to join the Peace Corps and a fraternity, but hasn't told anyone either of those things. He tells me everything. He really loves his sisters. And he's so much like my dad. With the smoking, I guess, but also with the way he Is, you know?
Plus. You know. I want him. And he wants me. And he tells me all the time. I can, like, feel him thinking about me.
STAR: OMG you have to be with him.
@SSHOLE: My parents met this way. He was with someone

else and she stole him away. It happens.

STAR: It sounds like he feels more for you than he does for her. Just a feeling I get.

@SSHOLE: That's exactly what my dad said. That eventually his feelings for my mom so outweighed the feelings for his GF that he had to just be honest with himself.

And then I'm soaring. It doesn't matter that Joe is going to bring a brownie to Sasha after school. It doesn't matter that Alison and Jemma and Elise and maybe the whole school kinda-sorta suspect something's up with us. It only matters that his fingertips feel like fireworks on my skin.

Three o'clock hits and Zed's said nothing about my secret.

When classes end, I catch sight of the red exclamation point that signifies an Assignment. My heart stops when I click on it. But it doesn't lead me to the page where I posted about my father and his smoking. It leads me back to the conversation about loving Joe.

ASSIGNMENT, Zed's written underneath the conversation. **Still mulling over your other secret, Bitty, but where there's passion, there's usually the need for action. So a follow-up Assignment with your guy.**

BITTY: I didn't know that was . . . an option.

People start responding right away, my page jammed with comments. This is what happens when an Assignment goes live. Suddenly everyone is on the site, ready to go. I can barely keep up. I turn toward my locker, open the door, and hide my head and phone inside. It's awkward, but at least no one will see what I'm seeing.

ZED: Everything's an option, once a secret is up. We gotta see things through, right?

I nod, even though no one can see me. I do remember that from other people's entries, but I hadn't thought about it when I posted mine. Does that mean he can make all the decisions from here on out about Joe? Does that mean I'm basically required to let him run that whole relationship?

I try to get my heart to slow and my hands to still. I want to trust in the power of the group, but I've sort of jumped into all this without looking to see what it is. Deep-sea diving without asking about sharks.

AGNES: That's the beautiful thing. All things are options. That's what you're going to learn, Bitty.
BITTY: But aren't there, like, rules?
ZED: Sure. That's what you've been doing this whole time, right? Rules. We're trying to help you get rid of those. More options. Less rules.
AGNES: And then, ultimately, no rules.

I check behind me, squirrel my phone, and head away again. No rules. I like that. And I like Agnes. Her breathless bravery. She's almost cool. Dark and angsty and weird but cool.

ZED: You ready for this? Here's the Assignment: Make him jealous. Tell him there's someone else. If you can, find someone else.

ELFBOY: Yes. This.

AGNES: I kind of hate that. But I'd do it. That's the thing. Sometimes the assignments you hate are the ones that end up best.

BITTY: Yeah . . .

I don't want someone else. I don't want him to think there's someone else. I only want him.

I want Star's happy love story and shiny red shoes and freckled knees and crazy talk of forever-ness.

I keep thinking about this one part of *The Secret Garden*. The Red Pen Margin Note Taker made an asterisk, a huge one, next to this bit of dialogue. Mary and her new friend Dickon are discussing the flowers Mary has planted in her newfound secret garden. Mary and Dickon are pondering what the garden will look like. "'Don't let us make it tidy,' said Mary anxiously. 'It wouldn't seem like a secret garden if it was tidy.'"

I don't know that I'd ever noticed that moment of dialogue before seeing it through the Red Pen Margin Note Taker's eyes. And I don't know that it would have mattered much to me if I didn't have LBC. But I get it now. It's good for things to be messy. It's not necessary to clean your life up all the time. You can let it grow wild.

"Tea Cozy?" Elise says, sneaking up behind me and grabbing my sides so that I drop my phone and have to scramble to pick it back up. "I could use some Elise-Tabby time."

I swallow. I should not be saying no to the only person in school who doesn't hate me. But my forehead is a Slip 'n Slide of sweat and I am in the midst of about a hundred life-changing epiphanies right now.

"How about tomorrow?" I say. "Bookstore and Cozy and catch-up?" I make it sound breezy.

"How about *today*?" Elise counters. She's hopping from foot to foot. "You look like you need sugar. And a pep talk. And, like, I don't even know. Ritalin? Where *are* you right now?" She taps my wrist with her thumb. I guess I've been twiddling my fingers and staring somewhere unfocused, not at her face. I shake my head awake.

"I think the word you are looking for is *nap*. I need a nap," I say.

"You need to be taking better care of yourself," Elise says. I know she's not talking about Assignments or anything, but she's right, of course she's right. I need to be doing better. I need to be more.

"Totally," I say, and take a huge breath.

I know I have to do the new Joe Assignment. Zed's right. They're all right. I've been living with all these rules and ideas of how to do things. I've been keeping my little garden tidy. And all it's doing is holding me back from the life I want.

My phone buzzes in my pocket, and I bring it out. It's another LBC update, a picture from Star: bare legs hanging off what I assume is her guy's bed. Boys' slippers on her tiny feet. The caption: **No one in their right mind would leave something that feels this good. Don't worry, Bitty. It all works out for the best. Promise.** If there were a swell of music, this would be a movie, and I'd be trying to keep tears in by holding my forefingers under my bottom lashes. Since it's not a movie, but actually my life, I take another lifesaving inhale.

"Um, hi?" Elise says. I'd completely forgotten she was even there. She cranes her neck to get a glance of what is distracting me on my phone, but I pull it away from her. "Keeping secrets?" She taps my wrist with her thumb again. She thinks it's Joe.

"We can hang tomorrow, I promise, okay?" I say. She musters a lame smile and walks me to my car.

And when I'm halfway through my drive home, I call him.

Joe almost never answers his phone, but this time there's a "Hello?" and the sound of his car, probably as it zips away from school to Sasha Cotton's sickbed or whatever.

There is nothing better than hearing someone grin over the phone. I try to convey that same warmth right back, hoping he gets an identical rush of warmth from the unlikely softness, the intimacy of dropping my voice and squinting my eyes and holding the speaker so close to my mouth that we are almost kissing, our lips meeting across channels. No one has ever wanted something so badly. If sheer will were enough, our lips would be touching.

"What if I came over?" I say.

Joe laughs low. It hurts. My spine feels that laugh, the sexiness of it. "Well, what if?" he says, and I know that's a yes.

When I get to the door of his house, I can smell garlic simmering and a salty seafood scent. It hits me hard—I'm hungry.

Once I am safely inside his home, we hug and I feel the whole of his body against mine. I am so not over him. Every piece of me seems to line up with every piece of him: my thighs kiss his, my chest to his, our bellies and collarbones even find each other. He is only an inch or two taller than me, which some girls would hate but I find sexy. The meeting of our bodies feels good; the parallel body parts and the way they attach when we hug is a revelation every time.

"Hi," I sigh out.

"Hi."

"Hi." It's hard not to kiss, since our mouths line up too, but we resist, letting our breath mingle but keeping an inch or two between our faces.

"Want early dinner?" he says.

"With . . . you?" I am stupider around him. Not always, but now.

"Mom made seafood pasta. It's really good. Her specialty." I lick my lips nervously and he goes on. "I'm normally starving right after school, so she lets me have dinner right away if I don't have practice. Weird, I know."

"Oh wow." I have not met Joe's family, since I am not his girlfriend. I've been to his house two times, but only when his parents were out to dinner and only in a group of people wanting to get drunk.

Seafood pasta and early dinner with the family is a new level of our relationship, and I can't wait to tell Star about this leap.

"I'm starving too," I say, and a smile finds its way onto my face. Then it grows into a grin. I'm screwed.

Fourteen.

If I thought the smell of garlic and Italian cooking was tempting before, it is nothing compared to the way it hits me once I'm actually in the kitchen. The onion-garlic-tomato-butter deliciousness practically knocks me over.

His mom is standing over a few pots: pasta, sauce, spitting simmering minced garlic. She's heavy and her hair is the same color as Joe's; just as thick, but wiry and knotted. She reminds me of a book Cate used to read me when I was little, *Strega Nona*, about an Italian pasta-making witch. Joe's mom is totally Strega Nona. Her apron is paisley and covered with tomato remnants and oil splotches.

"Hi, Mrs. Donavetti," I squeak out.

"Mom, this is Tabitha. My friend," Joe says. He puts a hand on my back and pushes me toward her. I stick my hand out, and she smiles and nods to the huge wooden spoons she has—one in each hand.

"Lovely to meet you, Tabitha," she says. "You'll be joining us for dinner, I hope?"

"Smells amazing," I say, nodding. She glows and exchanges an indecipherable look with Joe.

An hour later I know exactly what that look meant. Mrs. Donavetti *hates* Sasha Cotton. I know this because she talks about Sasha through the entire meal, wringing her hands and chomping so hard on her mussels and clams and al dente pasta that I think she's going to chip a tooth.

"Joe just shouldn't be with a girl that troubled," she says, spinning long strands of linguini over her fork with expert ease. "You know her well?"

"Not too well," I say.

"Not too close with her?"

"Oh, no," I say. She smiles and nods. Right answer.

"You're a good friend to Joe," she says. "He needs someone like you. Grounded. Smart. Good girl." I nod and don't look in Joe's direction. The conversation has gotten strange and I don't feel able to really participate in it.

"Mom, chill," Joe says at last, and Mrs. Donavetti shrugs and smiles my way. Like I am the girl she's been waiting for.

"Want a little more, Tabitha?" she asks. I'm not really hungry after devouring a whole bowl of her stupendous seafood pasta, but the sauce is so spectacular and the noodles so comforting that I can't say no.

"Yes, please."

"Good girl," she says, and again looks to Joe with that *I told you so* look. I guess Sasha never asks for seconds.

I am in Joe's house. I am smiling at his mother. I have found the one person in the universe who prefers me to Sasha Cotton, the one person immune to her long legs and dim smile and breathy lullaby voice. I am touching elbows with Joe because we can't hold hands, but touching elbows might be even better. My funny bone tingles with recognition: *This is love.*

Halfway through my seconds I duck into the bathroom and post to Life by Committee. I'm a pot boiling over, and I can't tell Elise. I can't tell Cate and Paul. No one I love would approve of this or give me the response I'm looking for. I want a squeal of delight and encouragement and stories about @sshole's parents, who got married after their shady start.

I want LBC.

I wish I could speak out loud to them, because capitalized words and emoticons and exclamation points aren't enough to convey what it feels like to be in this house playing Girlfriend and knowing that I never could have done this alone. Alone I would chicken out and stay home eating scones and texting Elise and watching Cate's belly grow and my life vanish.

> **BITTY:** I'm terrified. But it's sorta all happening. The life I want. Not the way I pictured it, but the way it has to be.

Mrs. Donavetti eventually leaves us alone, when she is sure we are stuffed full of pasta and shellfish and garlic. Joe and I stay at the kitchen table and she busies herself upstairs, and I want it to be this way forever.

"Your mom likes me," I say. I scoot my chair a little closer to his, and he doesn't protest.

"She does."

"She's not so into Sasha."

"Come on, Tabby," he says. He fidgets in his seat.

"Just saying."

"I don't want to talk about Sasha," he says. I scoot my chair in a little more. Fine by me.

"I just— Don't you want us to be . . . more?" I can't believe I'm actually saying it to his face, not hiding behind the computer screen or my phone or anything.

"Don't get like that. You already know how I feel." The words Joe says don't match up with the things his body is doing. For instance: he sounds like he is annoyed with me, but his hand has found its way to my thigh, and his face is now close enough that I can feel his breath travel across that sweet line from my ear to my neck.

"Sort of . . ."

"This is all really hard," he says. "Having feelings for two people at once." He keeps pressing his lips together and rubbing my thigh. I'm not even moving, but I'm out of breath from sitting near him.

"Yeah . . ." Even though I know he's with Sasha and I guess kind of loves Sasha, or at least likes sleeping with her, it hurts to hear him say he has feelings for "two people." It slips out of his mouth so easily, but it *thuds* in my head, the worst reality, the thing I don't want to believe.

That stupid kitchen clock almost sounds like it's speeding up, but I know it's actually my anxiety that's getting higher and faster. This is my chance.

"I like you for different reasons, you know?" Joe's musing. I don't want to hear him muse about his feelings. I get the sense a pro-con list could be coming, and I don't need to be lined up against the messy-sexy neediness that is Sasha Cotton, so I cut him off with the first and only thing I can think of that will shut him up. And the last thing I actually want to do.

"Yeah, I totally know," I say. "About liking two people."

My phone buzzes. I can hear it going crazy in my purse, but I know it's Cate and Paul calling to see where I am. I forgot to tell them about my impromptu after-school trip.

"You . . . do?" Joe says. His hand moves to the place between my shirt and the back of my jeans. It finds that little patch of skin and tortures me.

"I really, really do, actually," I say. "I know all about it." *Assignment completed?* the voice in my head asks. I could go further. I could push even more against all my impulses. His hand is rubbing my back. Tracing circles around the discs of my spine, and I am dizzy from the wonderfulness of it all.

"I don't want to share you," he says. And he comes in for a kiss, right there in his kitchen with his mom humming along with the TV commercials upstairs. The kitchen is still warm from all the cooking and Joe himself is warm, and nothing has ever felt this damn good.

It works. Doing something brave and strange and unexpected.

Because the aftermath, too, is strange and unexpected and brand fucking new. I am on cloud nine.

Until: Joe comments on the buzzing of my phone, in between kisses, and I go to shut it off. I can't stop myself from checking LBC for updates, while the phone is in my hand anyway. I want to find a way to type in *Assignment completed, update soon*, but I know Joe will ask what in the world I am doing. He's watching me from his chair. I open up the website and let my eyes linger long enough on the page to see the red exclamation point on my profile page. Zed has come up with the other Assignment for me.

I click the link and look, bend over my phone at a strange angle so that he can't see.

> **ASSIGNMENT:** Time to bond with your dad. Get high with him.

I gasp. I don't know that I've ever gasped in real life, but I do it now and it's loud. "Kinda insulting when your phone is more interesting than, you know, *this*," Joe says. I look his way, but my heart's pounding from the seriousness of this new Assignment. I almost give in to the terror of what I have to do.

But.

But.

But Joe's right there and his lips are still wet from the kissing and his mother calls out to say she is going to go out for groceries. And I'm going to do something terrifying and life-altering in the next twenty-four hours, so I might as well do something ecstatic and ridiculous right now.

I rush at him. Forget about my chair. Climb onto his lap. And dive at his mouth.

I keep one hand wrapped around my phone. I can't let it go. I can't let go. I want to be only in this moment, but right outside this moment, visible even from the gooey, sweet center of it, are Sasha Cotton and my Assignment and the fact that everyone hates me and that my parents both have hoarse voices from all the yelling. It's a crowded view, and impossible to ignore. The kissing is beautiful, but everything else we have to contend with is neon and unrelenting and loud.

"Tell me about this other guy," Joe says, when the kissing has subsided and my shirt is half off and my bra strap's pulled down nearly to my elbows. He is distracted too.

"Other guy?" I say. My mind is a black hole. I couldn't come up with the capital of our own state if it killed me, let alone grasp what Joe's getting at.

"You said you get having feelings for two people. . . ." He's rubbing my bare back, and his eyes are huge and maybe even brimming with real live *feelings*.

"Oh. Right." I'd momentarily forgotten that I was still in the middle of building a whole other lie. I'm not the best liar anyway. I shrug and lower my eyes and try to go in for a kiss.

"I need to know," he says. "It's only fair."

"He's a little older," I start, going nowhere. "Skinny. Sarcastic. Not like you at all. Likes weird music and, you know, readings at the bookstore. He reads a lot." I ramble on for a moment before realizing what I'm doing.

I am describing Devon.

It makes sense. He appeared. He's cute. I have a crush on him the way you have a crush on a musician or an actor. Not in a real way. He's convenient. He's on my mind because of this morning. I like that he flirts with me. And I miss being around him all the time. But that's not the same thing as having real feelings for him.

It's not like I'm considering completing the second part of that Assignment. The part where I actually start dating someone else, to make Joe jealous. That would be too far.

But there I am anyway, talking about the buckles on his boots and the fact that I've known him since I was six. Acting like I have feelings for him. Acting like he is my Sasha Cotton.

Joe nods and nods.

By the time we have finished kissing, it's dark outside and both of our phones keep buzzing and beeping and singing and blinking.

He's even ignored a call or two from Sasha. I can't contain the bliss I feel at that knowledge. I want to spend our last five minutes together staring into each other's eyes and making promises about What Happens Now. But Joe's hands are nudging their way under the waistband of my pants.

It makes me miss our conversations online. It is the thing I have been wanting: him close to me, him tugging at me, choosing me, wanting me most of all. But here I am, sweater discarded, top button of jeans popped open. And all I can think of is how sweet it was to hear the *ping* of his chats, and see the words as they appeared onscreen: halting, erratic, unpredictable. I didn't know where we were going.

Now, I think I know.

"I wish the drive home were longer," I say to Joe after he walks me out to my car and kisses me through the open window once I'm inside.

"Hm?"

"Never mind," I say.

What I meant was: everything changes after tonight, and I'm not sure I'm ready.

What I meant was: this is the last perfect moment before I do more terrifying things.

STAR:

Here are a bunch of secrets.

I want to get married.

Yeah, I mean, I know. I've lived in L.A. for less than a week, and maybe we don't know each other that well. But I want to know I'll never lose him. I want to know I can live this life and that it is mine.

There's a picture hidden in his bedside table, I think of an ex-girlfriend. She's a redhead and one of the skinniest girls I've ever seen. I asked him about it, and he said he meant to throw it away but never got around to it. Which is funny, because throwing something away isn't hard, isn't something that takes time.

I threw it away for him.

ZED: Propose.

STAR: What?

ZED: Assignment. Propose.

Fifteen.

BITTY: Assignment completed. I told Joe I have feelings for someone else, too.

ZED: What about the rest?

BITTY: The rest of what?

ZED: What about actually going for this mystery person? To make Joe jealous. Action's better than words, right?

BITTY: Right.

I am trying to be agreeable. But I am already so worked up about having to do *drugs* with my *father* that I'm not sure I can handle anything else. I don't want to say as much. I want to be steely and strong and spontaneous. I want to be an LBC-er. I want to be like Star, telling a million secrets and getting the world's biggest Assignment.

I mean, a proposal. Shit.

STAR: Jesus, Zed, give the girl a chance to breathe. One Assignment at a time, right?

ZED: She seems pretty formidable to me. Reminds me of you.

STAR: Still. Come on. Her Assignment today is for real. Don't overwhelm the new girl.

ZED: Is it possible you're projecting? I haven't heard any updates on your Assignment yet.

Star doesn't reply.

I wonder what smoking weed will feel like. If it will make me giggly or dizzy or sick. I wonder if Paul will coach me through it or, like, ground me for life or start wanting to smoke up together all the time.

Maybe I don't know him well enough to even guess what his response will be. Or maybe I don't know myself well enough to know what my own response will be either.

Paul's at the kitchen table with coffee and clear eyes when I wander down Saturday morning before I head to Tea Cozy.

"Little Bitty," he says with a sober smile. My heart rate spikes. Hearing my LBC name out loud makes my hands shake. I should not have used a name that Paul calls me all the time. He gets up to pour me a coffee and make me some toast. I love when Paul makes me breakfast, even when it's only toast or cereal. I like that sometimes he's in charge. I don't commit to sitting down. I don't think I can sit across the table from him and act like a normal person right now.

"Big ole Paul," I say, and do my impression of a person with a boring day ahead, smiling at her father.

"You feeling better today?" he says. It's a strange question, because it's not the question he actually wants to ask. I assume he wants to know if I'm still mad at him, if we can move forward without actually acknowledging the terrible things we said to each other.

"Are you?" I say.

"We gotta do better than this, Tabs," he says. He looks sheepish. He hasn't shaved still, and he shrugs and gives me big puppy-dog eyes.

"I know. Now that the baby's coming and stuff," I say. I crunch through the toast and crumbs fly everywhere. Paul doesn't make me sit down or use a plate or use margarine instead of butter or anything.

"Nope. We gotta do better than this because I am still going for Family of the Year, and we're not going to pull it off if we're yelling at each other in public."

I can't help laughing. Paul has long joked about our ability to win Family of the Year. Over the years it's become a thing we reference as totally real, like the Olympics. Like any day now they're going to show up with a trophy.

"Germany could pull ahead of us?" I say.

"I think the real competition is going to be from Australia this year. They're contenders," Paul says. He goes to put more toast in the toaster for me, but I shake my head and pour some of the coffee from his full mug into my empty one.

"We can't let the Australians win!" I say, and give him a little half hug before heading out the door.

Eleven hours to complete my Assignment.

By the middle of the day, I have a perma-mustache of stress sweat happening above my lip. I don't want to do drugs with my dad. But I also don't want to get high, period. I don't like the way Paul's eyes change when he smokes. I want my eyes to stay the same.

I want us to win Family of the Year and crush the Australians, and I'm scared.

But things are going to change either way. That's what I remind myself when I almost want to give up. Everything is changing whether I like it or not. I might as well take charge of the changes.

I have so much trouble focusing while making lattes that I check my phone behind the counter, even though Cate hates it.

Midmorning, Joe comes in with Sasha, but he stays by the door, actively avoiding me, and she is too busy texting and making moony eyes at him to chat with me. Joe's almost too much to take right now anyway. He's in a collared white shirt and a thick blue sweater and it's so handsome and unlikely on him, I have to wonder if maybe it's for me.

I focus on my countdown, the way the hours have moved all the way down to single digits. Five hours to go. I also want to see Star accept her Assignment. I want to know she's bought a ring. Or whatever it is girls do when they're proposing to boys.

I can't help it—I look at Joe again on his way out the door. He takes Sasha's hand and an essential part of my heart cracks. I can't imagine keeping up with the charade that I am interested in someone else.

AGNES: Star, couldn't you go to City Hall or Vegas or one of those places people go? White sundress. Silver flip-flops. Candy ring. One of those beautiful poems that Bitty recommended, spoken in a hush in front of some judge or Elvis impersonator. Hours in bed afterward. What are you waiting for, Star? You're the one who made us believe in love to begin with.

I scroll through responses under my desk, loving the romantic way Agnes writes and the way she pushes us all. I try to keep my head facing the line of customers. It's quite an impressive feat.

ZED: Four hours, Bitty.

He doesn't waste any time reminding me, at the end of the day, that even when I'm on a break, I have a lot of work ahead of me.

When I sit down, Cate brings me chamomile tea. She says I look sick and I have been staying up too late and we're all going to get healthy and responsible together. Paul is cleaning tables nearby, so he overhears and sighs.

I sigh too. Because I hate chamomile tea.

I want it to be the moment *after* I complete the Assignment. I want the glowing skin and wink in my eyes, the glamorous red high heels and the pride in who I am, and to report back on the ways my life is changing. I want the same rush of feeling in my gut and all the way down through my legs as when I took that half step forward and kissed Joe in the gym. I want that flicker of power that came from being the one who leaned toward him instead of being the one who was leaned on.

Elise breezes in moments later.

Our date to hang out at the bookstore and eat scones and catch up. Shit.

It's one of the few times she's been more dressed up than me. Worn-in jeans hang off her hips, but she's got orange cashmere on top, and a vat of gel worked into her hair. I wore leggings and a gray sweatshirt for my big day.

"Let's go," Elise says.

"I'm sort of not in the mood," I say. There's a wrinkle of annoyance between her eyebrows. I try to avoid looking at it, because I don't really have a choice about this right now. I need to get my Assignment over with.

"Come on. You promised the bookstore. I'm bored. And you're wearing your cranky outfit. So let's fix all the things."

"Yes!" Cate says. "She's been the crankiest. I can't take it. I have enough of my own hormones."

"The girl wanted coffee," Paul says, because he apparently has some kind of death wish. "You gave her the saddest drink imaginable. And called it good parenting. Come on, Cate. That's not the woman I married." He says it with a wry smile and a wink, but man, it comes out rougher than anything he's ever said to her. Elise swallows so loudly, it sounds like a dead bolt clinking into place. This is literally the worst possible day for me to smoke up with my dad, but I can't imagine being the girl on LBC who fails. I don't want to be Lucky15, alone and sad and looked down on. I can't let the idea in my head of who I could be fade away already.

I can't fail at this. I have to be one of them.

"Please leave the café until you sober up," Cate says. It's under her breath, I guess, but customers at the tables near us could definitely hear her. Elise takes a few steps to the door, and I do a mini calculation that tells me four hours is still totally enough time to go to the bookstore, get coffee and baked goods, wait for Cate and Paul to cool off, and then do what I promised myself and my new friends that I would do.

I can do it all.

"We'll be back," I say to no one.

"So? Heather?" I say when Elise and I are huddled in the poetry corner of the bookstore. The navy-blue polka-dot carpet is plush, and we've been known to sit on it for hours. "You like her?" I try to be really good about checking out who's around when talking to Elise about girls. Her eyes dart around too, and then she grins.

"She's so cool. She's really into making her own perfumes and soaps and stuff. And she's inviting me over, like, *all* the time. And she never talks about guys."

"But?"

"Don't be a downer, Tab," Elise says. She says it lightly, but her face grimaces. It's that extra step of actually making a move on another girl that Elise never seems to get over. So the crushes get to this place, and then halt when Elise can't nudge them along any further. She never says she likes them as more than a friend, never asks if they like girls, never leans in to try kissing them.

"Do you have a plan?"

She's looking right at me, and her dark eyes are blurry with feelings. "I have to just do it. Right? Tell her how I feel about her. I mean, either way, it won't freak her out, hopefully. Or if it does, she's not my friend anyway, right?"

"Totally," I say. And it's true. But I also love Elise enough to feel the nervousness that comes with that confession. The horror of it. The way it could emerge from her mouth and drop to the floor with a huge, hollow *thud*. It's hard enough to tell someone you have a crush on them. It's made even harder for Elise, who isn't totally sure if Heather's even gay. "Nothing ventured, nothing gained," I say. I don't usually speak in platitudes, so Elise looks at me funny, and I can't figure out where that came from, either. And then I realize it's in Zed's profile on LBC.

"People don't just do whatever pops into their heads, you know?" Elise says. "We're not all the way you are with Joe or whatever." I recoil. She might as well have hit me.

"What do you think I'm doing with Joe?" I say, not really wanting the answer but needing the answer anyway.

"I hope nothing, but I think you have a skewed sense of how romantic crap happens. I'm not going to, like, throw myself at Heather and see what sticks. I mean, it's cool. That you are being all . . . um . . . free. But that's not me. That's all I mean. I, like, totally envy your . . . way of being or whatever. But I'm going to feel it out and wait and see."

I try very hard to come up with the right response. I don't want to fight with Elise, but I also don't love the weird implication that I'm kind of a huge disaster.

"I meant it as a compliment," Elise says, I assume because the look on my face is one of horror and shock. "And, you know, thank you for wanting to help with Heather. I'll get there." She raises her eyebrows and plays with the collar of her shirt.

"People do get what they wants sometimes, you know?" I say, and Elise nods and that's basically it for that portion of the conversation. We both look at our feet and our phones to recover.

Mine reminds me I now have three hours.

"So. Informal poll. What's the weirdest book in this place?" Elise says. "I'm bored with poetry and self-help. Can we find something new?" She walks over to the religion section, but we've done that before, too, so it won't be much more interesting.

"I'd go for one from the 'local writers' section," I say. The bookstore features a whole display of self-published texts from people in town, and the people in town are pretty damn weird, so it's a good bet.

"Good call," Elise says. "Okay, I'm going to get some weird anarchist manifesto or something. What are you going to get?"

"*The Secret Garden*," I say. I want to find another marked-up copy. I want to know if everyone who reads the book has the same thoughts as me and the Red Pen Note Taker, or if we really do have the bond through time and space that we seem to.

"I thought you were into *A Little Princess*," Elise says. I love that she knows this about me. After only being friends since June, this seems like a huge accomplishment. She's really listening. I get that about-to-cry feeling in my chest and I'm not entirely sure why. I want to hug her, but Elise is not a hugger. I guess I've been thinking I don't have anyone, but maybe I sort of do have someone aside from LBC-ers.

"New fad," I say. "I'm falling for *Secret Garden* now."

"Haven't read it," Elise says. I take a step toward the children's section and breathe in the smell of mustiness and pumpkin candles that always fills this store. It's cozy and mine, and in a flash I don't want to share this particular thing with my best friend.

"You'd hate it," I say.

I end up with two more copies of *The Secret Garden*. Neither of them has very many notes. One looks like it was read by a chocolate-loving kid who was being forced to active read at Circle Community. The other is an old library book that some asshole wrote what looks like phone messages in. Not exactly inspiring reading material, but I can't let the books go to someone else, and I can't stop the flicker of curiosity at what this book does to people.

We head back to Tea Cozy but don't say hi to Paul and Cate. I have two hours left to complete my Assignment, zero extra inspiration from my new books, and a friend watching my every move. Basically: I'm screwed.

"Hey, can I ask Heather to come by?" Elise says when she looks up from a self-help weight loss book with intense underlines and erratic exclamation points crowding the pages. I nod my head without really thinking.

"I'm gonna check my email," I say, but Elise is already too into her text messaging to care.

"Heather'll be here in ten," Elise says.

"Wait, like, now?" I say. I have got to snap out of it, or I'm going to make this situation even worse.

"It's stupid, I know, but I want you to know her a little. I mean even if it's nothing . . . we can all hang out. She's really into baking, like you." I nod.

Elise is always doing this—finding random and mostly unconvincing ways for me to bond with her other friends or crushes. I mostly politely decline, but she's trying extra hard with Heather and I can practically taste her nervousness, so I give my most enthusiastic nod while watching my phone try to load LBC.

I try to get my head around Elise and Heather both being here while I complete my Assignment. It's like this whole situation is running away from me, and I can't get it under control again. It reminds me of the one car accident I ever got into. I lost control of the car because of ice on the road. I couldn't brake. I couldn't turn the wheel. The car drifted toward the middle of the road, veering to the wrong side, threatening to drive me against traffic. I kept turning the wheel, begging it to respond to what I was asking it to do. It simply would not listen. I've never been more terrified.

Then, all of a sudden, the ice let up and the car started working normally again, but it was too late. I'd turned the wheel all the way to the right when it wasn't responding, so I flew off the road.

I'm pretty sure that's what's happening right now. I'm moments away from flying off the road.

Zed: Document your Assignment if you can.

I've been waiting for this part. The photographs and audio files and grainy knee-down videos are cool and weird and random and I want to be part of that, too. I guess technically it's to "prove" we completed our Assignments, and I guess we can't totally be trusted to be honest, but I couldn't fathom lying on Life by Committee. What would be the point? Everyone else would be changing and growing and making a beautiful life, and I'd be hanging out, lying about how awesome I am.

I have to be better than that. But I have a sick feeling in my stomach and I can't make the pulsing, fearful headache go away. I try to get the image of my car crashing into an icy tree out of my head. I try to remember what Paul told me after that accident—that you have to ride with it, not fight against it. That the next time, I have to let the car drift, keep myself breathing, and ride it out.

I've stopped looking at my phone. I'm now looking around the café, all scared-animal-like, as if everyone in there knows what I'm about to do. Elise is looking at me like I'm losing it.

"Are you out of breath?" she says. "Tab? Do you need some kind of paper bag to breathe into? Are you having a situation?" She tries following my gaze, and we both realize in the same instant that it has settled on Devon.

He makes eye contact with me. He is all haunted blue eyes and skinny arms under his long-sleeve tee. He smiles and waves, and first I think: *cute*. Immediately followed by: *Is this a sign that I have to make something happen with him, like LBC told me to?*

My phone buzzes to tell me I have one hour left to complete my Assignment. I am now sweating approximately as much as your average marathoner. I guess I wanted a brand-new type of life, and this is certainly that. I have never felt this many things at once.

"TABBY," Elise says, loudly enough that multiple people turn around and give us *shut up, I'm working* glares.

"I'm okay!" I say, but I'm obviously not, so Elise shifts in her seat and moves her face closer to mine, like she will find something in my pupils that will tell her what's up.

Devon cocks his head and waves again. He wears his grandfather's old wedding ring on one hand and a leather cuff like Elise's on the opposite wrist. I can't deal with all of this right now. I have to find Paul.

"You're shaking," Elise says. Her hand reaches for mine, the smooth expanse of her fingers covers my trembling ones, and I twitch under the pressure.

"Do you know Devon, Jemma's brother?" I whisper. My knees are knocking against each other. It's a hollow feeling, a strange reflex that gives me goose bumps.

"Sure? The one who liked you?"

"Yeah. I mean, no. He didn't, I don't think. Doesn't. Anyway, that's him." I leave it at that, and Elise nods, like she now totally gets it.

"That is some intense eye contact happening," she says. I have not taken my eyes off Devon, and he has not taken his off me. His smile's gone crooked and a little goofy, like we're playing a game, but I am *not* playing. I'm trying to decide something big.

"He should not be here," I say. I mean it. I don't want to do this with Devon watching. But I'm trying to ride out the icy road, let the car go where it wants to go.

"He's supercute," Elise says, nudging me with her elbow and a smile.

"Should I talk to him?" I say. It's not the question I want to be asking, and Elise is giggling and nodding like this is all some ecstatic crush situation, and not a deliberate and exacting attempt to do what I've been told.

"Definitely," she says. "But I'd wipe your forehead first. You're a little . . . damp."

"Maybe I shouldn't talk right now, though," I say. "I have to do some stuff." I'm basically talking to myself, and I don't want Elise to ask questions, but there's so much happening in my head that I have to let little bits of it escape through my mouth. "Give me a second to think," I say, and I lean forward so much that I'm practically flashing Elise. My uncontrollable and super-objectionable breasts are at it again.

"Well, if he didn't like you before, he definitely does now," she says with a nod to my cleavage and then to Devon, whose long, skinny-jeaned legs are pacing toward us. Elise plays footsie with me under the table and can't stop the sneaky way her lips curl or the excited blush on her cheeks. "And seriously *so* much cuter than Joe, b-t-dubs."

"Am I still allowed here?" Devon says. I am dry mouthed from the traffic jam of things happening right now.

"I don't— I have to— I'm busy."

"You don't look super busy," he says, and there's his smile again, lighting up this corner of Tea Cozy and some tiny part of my heart. The non-Joe part, which isn't the important part. I shake my head to ignore it. If I do something with Devon, it's only to get Joe. He looks appealing because kissing him would make me even better at Life by Committee, would make Zed respect me more.

"Can I take a picture of your shoes?" I say. It is not a normal question.

I also am legitimately running out of time, so it is an ill-timed question.

"Tab, are you okay?" Elise says, as much under her breath as possible. She and Devon are giving me the same look of abject confusion and awkwardness.

"My shoes? Sure?" Devon says, but I'm not really listening to either of them. Paul has just stepped outside, out the back door, and that can only mean one thing.

"Maybe later?" I say, and too late realize that sounds insane since I'm the one who just super randomly asked to photograph his footwear. "Good to see you, though." I shrug. Forget to smile. Forget to sound cute. Forget how cute he is. Forget everything but the number of seconds Paul has been outside. If I don't go now, I'll miss my chance.

"Ah," Devon says. Takes another step back. "I'll come back

tomorrow, maybe? For a coffee?" A glance in his direction tells me he's trying to get that little smirk back in place, but he's fighting hard against the discomfort I'm obviously causing.

"I'm being weird," I say.

"We're waiting for my friend to stop by," Elise says, trying to save me from myself, I think. Of course, that in no way explains why I am acting like I have never participated in human interactions before. I take a deep breath, because I'd forgotten Heather was coming by too. I cannot take another person witnessing whatever it is I'm about to do to myself.

"Maybe you should meet Heather somewhere else," I say.

"Oh."

"Who's Heather?" Devon says, taking this all as some opportunity to stay involved in the conversation. His voice is too chipper.

"My parents are weird right now, Elise. They might do something embarrassing. I mean, I wouldn't bring my *own* dates here. So I don't want to ruin yours. Tell her we can all hang out a different time, okay? I think it'd be weird if she came here."

"*Tabitha*," she says. My name pinches her mouth and comes out a grumble. Her frown is turning into a line so straight it could be a ruler. Devon clears his throat like we need a reminder he's there, and holy *shit* we *do* need a reminder of that, because I just called Heather Elise's *date* in front of a total stranger.

"I'm sorry, I just mean, maybe it's too weird to—" I try. She's red-faced and glassy-eyed, like tears are only a few deep breaths away. Between me half outing her to Devon and implying that it'd be weird to have her bring a girl here, I've basically become the world's worst friend in under a minute.

But I feel Zed's countdown in my bones. As if I'm Captain Hook's crocodile and there is a ticking clock in my belly. I've got to get her out of here so I can focus on my Assignment.

"Anyway, you don't want me screwing it up for you," I try. I glare at Devon so that he takes another step back. I do not have to glare for long. He does a one-eighty and slumps back to his table. I am ruining people's days and their opinions of me left and right, but it will all get way, way worse if I don't meet my deadline.

"No, yeah, I get it," Elise says. She raises her eyebrows, widens her eyes a little in a challenge. Shoulders back. Aggressive.

"She'll like you better if she doesn't know how close we are." I'm rambling now. I'm doing that thing where I'm leaning forward and basically packing Elise's bag for her. No jokes about my cleavage this time, and Devon's not looking over here anymore anyway. I keep looking toward the door. I know I'm doing it and I know it's rude and I can feel Elise's eyes, hot on me like the Tea Cozy fireplace when it's really roaring.

"I don't think the problem is with Heather's opinion of you," Elise says. She's practically throwing her books into her tote, and I can see her jaw clenching and her hands shaking with anger. "*Heather* is super open-minded."

"No, I know. I'm sorry. I'm trying to help," I say. I have to get this Assignment over with, since it scares me so much. I told them I'd do it. I read the rules. I joined the site. I am one of them. Elise would get that, if I could tell her everything. Which I obviously can't. Won't.

"I said whatever, Tabby," Elise mumbles.

I'm going to have to fix it later.

"Have fun, okay?" I call out, but she doesn't turn back on her way out the door.

Cate's on me as soon as Elise is gone.

"Thank *God*," she says. "Your father is AWOL and I need someone to serve drinks. You game?"

I don't answer. She thrusts a couple of mugs into my hands and points me toward the table that ordered them.

"You're a doll," she says, and kisses my cheek before scurrying behind the counter. A few families have come in, and our policy with little kids is to get them out of the café as quickly as possible.

Cate hands over more drinks, and I drop off a green tea and a decaf coffee to some of the little old ladies who like table service, and then I go to get a better look, a few steps closer to the window. There's the top of Paul's head, graying red hair and a spiral of smoke sneaking up over his head and disappearing when it hits the sky.

My mind is raw enough right now to push me ahead. If I think about it any more, I might not go through with it, and I *have* to go through with it.

Cate's eating a scone behind the counter, having successfully rid Tea Cozy of tiny children, and the few filled tables are digging into cookies and coffees, so I can sneak out for a few minutes without being noticed. I take off my apron. Some weird logic has me worried that if my apron smells like weed, my mom will know what's up. I tie my hair into a bun (didn't someone say that helps with the lingering smell?) and ignore the *no no no* voice in my head that's telling me to just have a normal day doing normal things. Reading books. Pouring coffee. Replacing the honey and the skim milk on the counter. I could give up on LBC and Assignments and be Tabitha from Before. She was okay, wasn't she?

I have to do this, I think, and try to put all the fear and not-wanting-to in a box in the back of my brain.

The back door always sticks, and I have to push the full weight of my body against it to nudge it open.

"Tab! Jesus!" Paul waves his hand with the joint around. He can't decide whether to take another drag, hold it behind his back, or stamp it out into the frozen ground.

"You sharing?" I say. No pause. No intake of breath. No hemming and hawing while I figure out how to phrase it. Inside I am a mess, but on the outside maybe I am pulling this off.

I'm looking Paul in the eyes. Our secret rule has been that I never look at him straight on when he's smoking or high. It's funny how those boundaries set themselves up and keep us safe.

And it's even funnier how I'm out here kicking them down.

Paul's either so shocked or so stoned that he can't muster up an actual response.

"Do you have some for me?" I say. I pull my shoulders back like I'm all confidence. I reach my hand out, and Paul almost hands the joint over on reflex, I think, before shaking his head and remembering who exactly I am. You know. His daughter.

"Go inside, Tab," he says. His voice is small and sad, and he shuffles his feet in the pile of icy leaves he is standing in. They crunch and the wind whistles and I pull my wool blazer more tightly around myself.

"I accidentally outed Elise. I have officially lost my last friend," I say. I'm not sure making a plea about how shitty my life is currently is the best strategy, but I have to fill the silence with something, and the truth is what is most readily accessible. Paul reaches out his free hand to squeeze my shoulder, but I wince away from the touch so he knows that's not what I want.

"Also, the school counselor, your good friend Mrs. Drake, basically called me a whore."

"That is completely not okay. Cate and I can go in and—" Paul loses his words in a hefty cough and then seems to forget what he was saying. "Bad" is his epic conclusion.

"I'll do it regardless," I say, pointing at the joint when he has neither taken a drag nor handed it over to me. The joint hangs in the air between us, an unanswered question. "This guy I sort of like does it. Everyone does it. I thought you'd want me to try with you first." I don't say it like a threat, but I guess that's what it is. Paul looks at me with his drooping eyes and pulls his winter cap farther down over his ears. He likes that I'm telling him things about my life, though. I can tell.

"Your mother will hate me," he says at last, in a morning voice, groggy and slow. The pile of leaves gets picked up in the wind, spins around frantically, and drops down somewhere else.

"I'm not telling Cate," I say. "I'm not crazy. This is a Paul and Tabby thing." It's a phrase Paul uses. It refers to used books, strong espresso, science fiction movies, staying up way too late, adding crazy garnishes to Cate's perfect recipes, singing along with country singers using opera voices and cracking ourselves up, eating an entire block of cheese in one sitting, collecting photographs of New York City. And if all goes my way, smoking pot together.

Paul brags to his friends about Paul-Tabby things. "I'm not one of those distant, secondary-parent dads," he's always saying. "This one here's my best friend. We've got something special. Cate and I have very separate relationships with her. Like it should be." It is maybe the only thing Paul ever really gets on a high horse about.

It does the trick.

"I appreciate you coming to me about it, instead of going to some party and doing it there," he says.

"Family of the Year," I say. "I know I can trust you."

"Okay," he says. He rubs his forehead, like maybe he can dislodge some thoughts. "Okay," he says again. He drops the last bit of his joint on the ground and rolls a brand-new one, his fingers moving confidently in spite of how high I'm sure he is. "Your mom's busy in there?" He nods to the back door of the Cozy, and I nod back. He has got to know what a horrible idea this is, giving me drugs in the back of his family-owned business, pregnant Cate a few feet away. But Paul has never been much for carefulness.

"You're the best," I say without even trying to smile. I'm too scared and shocked and uncertain to muster up a normal facial expression. I've never even smoked a cigarette. I hear it burns on the way down. I've seen the way people cough it up, and I don't like the strange, earthy smell.

Paul hands me the joint, and I suck at it the way I've seen him do.

It tastes like it smells, which is to say not great, and there's the burn I'd heard about, a rockiness as it goes down my throat, and a screaming insistence that I blow it right out even though I know the people who know what they're doing hold it in. So I shut my eyes tight and focus all my energy on keeping my mouth closed. Smoke spins around in my mouth, the roof getting too hot to handle.

Paul can't stop himself from laughing, but he opens his mouth to have me mirror him, and I do. I sputter and cough and wait for something to feel actually good. "Another," he says. What was awkward only a moment ago is now something he wants even more than me. I shiver in the cold and look at the mountains. Something to anchor me.

Paul's eyes have lit up, and I'm not his daughter anymore but a project. He is taking it seriously and wants to do it right. I do what Paul tells me and take another hit, and another.

I finally keep a little down and go light-headed. I giggle.

"There it is," Paul says. He's full of pride for about a second, and then his forehead creases and it's something else: fear of what he's done, of what it means, of who he is. Maybe even of who I am.

I wonder if even the mountains shift, in this moment. Maybe a little snow melts and slides down. Nothing is quite as stable as it might seem.

Paul puts an arm around my shoulder and pulls me close. And that's nice, the closeness, but my chest squeezes a bit when I think about sitting on his lap as a little girl and coloring my baby dolls with Magic Markers and having him take me to gymnastics on Saturday mornings.

I'm high, he's high, and the best things about having a father have vanished.

There are things you should not do with your father, even if you call him by his first name.

Immediately, I miss the time before this exact moment.

I think Paul does too. He is frowning and we're shaking from the cold and our decisions and the fact that we have probably officially taken ourselves out of the running for Family of the Year.

I want it to be a year ago. I want it to be three years ago, five even. I want it to be thirty minutes ago.

The door does its slow push forward, and Cate's face appears where it shouldn't.

"Tabby, your tables are—" Her voice is edgy and impatient; she's been looking for me for a while. She sounds even a bit relieved, at having located me, I guess, but then she stops short.

The joint is still in my hand, between two fingers like I'm some expert.

I know I'm high because the thought occurs to me in slow motion. The slowest, most detached realization I think I've ever had.

"Oh come *on*," Cate says. "Some fucking father you're becoming, asshole."

The words hit me so hard I trip, even though I am standing still. This is not how Cate and Paul speak to each other. Not ever. Not even with pregnancy hormones and stuff.

"Hey, hey, hey," Paul says. If he's as high as I am (which, let's be honest, I'm sure he's way higher), he simply can't come up with anything more compelling to say right now.

"Hey?" Cate says. She is fuming, and no one's manning the counter, which means she must be *really* freaking out. She takes Tea Cozy seriously. "HEY? You are giving *drugs* to our *daughter.* What the *fuck* are you thinking, dipshit?"

Now I'm sweating. Pouring sweat. People inside the café are listening in and Cate is railing at Paul and I'm still stuck here with the joint in my hand, which is still strangely funny so I'm trying simultaneously not to laugh *and* not to cry. Leaves blow around and get displaced again. Every little gust changes everything.

I can see, beyond Cate's pregnant body crowding the doorway, customers craning their necks to watch. Whispering to one another. Scooting their chairs closer to the door, hoping to get a glimpse of the excitement. I reach forward to close the door, but Cate's not budging, and I don't want to make her even angrier.

This is bad. Not just bad for the family, but bad for business, I would think.

"Ummm," I say. It does not stop Cate from yelling at Paul.

"Don't even think about coming home. You hearing me? I am having another kid, and we are raising this one right, and I will not have you pulling this crap with—"

"Okay, okay, show's over," Paul says, cutting her off. He grabs the joint from my hand and throws it to the ground. Hands me the keys to his car, which Cate rushes to grab back since obviously I'm not driving when I'm high. Paul blushes. He'd been trying to do the right thing. He says a literal "Oops," which I don't think I've ever heard an adult man say in real life.

But he keeps going, like he has something to prove. He removes Cate from the door and starts picking up empty glasses, asking customers if they want more coffee.

"Stay," Cate says to me. She points a finger. Not only am I the crappy child they raised all wrong, not only am I their guinea pig preparing them for their *real* baby, I am also, apparently, a dog.

I stay.

BITTY: Assignment completed.

STAR: Someone's high!

BITTY: I didn't like that one.

AGNES: Sometimes it's unclear why we do something until much, much later.

BITTY: I feel worse than I did yesterday. And being high so far is mostly annoying.

ZED: Feel the way you are losing fear? The way you are gaining control?

STAR: You can't see everything right now. I promise. One of my least favorite Assignments led me to the party that I met Moon at. I was miserable for months after. And now, I'm here.

Also, I'm gonna do it. My Assignment. Propose. And Bitty, you helped me decide that I could. If you can do it, I can do it, right?

Star posts a picture of her feet and what I assume are Moon's feet. Barefoot, pinching blades of grass between their toes. The hope that's been bubbling more and more since I joined LBC rushes into a boil. I can have that. If I power through the unsettled feeling and the intense desire to vomit, I could be that girl.

I'd almost forgotten to take my own picture, but luckily I have my phone stranded out here with me, so I stand next to the joint that Paul discarded into the pile of leaves. I'm in ugly yellow rain boots and I don't know how to make it interesting, so I line everything up in a straight line: my two feet, the joint, the lighter, which I drop onto the ground also.

Snap.

Sixteen.

STAR: I have to be honest. I'm scared. What if he says no? What if I learn more about him and don't like it? What if I don't understand everything yet? What if he says yes?

I can't stand Star having doubts. Not now. Not so quickly after she agreed to her Assignment. Not when she only has a few hours to go.

I shiver from the chill but thank the sun for settling in right over my head.

I wish I could say I am simply enjoying the sounds of nature once Cate strands me outside: tweeting birds, the oceanic sound of wind hitting leaves, the occasional crack of twigs breaking in half under the weight of tiny animals. It looks like a woodland November wonderland out here: the sun breaks through the pumpkin-colored leaves and makes odd patterns on the grass, and there's the persistent optical illusion of close-looking snow-topped mountains that are actually sort of far away.

But. After hanging out on LBC for a few more minutes, all there is to do is listen to Paul and Cate scream at each other.

"You *fuckup!*" Cate yells. Since I can't see her, my mind gives me a moment of relief when I don't have to believe it's actually her. I smirk, like some other family is causing a scene. But then: "Not only are you ruining our business with your ridiculous . . . stoner-ness . . . you've also decided to ruin our *daughter*?"

Yeah, that's me. The ruined one.

I kick a pile of leaves. Grind one under the heel of my yellow boot.

"How many warn—chance—warn-chances did I give you? You really needed me to be more clear about what I wanted? You can't be a father and a . . . a . . . trouble-pot-stirrer."

Cate makes up words when she's mad. Her level of anger almost always directly correlates to how many nonsensical or cobbled-together words and phrases she peppers her speech with.

"She—Tabitha—she was going to experiment—" Paul starts. "She finally started talking about some of the things happening in her life—" He stops cold. I am clenching my jaw so tightly, it aches. I am grinding my teeth with such ferocity, I swear I can feel little shards of them coming off in my mouth, like I'm sandpapering them down. I'm wishing the walls were thicker and soundproof. Because next I have to listen to Paul asking customers to please leave. Plus it's freaking cold.

"I'm so sorry," he says, and I know without seeing his face that it is crimson and grimacing, like mine, but worse. That floating, giggling feeling I had a few minutes ago has tempered, too. It's still there, but only in the back of my head, and I can't crawl inside it. It feels like I got suddenly shoved outside that warm, silly, cloud-insulated place and back into the cold November air. I wish I had a jacket and some headphones.

Cate is silent.

"We'll open back up in a few hours, okay?" Paul says. There's a pause, and I think I can hear Cate's words biting the air. "Or tomorrow," he corrects himself because of whatever Cate said. "We'll be open again tomorrow."

I could sneak away, obviously. There's no electric fence or Great Wall of Tea Cozy keeping me locked into the café's overgrown little backyard. But there's nowhere to *go.* I pissed Elise off and weirded Devon out, and my house is too far away to walk to. I'd like to talk to Joe and see if he likes Stoner Tabby. If we are even more connected now that I've done This Thing. But I don't want him to hear my parents screaming at each other in the background.

"We can put the rest of your hot chocolate in a to-go cup," I hear Paul saying. Cate must be throwing things around, or at least clanging them together, in the kitchen, because there's a metal-against-metal symphony rocking the little cottage that is Tea Cozy. " . . . I'll throw that cake in a doggy bag," Paul continues. A little bit of the giggly high sneaks back in, and I have to cover my mouth so as not to let out a big belly laugh at this one. On any normal night, Paul, Cate, and I would eat burgers at home and imitate the cranky old lady who won't leave the café even when the owners are openly brawling.

I know this won't be a normal evening.

The reindeer bells attached to Tea Cozy's front door jangle, and then it's just Paul and Cate inside, and me, forgotten, outside.

"I'm so sorry," Paul starts. "I wasn't thinking. Obviously. And you have every right to be mad—"

"You *never* think!" Cate screams. "When's the last time you thought? A gatrillion hundred years ago? We said this would be different! We said we'd be adults! Parents! Real ones! You promised!"

I wonder if I should go in and join the fight. If I'm taking the power out of the Assignment by hiding out here. I try to access that part of me that surges with pride when I complete an Assignment. The part of me that is brave and strong and taking control. It's there, but it does not like hearing Cate and Paul yell at each other.

Paul must be cowering in the corner, because I can't hear a response from him even though I can hear Cate's heavy post-outburst breathing. Music starts pumping through the speakers, and it's loud and clear from out here: Whitney Houston, which Cate only ever resorts to when she needs some serious strength. She sings along at the top of her lungs, and after a few verses, the bells on the door jangle again, meaning Paul's left without me.

I listen to Cate sing the entirety of *Whitney: The Greatest Hits*. Sometimes her voice breaks halfway through a song and she cries in an angry, openmouthed way. I have heard her cry that way when her sister refused to have her over for Christmas, when she thought she might have to close Tea Cozy because a customer reported them to the IRS, and, most recently, when she found me curled up in the fetal position, crying after the dance where Jemma told me I wasn't worthy of being her friend anymore.

But I have never, ever heard her cry that way about Paul.

When the album's over, the front-door bells ring their Christmas cheer again, and I'm just a forgotten girl in the backyard without a coat. But at least it's safe to reenter.

Back inside, my laptop's right where I left it, but the rest of the café is sparkling clean and tidy. They remembered everything but me. Or the other (even worse?) possibility: they remembered me and chose to leave me.

Joe has chatted me a bunch of times.

5:17: Let's talk.

5:23: You at the Cozy?

5:32: Okay if I come by?

5:51: What is going ON in there?

5:52: Uh, people are on the sidewalk listening to your parents rip each other apart. . . .

5:53: Hope you're okay.

5:55: Please let me know you're okay.

6:10: I assume everything's okay. Other stuff happening. Gotta run.

For a second, I think I had him. The drama of my parents screaming at each other, the anxiety created by him not being able to get in touch with me, the idea, maybe, that he could help. But then, I assume, Sasha got in touch and he had to take care of her. Because in the battle between my issues and her issues, hers still win. "Other stuff" means Sasha. It's like the world's worst code name.

At first it's only a theory, but she's got a status up, just Joe's name and a heart, and a bunch of my ex-friends have "liked" it. Joe saves Sasha, again.

When Tea Cozy is empty, I think it's almost louder than when it's full. The building is old and creaks, settling in on itself. I'm rarely here alone, so I want to enjoy it. I lean back in one of the paisley armchairs, slip off my shoes, and try to find something wonderful in the solitude. When I was little, I'd sneak to the Cozy: steal my parents' key rings, hop on my bike, and let myself in at odd hours. I want it to feel like that again.

It doesn't.

Not to mention there's Elise's status, *SOME PEOPLE. UGH.* I know it's about me because I can't think of anyone else it would be about. Elise isn't like me—she doesn't get angry easily, doesn't have a litany of awkward relationships with former friends, doesn't trash-talk or tell people her problems or complain online about her sorry life. But when she wants to tell me something and doesn't want to do it directly, she goes online to vaguely vent. The things she can't say to me out loud, she can hint at in public. I can't even fault her for it, given how messed up I am.

There's a knock at the window. I want it to be Joe so badly that I take a few seconds before looking up to see who it is. I just want a few moments when I can believe that it's him, that he'll be out there in his red North Face and wind-whipped cheeks waiting to rescue me, or maybe fool around in the empty café.

So there's an even bigger shock when it's Devon's face I see in the window. Big blue eyes and long lashes, a wiry frame, an oversize striped scarf, a furry hat that must be from Russia. And that face: the only word for it is pretty. His face is a perfect, slender oval, and there's something to love about his super-straight nose and freckled cheeks. Not love, but you know, find pretty cute.

He waves. He's more than a year older than me, but the way he moves is more like a little kid. I let him in.

"Hey there," I say. It doesn't sound like me. It especially doesn't sound like me in the state I'm in right now. I'm sad and stressed and scared, but he has a look on his face like he wants me to smile at him, so I do.

I could do more. I could be the girl Zed is pushing me to be. I could do all my Assignments, go further than I ever imagined. Maybe I could kiss Devon, and Joe could walk by and see us lips-to-lips in the window, and then Joe would burst in and wrestle me from Devon's arms so he can have me for himself.

Or something like that.

But I feel bad that my impulse is to use Devon. He's so cute all bundled up and unsure of how I'm going to respond to him.

"I needed a friendly face," I say. My nerves are under control, compared to earlier. Or maybe I'm high.

"I came by to apologize," Devon says, oblivious to the intricate fantasy happening in my head right now. "I mean, that's why I was here earlier too, before you got sort of . . . nervous. Do I make you nervous?"

"Yeah. I mean no," I try. I sort of shake my head and twirl a strand of hair and shrug at my own silliness. "I'm nervous a lot lately. So it's not you."

"Anyway. I'm sorry," he says. He doesn't laugh at how incredibly not smart I sound.

"Why? What'd you do?" I say.

"I guess I want to apologize for Jemma," he says. "It's partly my fault, I think." He stares at the tips of his shoes, so I do too. "I kept teasing Jemma about how hot you'd gotten, and I think it sort of freaked her out, you know?" He isn't blushing red like me, but he is sort of shifting from side to side, so he's got to be at least a little nervous.

"Teasing her," I repeat. I don't want to talk about Jemma. I don't want to ignite the pocket of sadness and nostalgia and confusion I feel when I think too much about what it means that we're not friends anymore. "I don't think it's your fault," I say. I mean to dismiss the conversation, but because being around him makes me smile, it comes across flirtatious. Like, it's not his fault that I'm so supercute. How could he help himself?

"Jemma seems younger than you, you know? I mean, she doesn't think so. Jemma thinks she's about forty. But in some ways, she's a kid and maybe in some ways . . . you're not?" He steps closer to me. My heart pounds. Good pounds. But maybe it's the weed.

"I'm not really a kid," I say. I let myself take a step closer to him. So close my shoulder is an inch away from pressing against his chest. So close it would take nothing more than a little breeze for us to be hugging.

Or kissing.

I wonder what would happen if I leaned into his lips. How would my life change if I completed another terrifying Assignment? If I did something I'd never do without Zed's or LBC's urging?

Mostly I think of Joe and how badly I want him to want me, and I stay put. I stay close to him.

"Are you okay?" Devon says. He touches my shoulder, but I can't decide if it's sweet or pitying. "You're going to hate this, but I sort of . . . heard everything."

"I don't know what that means," I say, but the second it's out of my mouth I obviously do know what he means. He heard Cate and Paul and the screaming.

"I sort of stayed. You seemed . . . off. And I was worried. Apparently I'm worrying about you a lot." Devon shrugs. "If I'm being weird, tell me, okay?"

"Okay," I say. I can't decipher what the hell I feel. I went to a therapist once, with Cate and Paul when they were in a phase when they thought everyone should be in therapy. There was a chart of cartoon people making different faces. They were labeled with emotions. *This is what angry looks like; this is what surprised looks like; this is what happy looks like.*

I try to think through the faces and see if any of them match.

There is no corresponding face for the way I'm feeling. It is unrecognizable and jumbled. It is maybe all the faces combined.

"It's nice. To have you . . . thinking about me," I say at last. Because I can't figure out how I feel.

I can feel drops of sweat prickling to the surface, one bead for each vertebra on my spine. It's a slow build at first, but then just a wash of humiliating *wet* all up and down my back. I ignore it so that I can stay sexy.

This is what scared looks like.

"Want tea?" I say. I touch my phone in my pocket. They're all here with me, pushing me along, helping me. Star, @sshole, Roxie, Zed, Agnes.

"I love tea," Devon says. It's a lie. No teenage boys love tea. "You know, I really am sorry," he says when I'm walking away from him to get started on the tea. People always say the big things when your back is turned to them. It's easier to say stuff when you can't see the other person's reaction.

"I hate your sister," I say, which isn't in any way an acceptance of the apology, but it's the truth, and I'm getting really, really good at telling the truth.

"That's cool," he says.

"Green tea okay?" I say from the back.

"Sounds disgusting."

"It kind of is." I smile, putting the tea bag in, letting it steep before I go back to Devon.

"You're gonna hate this," I say, and hand the steaming mug to him. It smells like hot seaweed and cut grass, and his nose wrinkles but he chokes down a sip anyway.

"So, what are we reading?" he says.

I make a gesture like he should look through the bag of books from my bookstore outing earlier, but he goes right for *The Secret Garden*, which I've left on the table. Not one of the new-old copies I bought today, but *the* copy. The red pen one.

"I like your thoughts on this," he says, tapping the page. He's going to do great at college—he's a natural at academic-looking frowns. I'm eyeing my laptop, wondering if I can log in, type out some updates about Devon and Joe, and log back out before he sees anything.

"Oh, those aren't my thoughts," I say. I don't say more and he doesn't ask more, but I don't pull the book away from him either. It makes me nervous—it's very much *mine*—but I like that he likes it. I watch him read for a moment, then turn my focus to my computer. Pull up LBC.

I know I shouldn't, in front of him, but I can't help myself. I feel too untethered to be here alone with Devon.

"You're a mystery, Lady Tabitha," Devon says. He moves his hand, like it might touch my face or my back or close my computer so that I focus more wholly on him. His hand lingers in the air, undecided. I watch it until it drops to his side, and he takes a step back, as if to give me and my computer some space.

There's only one new comment for me.

ZED: What's next?

Next.

Because I only have a week in which to post another secret, complete another Assignment.

Next time. Something bigger, badder, scarier.

Next. Time.

"What's that?" Devon's voice interrupts the loop of *next next next* spiraling in my head. He has snuck around behind me. His elbows are on the back of the armchair, and he is bent over so far that I can feel his breath as it hits the top of my head. It's warm and blows around the little stray hairs that have escaped from my ponytail.

"Hey!" I say, the noise popping out, the sound version of a jack-in-the-box. I close the computer and hug it to my chest, but when I turn around, the look on his face says he's seen too much.

"Who are those people?" he says, drawing his words out slowly. I don't say anything, because I don't really *know*. "Assignment completed?" he keeps going.

"Could I get a ride home?" I say.

"What are you doing?"

"Making sure no one is reporting my parents to the police for, like, a domestic disturbance," I try to joke. He doesn't laugh.

"No, what was that site?"

"Is this what having a sibling is like? Spying and butting in and stuff?" There's a shake in my voice that I have to hope he misses.

Devon clears his throat, puts his hands up to surrender, doesn't say anything else.

Outside the window, it starts to snow.

Seventeen.

Devon holds my hand to walk me to his car. Because of the ice, he says. We both have mittens on, so the grasp is soft and clumsy and reminds me mostly of being a little kid. Devon in general reminds me of when I was a little kid. So does snow.

We don't speak on the ride to my house, except when Devon asks me if I'm sure I don't want to grab a pizza, and I shake my head really fast back and forth. Zed will be disappointed when I share this part. I should say yes. To everything, I think.

As I'm getting out of the car, Devon tilts his head. He can't see my mouth or my forehead—I'm all wrapped up in a scarf and an oversize winter hat. Safe from scrutiny.

"Call me if you need another ride," he says.

"It was nice of you to come," I say. He has to ask me to repeat myself, the sound is so muffled by my thick fleece scarf. "Or stay. It was nice of you to stay and make sure I didn't, like, implode or whatever."

It looks like there's more he wants to say, but the snow's coming down harder now, so I pretend it's urgent that I get out of the car this instant.

"I like hanging out with you," I say after a big breath.

"Everything is going to be okay," he says. It's a funny response. I expected him to say he liked hanging out with me too, or even that he is into me or wants to take me out next weekend or something. But he sounds certain, when he says it will all work out, and for a moment I don't feel the snow somehow finding its way under my scarf or blurring my vision when it sticks to my lashes. I feel only his sureness and the flipping in my stomach that is different from the pounding that comes when I am near Joe. But it's something.

I nod and wave and kick snow up, walking to my front door, and Devon doesn't drive away until I am all the way inside the (very quiet) house.

"Hello?" I call out.

There aren't calls back or feet scuffling or showers running. There is no one waiting for me by the kitchen counter with pamphlets on teen drug use or stern talkings-to. "Hello?" I try again, louder and faker, a sound that doesn't expect a response. I wander from room to room, some part of me thinking maybe Paul is passed out, but he snores and I would have heard the buzzing breath of his sleep if he were conked out on a sofa somewhere.

I don't mind the house all emptied out like this, except that I think it's intended as a punishment in this circumstance. I am supposed to think about what I have done. They didn't need to leave the house empty for me to do that. It's all I can think of anyway.

I get online and look for Joe. He pops up immediately, and I think maybe I can distract myself with him.

Long day, I type in. I've only turned on one weak lamp in Cate's office, and it's mostly lit by winter moonlight reflecting off the thin layer of snow gathering outside the window. It's cozy and warm and pretty as fuck.

What happened? he asks.

Pregnancy made Cate crazy, I say. Smiley face. LOL. Anything to lighten the mood. If Sasha Cotton is the troubled, fragile sex kitten, the least I can be is bubbly and peppy and fun.

Sounds like it. Joe isn't talkative tonight. It happens from time to time, but I hate that it's happening now, when I need to give my heart something sweet to spin around. *I'm busy, talk later?*

Busy means Sasha is there. Or on the phone. Or on his mind. I hover my fingers over the keys, trying to think of something to type that will keep him chatting for even another second. But before I can get any words out, he logs off, his name vanishing from the computer screen and leaving me alone. I listen to the nothingness for all of three seconds before it's too much to handle. Where the hell are my parents? I choose Indie Dance on Pandora and turn the speakers all the way up. Keyboards, echoing percussion, and feminine male singers fill the room with sound, and I sing along at the top of my lungs. Dance a little in my chair. Tell my heart to stop leaping in every direction: love, fear, nostalgia, boredom, interest, thrill, loneliness.

I fall asleep before either of my parents makes it home. My new life is wearing me out so much that I can't even make it to my bedroom, so I curl up on the couch fully clothed with late-night television and a worn green quilt and probably drool all over the pillow, and when I wake up the next morning, it's only Paul who has returned.

> Elise,
>
> I am the worst. THE. WORST. I'm so sorry.
>
> I'll make sure we have chocolate chip scones every day for the next YEAR if you don't stop talking to me. I'll tell Devon . . . something. I'll make it go away.
>
> I'm the worst, the worst, the worst.
>
> I can't even.
>
> I love you. You're amazing. You're better than me. I will fix it.
>
> Me

She doesn't respond.

I did not know it was possible to have even fewer people like me than I did twenty-four hours ago, but there you go.

Eighteen.

Ethics is my least favorite class. Not only because Jemma is in it with me, but also because I never agree with anything the teacher says. Or anything the writers and philosophers we read about say.

And this morning I hate it even more because I am sleepy-headed and strange, coming off everything that happened over the weekend. Yesterday, Paul and I stayed in separate corners of the house, not speaking. I didn't do homework or watch TV or go online. I slept and felt sorry for myself and listened for Cate to walk in the door. She didn't. This morning, I couldn't get it together to shower or do my hair or put on makeup, so I'm messy and feel my own grossness under my red cashmere sweater and too-tight black pants. I feel Luke and his cohorts looking at my ass like it's a freaking hamburger when I'm getting into my chair.

I haven't had coffee, either. No stopping by Tea Cozy this morning. No Cate making me a home-latte. Instead, it was me and Paul frowning and pretending to eat cereal and avoiding eye contact.

Ethics class and the overheating of Circle Community in general are making everything worse.

"Hey," Jemma says before Ms. Gilbert has gotten to class. I can't imagine she's talking to me. No one is talking to me. I have LBC and that's it and whatever, that's all I need, anyway. I make my mouth a steely line so they all know I do not care what they think about me.

"*Tabitha*," Jemma says, already full of exasperation.

I barely recognize her voice. Or the classroom. The whole world is unfamiliar. Conquerable. Mine.

I'm wearing red shoes today. Shoes like Star's. With a little heel and a strap over the ankle and a vintage, awkward patent-leather sheen. I am now a girl who wears red shoes and doesn't care.

"Oh," I say, turning to Jemma. "Hey. What's up?" I look her dead in the eyes. She must not be expecting that, because she blinks, like, a thousand times.

"What are you doing with my brother?"

"Huh?"

"My *brother*," Jemma says. Did she always talk to me like I didn't speak the language, or is this a new mode of communication she's adopted?

"You know," I say, and take a deep breath, "we're not friends now. So you don't really get an opinion anymore. On my life. You know? I mean, hate me from afar or whatever. But don't talk to me about it."

Other people are listening now. Not a few. All. All the other people are listening. I cross my legs, my stretchy black pants rubbing against themselves, and my red shoes glinting under fluorescent lights.

I hate them all. I straighten my back and smile, knowing that they all live their stupid Vermont lives, and I'm doing something Important and Real.

"That's awesome, except you are throwing yourself at my brother. You should have heard what he said to his friends on the phone yesterday. I mean, it's disgusting."

Luke snorts out some obnoxious jock laughter. I cannot for the life of me picture Devon talking trash about me on the phone after the hour of time we spent together Saturday. I raise my eyebrows at Jemma, who obviously wanted me to blush and look away.

I have a shimmer of pride, or a whole flame of it, at being better than that now. At how much I'm growing.

"Huh. What'd he say, exactly?" I say. I flip some hair behind my shoulders. If she's going to hate me, she might as well really hate me.

"That, like, that you, whatever." Now it's Jemma who is blushing and looking away. Alison elbows her, like she's supposed to be doing a better job at making me feel awful about myself. "Don't make me say this stuff," Jemma continues after clearing her throat. "Please stay away. Please? You don't need to go after him, you know? You can get someone else." She looks around the room at Luke and his cohorts, who are all laughing and chewing gum and drawing pictures of boobs on their notebooks.

I rub my eyes. The truth is, I'm still so exhausted and I have a knot of anxiety in my stomach that will not untangle.

"Stop talking to her," Alison mumbles. It's not like the rest of us can't hear, though, so it's especially lame.

"Yeah. Stop talking to me," I say. The smallest, weirdest part of me wants to know what Devon *did* say about me and who he said it to. Because even though I don't buy what Jemma's saying, something has set her off. "I've never done anything remotely terrible to you. And you know it, too. That's why you're blushing right now. Because you know that I may look like some slut, but you're a huge bitch."

It's like the words came out of someone else's lips. My heart races, and I cover my own mouth for a moment. The room is absolutely still. Luke isn't laughing anymore. The other girls aren't whispering. Absolutely no one is doing last-minute homework catch-up.

I kind of can't breathe. I'm caught between feeling amazing and terrible about what I said. I can't decide if it's a jolt of bliss or regret. It's like those two things are located too close to each other to tell.

"I—" Jemma tries, unsuccessfully, to get some more words out.

"You can't rewrite history to make yourself feel better about what you've done," I say. "I mean, isn't that what your therapist would tell you?" Now that I've jumped over the line from polite to terrifically, terribly honest, I might as well stay there.

Jemma's eyes go so wide and wild, she looks like a cartoon. She is the Donald Duck version of herself: angry, tongue hanging out, spirals instead of eyeballs, smoke whistling out of her ears. There are some barely disguised giggles.

"I'm not in *therapy*," Jemma lies. She may be my personal mean girl, but she's still pretty low on the Circle Community Day School totem pole. Plus now that's she's all tight with Sasha Cotton, it won't surprise anyone to hear she's in therapy.

I don't respond. Like Star said one time, sometimes it's best to let someone dig their own grave.

I feel absolutely full with new knowledge. It's like suddenly I can do everything in a completely different way than I would have before, and the stability of the Vermont mountains and cold and my scared self are up for grabs.

My red shoes pinch my toes a little, truth be told, but they are worth it.

"I'm *not*," Jemma says again. "I don't have a therapist." Her eyes are pooling with tears. "You should be in therapy. For your problems. With guys," she says. With the eyes of the entire class on her, she's getting more and more awkward. I sigh and shake my head, since I've heard it all before. "You want attention from all of them. People's brothers. People's boyfriends. It's disgusting, what you're doing with Joe. Like, completely. Awful. In the worst way."

She said his name.

"Good ole Joe," Luke says, his smirk back on his face, his eyebrows raised and jiggling when I accidentally look his way. It's his way of confirming, for everyone else in class, what Jemma's accusing me of. That I'm hooking up with Joe Donavetti, one half of everyone's favorite, super-strange couple.

Girls wrinkle their noses. This tall, skinny, almost-pretty girl named Ginger tears up. Literally tears up. My mind rushes, waterfalls, with things to say in response. Denials and defenses and comebacks and distractions.

But before I can choose which one to use, Ms. Gilbert finally comes in, all flustered and red-faced and apologetic.

"I didn't," I say to the room. None of them are looking at me anymore. Except Ms. Gilbert, who wrinkles her forehead in confusion. "I mean, I'm not. Doing that. With whoever."

"Tabitha?" Ms. Gilbert says. I get the feeling, from her tone of voice and the way she's blushing and watching my classmates, that she knows about my growing reputation. I get the distinct impression that Mrs. Drake has been making the rounds with her thoughts on me, and that the most popular teachers are in on it too now. They have these group meetings to discuss Student Life every week, and I'm suddenly super sure I've been on the agenda.

"It's nothing," I say. "Rumors." I gesture to our ethics book. Like, I don't know, as a defense against them. As if I'm ethically right and want Ms. Gilbert to know it. I sort of give up on the gesture, though, because I don't think I know whether I'm ethically sound or whatever.

Ms. Gilbert shakes off my awkwardness and starts a heated class discussion on the difference between ethics and morals. Jemma keeps looking at me, like I'm the example of someone with neither.

I make a note in the margin: *What about your moral obligation to yourself?*

I tap my pen over the note.

Zed would like that. I have to remember to post it onto the site later today.

Ms. Gilbert is saying something conclusive and diplomatic and thought provoking, and I am putting the pen back to the page. I write the Life by Committee address next to my little margin note.

It's not exactly a safe thing to do, but it feels right.

I smile at the idea of some girl in a few years using my old textbook and needing to discover a new world, the way I needed it. Cycle of life, or something. Sort of beautiful.

Nineteen.

I curl into a couch at Tea Cozy when school is over and watch my parents make awkward paths around each other. They pass off dishes and shout out orders over the rumble of the espresso machine, but otherwise they avoid eye contact and keep at least two feet of distance between their bodies at all times, which is particularly impressive given how narrow the space behind the counter is.

It's hard not to feel doubt at my decisions, seeing them like that. Knowing that I caused it.

Tiny, tiny seeds of doubt that Zed promises are natural, are part of the process. He's said so over and over to other members who have struggled. I've seen it all over the site.

Growing pains, he calls them.

I type out what I wrote to myself in my ethics textbook, about my obligation to myself, and ask if that's right, if that's part of LBC and this new way of living. Zed responds right away, happy to see me back after my day off yesterday.

ZED: It's a moral obligation to have us ALL live our best lives. There's doing the right thing and there's doing the best thing. They're not always the same thing.
The best thing is a challenge. The right thing is often a submission.
We do the best things here. We do the unlikely things.

I nod along with what I'm reading, even though I don't completely understand it. Sometimes when I'm really deep in LBC, I think I am seeing some new shade of life, like a color I didn't know existed and maybe isn't as pretty as blue or green or yellow, but is still worth knowing. I've never worked so hard to understand something. All those years of math class, I thought I was really pushing myself. Turns out I wasn't even close.

I try to picture Zed, and hope, hope, hope that he is tall and strange-looking with light eyes and strong hands and broad shoulders. I hope he wears sweaters. I hope he drinks coffee. I hope he walks barefoot. I hope he reads long books and short haiku and has glasses and a deep but soft voice.

I rub my eyes and rock back and forth in my seat a little. I sigh too loudly for public, and eventually, Cate comes over with a cup of coffee. At first I think this is a kind of peace offering, but from the shrug of her shoulders when she places it in front of me, I know that it's actually a sign that she's given up on me. Up close I can see the redness of her eyes and the frizzy, unwashed texture of her ponytailed hair. She smells like her mother's outdated, too-floral perfume. I press record on my computer, thinking maybe I'll post the audio of some of this conversation on LBC.

"We're not going to talk about it," Cate says instead of hello. I almost hit stop on the record. This isn't the kind of thing I want people knowing about my mother. That she can be cold and harsh and leave the most important things undiscussed simply because she doesn't feel like addressing them. But it's real. And Zed says real is the whole point.

I keep it recording.

"I think we should talk about it," I say, angling my words toward the computer. I sort of want to apologize, though it seems like the LBC-ers wouldn't like that. I am probably supposed to stick by my actions and ride them out fully. "I am so, so sorry. I know I messed up. And I know saying I'm sorry is the lamest, but Jesus I really am sorry."

"You know I love you, okay?" she says, but there's no hiding the fact that she did not accept my apology.

"I know you love me."

"I hate being mad at you," she says. Which means: *I am mad at you*.

"Both of us," I add, meaning Paul but remembering not to say his name in the recording. She nods.

"But I am. Mad. Right now. And pregnant." She looks at me like I'm supposed to know what's coming, but I don't. "I'm going to stay with my parents."

She doesn't say for how long. I don't ask, because I'm scared of the answer. I wait, thinking maybe she forgot to finish the sentence, but nothing else comes.

"I know why you're mad," I say, trying my best to sound Together and Composed. "I don't want to, like, be a stoner. I'm not going to let the baby smoke up. Or smoke near the baby. Or smoke ever again." Cate nods, but there are deep worry lines in her forehead, and I'm not sure she believes me. And she definitely doesn't believe whatever version of that Paul said to her.

I need to say more. I need to say something unlikely and new.

"I can't be just your daughter and nothing else, you know?" I say. Cate looks at me funny. I can see a sentence forming behind her eyes, but she shakes her head and I guess decides not to say it. She shrugs, like she has no idea what to do with what I've said, or what I've done, or who I'm becoming. That's fair. I'm not sure what to do with who I'm becoming, either.

"Look. I love you more than anything," she says, too calmly. "I'm right down the street. And here, of course. So it's not a big thing. Just need some pregnancy space," she says. "I don't want to be that crazy, angry pregnant lady, you know?"

I nod, but I don't know what it means. Cate kisses my forehead and gets back behind the counter. As soon as she's back there, she nods in my direction, giving Paul the go-ahead to have his part of The Talk with me. We've never had family talks in succession like this. We've done everything the three of us.

I check the computer. It is still recording.

"What you got there?" Paul says, taking the seat that Cate was just in. He has brought another mug of coffee, and when he realizes I already have one, he get flustered, eventually choosing to put it next to the one I'm drinking, like it's backup.

"Ethics," I say.

"I could have used that class, huh?" He grimaces. He is not so good at this on his own.

"I think you do pretty well," I say.

"I made a huge mistake Saturday," Paul says, sighing so the words are a kind of waterfall of noise.

"Isn't she supposed to kick *you* out?" I ask. In the two minutes since Cate spoke to me, I've thought of seventeen different important questions. Like, isn't it totally counterintuitive to leave me with Paul after what happened? Shouldn't Cate be vehemently stepping in to protect me from his influence? Isn't she concerned about my new rebellious attitude? I look up to catch her eye, but she's facing the other direction.

"This new baby . . . ," Paul begins, but he can't seem to get past those three words, and he starts picking off pieces of my peanut butter cookie and channeling all his energy into that.

"I know," I say. "You want to do it all differently. You want to do it right. I got it."

"Your mom's ready to be an adult," Paul concludes, not answering a single one of my questions but creating space for more to pop up.

The line at Tea Cozy is getting longer, snaking past my little table with Paul. He tries to ignore the crowd and turns my papers toward him, checking out what I'm reading and writing with fake interest. "I can look over your paper tonight," he says. He has not checked my homework for me since fifth grade.

"Yeah, okay."

"Don't bother her about this stuff, okay? Let her do her thing for a few days."

"Yeah, okay."

"I'm going to cut back," he says.

"Yeah, okay."

"Definitely will stop before the baby comes," he says.

I don't say *yeah, okay* again.

"She thinks I'm a lost cause," I say, clearing my throat before finishing. I take a sip of the coffee Cate brought over, to prove my point. It's more bitter than usual. "But we all grow, all the time, you know? There's no such thing as a lost cause." My voice rises, to make extra sure this last thing has recorded. Life by Committee needs to know I get it.

"You're my girl, Bitty," Paul says, which is maybe him admitting that Cate does think I'm already lost to her, the way he is.

"I'm my own girl," I say, and I don't mean it cruelly, but his face collapses a bit when the words hit him, and I hear it the way he must have. Like I'm leaving them, like I'm not one of them anymore.

Paul gives a sad little nod and kisses my forehead on his way back to the trenches, and he doesn't smell like weed, which means he at least hasn't smoked up today.

I post the audio on LBC that night. I play with the sound levels a little, to distort my voice and my parents' voices. It's more fun than anything else, plus this could be my signature style. I want to have artistry in my postings, like Star.

The first response is not a usual supportive message.

STAR: Hey. Careful.

ZED: What's that?

STAR: Just saying. Anonymity and stuff. Bitty's new still. Naive.

ZED: We aren't careful here. Are you being careful? That why you're past deadline? You have a completed Assignment yet?

STAR: Living life, Zed.

The conversation ends abruptly, after that comment. I stare at it for a while, wondering if I should participate. Wondering if Star is getting into trouble. Wondering what happens next. I consider asking Star what I should be careful about, asking Zed if we are ever allowed to stop, if we ever graduate, proclaiming my devotion to the site, to This Way of doing things. Telling Star to push through and propose already.

I say nothing, though. I listen to my semidistorted audio file again and picture people all over the country doing the same. Only a few people, of course. Only my people.

I start a new post. Because it's time. I have more work to do.

SECRET: If my best friend would take me back, I'd be her best friend again, even after all she did to me.

ZED: Hmm. Maybe you should destroy her. Get her kicked out of school. Do to her what she did to you. And then stop missing her, because we can't live in the past. We have to move forward. Thoughts, everyone?

I have a different kind of sick feeling, reading the comment. Not the adrenaline, not the heart-leaping courage. Not even the nauseous fear. I don't know if it was Star's strange almost-warning, or the idea of letting go of Jemma for real, or having to do something large and aggressive and destructive, but I feel tired and ill, not inspired.

I don't reply. I don't even know what I'd do. I'm sure Zed would have ideas. I'm sure they all would.

Twenty.

"There she is," someone says to my back when I'm heading into assembly the next morning. I turn around, hoping it isn't actually being said to me, but there's Luke, grinning, glowing practically. He raises his eyebrows. Wiggles them. Apparently that's his signature move. Even more depressing is the knowledge that it is currently working on a good half of the Circle Community population.

"Who's your next target?" he says.

"Excuse me?"

"You don't think he'll keep hooking up with you now, do you? Cover blown. No way. He's gotta cut his losses to keep his girl."

I hate the way Luke talks. I'd have to actually get stupider to understand it. I give him a look that hopefully verifies how completely idiotic I find him to be. It doesn't seem to register, though, because he puts a sweaty hand on the back of my neck, underneath my ponytail. It's a place Joe has touched with his fingertips and his lips and even the crook of his arm, and I hate it being touched by Luke.

"You know what I'm saying," he says into my ear. I jump away from him. Elise is walking by at the same moment, and I try to give her a *help me out of this* look, but she gives me a *you like the attention, don't you* look instead, and I'm so shocked by it, I can't even squeak at her.

"Get off me," I finally manage, when Elise is in her seat and I remember I have no one but myself to protect me against things like King of Hockey and Tool-ness, Luke.

"Don't kid yourself," he says, but he does get off me and head toward his own seat. I wipe the back of my neck, like somehow I can wipe away the memory of him or at least the physical sensation of his hand on my skin, a feeling that lingers too long and makes me queasy.

It's already basically the worst morning ever, but Jemma's been watching the whole thing with a pinched, horrified, just-tasted-sour-lemon face. And I am that sour lemon.

"No one told Sasha," she says. It's a whisper, and judging by the way she flips her hair with the words, a massive favor she thinks she's paying me. And maybe she's right, but I hate that she wants me to owe her, after everything.

"I don't know what you're talking about." We both know it's crap, but it's, like, the only thing I can possibly say at this point.

"I used to be jealous of you, you know," Jemma says. The lights are dimming in the auditorium, and in a minute the teachers will instruct us to find our seats, but for a moment it's me and Jemma and a decade of feelings between us. "Seems like a long time ago now. Nothing to really be jealous of anymore." She says it like she's only now figuring it out, like she's putting together her deepest feelings right in front of me, in real time. "I mean, you look pretty. Don't get me wrong. Obviously you look pretty. Or hot or whatever. But look what you had to do to get there."

She heads to her seat, not giving me a chance to respond or breathe or blink or anything, really. She's wrong, of course. But goddamn, it hurts.

The day gets worse from there.

I sort of think everyone except, apparently, Sasha Cotton knows about me and Joe. And Sasha Cotton *really* doesn't know about me and Joe. She compliments my purple polka-dotted scarf and asks me if I got a haircut, because my hair looks "like, swingy." Elise lets me sit with her at lunch but she doesn't say a single word, and when I try to take one of her fries, she actually pushes the tray away from me. Mrs. Drake approaches me in the hallway and says we need to have an appointment later in the week.

And Zed has come forward with a specific idea for how to take down Jemma, thus starting the twenty-four-hour ticking clock.

ASSIGNMENT: Weed. Your dad's weed. Tell that counselor at your school. Show the evidence.

@sshole: Dude.

BRENDA: I don't feel like that will necessarily work.

ZED: We can't control the outcome. We can only control the journey.

AGNES: There is no right.

ZED: There is no right. There's only best. There's only going far and reaching forward. Together. We'll be right there with you.

I read it in my car at the end of the day, blinking back tears. I grind the palms of my hands into my eyes, like that will stop the feelings, but it doesn't. I shake my head, but Zed and the rest of my friends can't see it.

Star doesn't say anything. I refresh and refresh and refresh, but she's nowhere to be found. I even go so far as to give her a specific shout-out, asking her opinion of my Assignment, which I'm pretty sure is completely against the rules, but I need something to hold on to, and I have so few options left. Zed hasn't posted on her page again, and I hate being left out of her life. I thought we were in it together. I'm scared for her. And for me. And for Jemma, sort of, too. I guess I'm scared for us all.

I'm down to twenty-three hours to basically destroy my former best friend.

I look in my glove compartment for my copy of *The Secret Garden* with all the notes that I so, so hope are Star's. But it's not there. The feelings, all of them, every feeling I've ever had maybe, are boiling in my stomach, and I'm going to tell Cate and Paul, I'm absolutely 100 percent going to tell them everything, and tell Elise everything too, because I cannot take the pressure on my own for one more second, with my life kind of in shambles around me.

But.

Joe texts me.

Come over. Now. I miss you.

Six words, and the whole world changes. I don't even think. I drive. I drive fast and straight and smiling until I'm in his driveway. If it's not a sign of our soul-mate status, it's at least a sign that things are coming together, that the things I'm doing are adding up into something beautiful.

Joe and me together is something beautiful.

His mouth is on mine before I can say hello.

He tastes brand-new, like he just squirted a tube of toothpaste into his mouth and doused himself in cologne and aftershave. I can taste the effort, and it doesn't have the appeal of Joe's messier side. I pull back.

"Hey there," I say, and touch his face like it has all the answers written in braille on it.

"Hey, sexy," Joe says, but the words are lost in my mouth and accompanied by his hands squeezing my ass.

"It's been, like, the worst few days," I say. He helps me out of my coat and I take a few steps in the direction of his kitchen, with the idea that he'll offer me some water and we can sit at the breakfast bar and talk for hours, the way we used to do online but haven't been doing lately.

"Been missing you," he says. His tongue lingers over the *s* of *miss*, and the little whistle of breath makes it sound like a huge lie. He has a shit-eating grin and he wraps one hand around my waist, pushes me gently against the wall. We kiss for a minute, so hard I forget to breathe and I think, yeah, okay, I could get lost in this instead of talking. This is the swooning part anyway, right? This is the passion. I wrap my arms around his neck and pull him in closer, think about relaxing my shoulders, which keep inching up to my ears like they have a mind of their own when they're under this much stress.

I pull back again, try to do it the way a sexy person might. Slowly and looking into his eyes, with a little sigh like, *I can't really handle how great this feels so I'm going to take a quick breather.* It works, and I get some eye contact, and there's a crazy spin-cycle feeling in my stomach at how much I think I could really love this guy whose hands are holding me steady as tiny bits of my world fall apart.

"People sort of, like, know. About you and me. And they all are hating me. Are they hating you?" It's not exactly a romantic thing to say, but he rubs my back and kisses my earlobe like it totally is.

"Don't you worry about me. I'm fine. Okay? I've got it under control." He moves his lips to my throat. He doesn't ask me if I'm doing okay. I don't tell him not to worry about me. If anything, I'm trying to tell him *to* worry about me. He pushes his hands into my hair. My whole scalp tingles in the most incredible way. I wonder if I could faint from my hair being touched.

"I mean, honestly everything is sort of falling apart at once, you know?" I say, doing my best to not give in to how good his hands feel. I want to talk, not make out. I want him to hear me. "My parents are totally freaking out," I say. "Like, get this, my mother is taking some time off from, um, *living* with us. What is that? That's not normal, right?"

"Totally weird."

I sort of wiggle out of his arms so we can look at each other and have an actual, nongroping conversation. It works for about a second.

"Is everyone talking about it?" I say. "Do people know? It's so weird. They're so weird."

"Yeah," Joe says, but his eyes are looking down into the space between my breasts. "I don't know, you should ask your friends."

"My friends?" I say. The word, even, is a punch in the stomach.

"Your friend, I guess," Joe says. I think it is supposed to be a joke. He gives a laugh that is mostly breath and assholery, and shrugs. A month ago, online, I described what happened with Jemma the night of the dance last spring. I described every detail, down to the dress I was wearing (yellow, vintage chiffon, scoop neck, knee-length), the song that was playing (Beyoncé. "Single Ladies." Practically mocking me.), the relative temperature (so hot I had to put my hair into a terrible makeshift bun) and the look on Jemma's face (contempt mixed with envy and topped with an extra sprinkle of total disappointment in me as a human being).

The point being, Joe knows how it is I ended up with no one but Elise on my side, and the idea that he would joke about it makes my head spin. I give him this look I think is maybe meant for just the two of us. The kind of look you give your boyfriend in the middle of a crowded room that communicates something particular and sacred between the two of you.

"Let's go watch a movie in my room," he says. Like the look didn't even hit him.

"What movie?"

"Any movie. I just want you in my room, pretty girl." His hands run up and down from the top of my rib cage to my pointy hip bones, and he smiles at the curve they find there. I go in for a kiss. I want a little one, the kind that is mostly lips and nothing else. The kind that says, *I care*. I put a hand on his cheek and another around his waist and keep my lips pressed together, but he probes them apart. It feels good, the warmth, the hitch of desire, the swimming feeling in my head. But it's not what I wanted. Today is not what I wanted.

"You're so hot," he says when I pull away. I miss our first kiss, and the way it seemed like it meant something. Without warning, without even the preliminary pulse of heat behind my eyes, I start to cry.

"Why'd you say that, about my friends? I can't talk to you about stuff?" I try to keep the tears in the realm of pretty. I don't sniff or snort or let the crying make its way to my mouth, where it would get all wet and distorted. I let the tears fall down my face and drip from my chin to the space between my body and Joe's.

"I didn't think you came here to talk," Joe says. He keeps his voice in a whisper, like that makes the words he's saying nice, somehow. He takes my pinkie finger with his hand, but that's it. Just hangs on to that one tiny finger and rubs it with his thumb. "I do a lot of talking already, you know? I sort of . . . you're sort of . . . a break from that stuff. Like, a vacation. Like the best vacation."

I am a vacation. I am the Caribbean, and a fruity drink and a sunburn and a break from real life. But I am not real life. No one lives in the Caribbean. No one wants a fruity drink every day. I'd rather be water: necessary.

"Oh," I say. The tears do not stop. Joe rubs his forehead like there's an ache there.

"I have a girlfriend." Whispered again. Thumb rubbing pinkie. Eyes on mine. He lifts his other hand to my face and brushes away some of the tears, but it's a sloppy effort. He uses the rough back of his hand instead of one single, gentle finger, and he uses so much force that it hurts.

"I thought Sasha and you—"

"I mean, you know how stressful that all is for me. I have to be a total rock for her, and I've always liked how independent and confident and together you are."

"I'm really not," I say, hoping he will see me and hear me.

"I think you're so awesome, you know? And I love hanging out with you and not worrying about anything." Joe closes the little space between our bodies and comes in for another kiss. One hand snakes around to my ass and squeezes.

"I think I should go," I say. It takes everything in me to say it, because those strong hockey-player arms are tight around me and kissing is the only thing I can think of to distract myself from the mess I've been making. I don't know how I force the words out, except that the way he's talking to me is suddenly so *not* the way you talk to the girl you are going to leave your girlfriend for.

"Come on . . ."

"I mean, you're already sleeping with Sasha, right? And, like, comforting her and being at her beck and call and having sexy poems written about you. So I'm not really sure what you actually need me for, now that I think of it." I'm saying it to the floor, mostly, but at least I'm saying it.

"I have feelings for you—" Joe sounds flustered, and his voice cracks on the word *feelings*.

"But not like your feelings for her," I finish for him.

"I'm in love with her. It's different." He shoves his hands into his pockets and sighs, and I know that this is it, this is the place where we end. It might be the place where my heart stops beating, too. Everything stops, for thirty seconds following that statement. Then the hurt comes, fast and hard and shocking as hell.

"Right. Cool," I say. I cannot believe I am able to say anything at all. He reaches for me again, even after that, but I don't hug him good-bye. If I step into his arms and let my nose find the place near his collarbone that feels like some kind of home, I will forget why I have to go.

I listen to "Rainbow Connection" on the way home. Maybe most girls wouldn't have the Muppets on every playlist on their iPods, but I am not most girls.

BITTY: It's not a secret, but I'm a lot fucking stronger than I thought. Or maybe it is a secret.
And this is no secret either, but he loves his girlfriend, not me.

There are some replies, but not many. Agnes has posted a secret; the LBC spiral lights up to inform me that I can check in on her Assignment, but I don't. I'm sick of Agnes, and I have enough going on in my own life.

I'd love an update from Star, so I can, like, believe in love again.

Twenty-One.

ZED: Seventeen hours to complete your Assignment, Bitty.

ELFBOY: Bring her down.

BRENDA: It's gonna feel good. Seems mean, but there will be some look on her face at some point that will make it all worth it.

STAR: It's real, you know? The things you're asking us to do, Zed. They're real. They have effects.

ZED: Did you propose yet, Star? By my calculations you are way, way behind on your Assignment.

STAR: Getting married is, like, real. Big. A decision. Not an impulse.

ZED: I assume that's a no?

STAR: I'm taking life seriously. That's it. Bitty should too. We all should.

ZED: What do you think we're doing here?

STAR: I sort of don't know anymore. Did you hear Bitty's post? Her parents? We, like, destroyed a family.

I wait for Zed to reply, and explain how destroying something ultimately fixes it. Creation from destruction, or something. I think that's from the Bible. Or science. Zed doesn't reply. I have about a million questions for Star, mostly: *Why are you hating on LBC when it got you everything you want?*

BITTY: I thought we had to take risks to move forward. I thought that's how you ended up in L.A. with pretty shoes and long kisses and a guy who wears Converses and loves the craziest parts of you.
STAR: I'm homesick.
BITTY: Homesick seems small compared to everything else.
STAR: Not every decision can be bigger than the one before. And not every decision is better because a dozen other lost people are telling you what to do.

Still no Zed. No one writes anything more. I turn Star's words around in my head, and I can't quite decide if they're true or not. I think I hate her, for saying it. I want to see her on bended knee. I want to see the bottom of her lacy, linen-y, beachy wedding dress. I want the world's strangest, quirkiest fairy tale. I want something I can believe in.

* * *

A half hour later, Star says one more thing:

STAR: Where does it end?

I'm dizzy from the question. From all my questions, too.

I'll complete my Assignment. I have to. I want to. I need to see this through. I click around LBC for another few minutes and the rules follow me onto every page, and that third rule, the one I'm the most scared of, seems to be getting larger and larger. "An active membership is the only way to protect your secrets." I don't see how Zed could ever follow through on that threat, but Star is right that I should at least be careful with identifying details. Especially since I'm pretty sure what I'm about to do to Jemma breaks the law.

I sign out of LBC. It doesn't feel like enough. I turn off the computer. My heart won't stop racing. I unplug the computer and leave the room, and a really illogical part of me feels safer, less overwhelmed.

If Cate were here, I'd ask her to go on another late-night walk, but without her around I have to go by myself, which I've never done.

I bring a flashlight and pay attention to where I'm walking this time. Without Cate I don't want to get turned around, especially if it means finding myself in front of Sasha Cotton's house again. When I reach a fork in the road, I take a step toward town, but then backtrack and go left instead. It's not some huge diversion. Turning left isn't exactly bringing me to the next dimension or anything. But it's not leading me to Tea Cozy or Elise's house or any of the places I usually go.

It's cold. It's always cold, but tonight it feels like it's about to snow again. I forgot a scarf, so the chill hits my neck. There's not a single car on the road, and animals and birds rustle in the treetops. I didn't even bring my phone, so I'm especially alone.

I take another turn, one I haven't taken for a while. I'm warming up, walking at a clipped pace like I have somewhere to go, which I guess I do. Because I find myself in front of Jemma's house. Which is Devon's house. It's too late to knock on the front door. Her parents may miss me, but they won't be pleased to have me waking them up. I'm not sure which window is Devon's. I'm not even sure I want to see him. But there's a light on in their third-floor TV room, where I used to hang out all the time. I imagine that Devon's in there. That he's as awake as me. I imagine he's even worried about me. That he's the kind of guy who would have held me and rubbed my back if he heard something in my life had been dismantled.

It's not like I can't comfort myself. It's not like I need some guy to hold me and tell me I'm pretty or whatever it is I think Devon might do. It's not like what they think about me is right. I'm not boy crazy. Except that maybe I am, because now that Joe has turned out to be a total Sasha Cotton–loving asshole instead of my kind, caring soul mate, I find my mind occupied by what it would feel like for Devon to look right in my eyes and tuck my hair behind my ears and kiss the place where my earlobe meets my neck. It's been, like, a few hours, and I'm looking for another guy to fix everything.

I'm clearly messed up. I'm clearly not capable of taking care of myself in any real way.

Maybe Jemma and Alison and Mrs. Drake were right about what kind of girl I am. I wish I had my phone, so I could check in with LBC. I shouldn't be out here alone. Not in the cold Vermont night and not in my life.

But it feels like it's too late to walk home, like I can't turn around and forget it. My legs hurt, my nose is stinging from the cold, and I can't stomach the idea that I did this all for nothing. I step onto the lawn, and that step feels bigger than all the little ones that came before it. I take another tiny little step, but nothing clicks into place. Without LBC I'm just a girl on the lawn filled with the worst kind of indecision.

I don't want to be that girl.

And that is when I decide to go into Jemma's house.

It goes something like this: When Jemma and I were friends, she was really into photography. Actually, everyone was really into photography. There was a new photography teacher at Circle Community a couple of years ago. He had long hair, which normally could be kind of gross, but he tied it back in this messy-sexy way, and had just enough light-brown stubble, and I liked the way a few hairs would escape his artist ponytail. The other girls liked his forearms and the way he smelled like toxic chemicals and woods. He was young. He let us call him by his first name. He swore sometimes. He called us all artists.

I was one of Jemma's many subjects. We'd go into the woods

behind her house and I'd roll around in the leaves or stare pensively at the sky and she'd tell me to move my head or shift my weight or stop giggling, and she'd take dozens of photos. Sometimes she'd set the self-timer and get us both in there. We'd press our cold cheeks together so we could fit into the frame, and each look in slightly different directions to make it artsy.

Alison hated having her picture taken, so she'd talk about light and shadows and then disappear into the house and come back out with snacks. Like a mom would.

This went on for over a year. Jemma took every class available with Tony. But the photographs were taken almost two years ago now, so I was still slim all over, flat and straight and into worn-in T-shirts and hooded sweatshirts and Dove soap and ChapStick instead of makeup. I was the kind of girl Jemma and Alison approved of.

I want to see that girl now. Cate and Paul aren't into photographs, so we don't have albums of nostalgia in the living room or on the computer or anything. I'm sure for the new baby they'll buy a new camera and plaster the fridge with snapshots and set up a blog to show off her sure-to-be-adorable face, but it wasn't like that for me. If I want to catch a glimpse of the Life I Used to Have, those black-and-white fake-artsy photos are my best bet.

Jemma's parents keep their key in a fake rock, like every other family in every other neighborhood in this ridiculous town. It doesn't take long to figure out which rock is hollow and fake.

The sound of the door unlocking is monstrous in my head. It

echoes, and the door screeches, and I'm positive the whole Benson family is going to run down the stairs with flashlights and stricken faces, but nothing happens. I try not to breathe on my walk from the front door to the living room. There are bookcases filled with Jemma's and Devon's accomplishments, and there, knee-height, is a leather binder. Label-maker label glued onto the spine. JEMMA. PHOTOGRAPHS. AGE 13–15. Exactly as I knew it would be. Because Jemma and Devon have the kind of parents who label and display every single accomplishment.

Heart pounding, I reach for it. I close my eyes, like that will help me escape the sheer intensity of anxiety in the moment. My fingers twist my thumb ring, something I do when I get nervous. But my hands are so sweaty and my fingers shaking so tremendously that it slips from my knuckle to the ground. It's a heavy silver thing, and it hits the hardwood floor with a crash. I gasp, and forget to quiet that sound, too. The sounds cause other sounds in the house. A creak upstairs. A shuffling of feet. My own heartbeat's acceleration.

I'm so scared I can't move. My arm is stuck in midair, still reaching for the book of photographs, but not actually grabbing it. I tear up but don't move a muscle. And that is how Devon finds me.

"Hey," he whispers. He looks confused, but maybe not as stunned as he should be. Which tells me I have been acting pretty weird the last few weeks and people are noticing.

"Yeah. Hi," I squeak out.

"It's, uh, late."

"Oh my God, I know. I know. Yeah." It's nice to whisper. Intimate.

I manage to get my hand to my side and my back straight so that at least I'm standing upright and facing him head-on.

"Did . . . Jemma . . . invite you?"

I so want to say yes. I want to say yes so badly that I start to say yes, get out the initial *y* sound, and then clamp my mouth shut and shake my head no.

"So you just . . . thought you'd stop by?" Devon is trying so hard to make sense of this moment. I can see the effort on his face. He grimaces and blinks a lot and rubs his eyes and moves his chin in little circles, like he is caught between a head shake and a nod and a total seizure.

"I was looking for something?" I try to stop myself from up-speak, but now that I've started, there's no way I'll stop.

Devon takes a huge breath in. So large and deliberate that I watch his whole abdomen fill, watch his lungs expand under his almost-tight-but-not-quite gray T-shirt. I notice his red plaid pajama pants for the first time and get an unexpected surge of pleasure. One side of my mouth lifts into what could almost be considered a smile, which is an epic feat, considering.

"Are you okay, Tabby?"

"Yes?"

"You seem a little . . . off. Lately. Not in a bad way. But in a . . . noticeable way."

"Life changes?" I say.

"Right."

We stand in silence. There's eye contact. The extended kind, where you almost don't want to blink, so as not to break the connection. I'm afraid if I look away, even for an instant, we won't ever find this steady gaze again.

I love the slow, unsurprised way he reacts to my total insanity. Like it's okay that I'm a little crazy.

"So. What were you looking for? Let's at least make it worth your while," Devon says at last. He doesn't take his eyes off me. He smiles. He has a tiny dimple in his chin and one in each cheek. He smiles like he's holding in a laugh. Maybe it's the pajama pants or the fact that he isn't calling the police, or maybe it's the rockiness of his voice this late at night, but he is gorgeous. All of a sudden.

"It's dumb." We're both still whispering, but I go even quieter now that we've started this portion of the conversation.

Devon shrugs and flashes that smile again. Lets out a hushed chuckle. A bit of my heart lights up. It's strange how easy it is for me to feel this way, pretty and alive.

I think a thought that makes me hate myself: *Maybe if Joe got jealous, he'd realize he could love me, not her.* I swallow. I have no idea what to do. Those photographs are so close to me, and maybe if I could get even the quickest glimpse, I'd have some vague idea of who I am.

"You don't seem like the breaking-and-entering type," Devon says at last, trying, I guess, to help me figure out how to explain myself.

"You can call the cops. Seriously. I probably need the consequences, you know? It'd probably be good for me or something." My voice is shaking so much, I barely recognize it.

"Naw, I'm an accomplice now," Devon says. He takes a step closer to me, looks at the bookcase, like maybe he'll be able to figure out what I wanted. "Helping you steal. Aiding and abetting. I don't know all the legal jargon, but it's a serious offense."

"Well, as long as we go down together," I say. I don't blush. I flame.

Devon does his low breathy chuckle again and picks out one of the family Bibles. "This what you wanted, I assume?" he says. I am going to kiss his dimples if his face gets any closer to mine. I've never kissed a dimple before. I giggle, but it comes out all choked.

"The photographs," I say, and point at the binder. "I mean, I could just look at them. I don't need to take them."

"Don't come this far and then give up," Devon says.

The words make me shiver. He's right. He doesn't know how right he is.

Devon grabs the binder and opens it, and there I am. Me, but not me.

The me I used to be.

The very first picture is me in a pile of leaves. I could be six, but I'm fourteen maybe. I'm sitting, and the leaves cover most of my lap. I've thrown half the pile in the air, and they are raining down on me as I look up at my hands, still lingering above me. I am grinning. My ears look bigger than I think they do now, like I grew into them a bit, but not enough. In the photograph I'm wearing an oversize sweater and French braids and my eyes are squinting and mascara-less.

"That's you," Devon says. It's almost a question.

"It used to be."

The tears come back. I sniff and bite my cheeks and blink really fast to try to keep them inside, but they are the reckless kind, and by the time we're on the next page, they are running down my cheeks. My face next to Jemma's stares up at me. My mouth is wide open, my nose scrunched, my hands blurry with movement. I must have been telling some story. Jemma's mouth is open too, and I can almost hear the laughter.

Then I'm sobbing. Into Devon's T-shirt. He is not a perfect boy. He pats my back awkwardly, and I know he has no idea how to deal with a crying girl. "Shhhh," he tries.

I take the binder from his hands and hold it to my chest, like maybe it will help me gain control of my breathing. It doesn't, so I let myself outside, and he follows. I can't risk Jemma finding me here. As much as I want to not care, I can't take things at school getting any worse. So we stand on the porch. There is a not-quite-full moon and a cold wind rustling the trees. Devon puts his hands in his pockets. I can see his fingers moving beneath the fabric, and I like that he can't completely hide his nerves. I look up, tilt my head back a little, and try to maintain eye contact for as long as my heart can handle it. He takes a step closer and I think maybe he will kiss me and maybe I want him to, but maybe I don't. Yet. There's a breath when I could move toward him too, but I don't take it. I let my chin drop, my eyes drift to the trees instead of his mouth, and the moment's over.

For some reason, this is the Assignment I cannot complete.

"Are you gonna be okay?" he says. I take a step from his porch back to his lawn. I look up at Jemma's bedroom window and for a split second wonder if I could plant the weed in there. Direct her parents toward its hiding place.

"Yeah, yeah, we'll figure it out," I say.

"We?" Devon says.

I'm so dizzy from the crying and the overwhelming weirdness of tonight that I'm not watching my words carefully enough.

"Like, me. And my friends."

Devon looks at me funny. Like Jemma has told him that I have no friends. Which I'm sure she has.

"Maybe I'll come by the Cozy tomorrow?" he says.

But tomorrow I will be busy ruining his sister's life. So I shake my head no.

"I have an Assignment I have to do," I say. I take a few steps farther away from him, and it's sad to know the night's basically over, that whatever adventure I was on is over, and all I'm left with is my own failure and a book full of pictures of a person I used to be. Devon's eyes are the kind that make me want to say all kinds of things, and I have too many things I'm not allowed to say.

"Hey, Tabby?" he says, before I am totally in shadow on the street.

"Yep?"

"Don't give up on us. On me. Or Jemma. Or just people, you know?"

"Why would I?" I say.

"I don't know," Devon says, taking a big breath and focusing those incredible blue eyes on me like he knows I already have. "That's what I'm trying to figure out."

Secret:

It wasn't love.

—Star

Twenty-Two.

The next morning, eight hours to go, I treat myself to three cups of coffee at Tea Cozy. It does not help me forget about the weed in my backpack. For something so light, it is unusually heavy. I wait to go into school. I skip first period. Paul is working, but there's no sign of Cate. For all I know, Paul thinks it is Saturday. His beard is neat and trimmed, though, and his flannel shirt tucked into his pants. His eyes and hands are steady, and he's listening to Aerosmith, which I know he can't handle when he's high.

Still, he doesn't see me. Not enough to do any more than wave at me and ask me to clean up a table.

I stare at LBC until my eyes hurt and my father starts to get a look on his face like maybe he has realized it's not the weekend and I should be at school.

BITTY: I would rather stay home and read.

AGNES: I would always rather stay home and read.

ZED: Cold feet on your Assignment? Don't trust us yet?

BITTY: I'm scared.

ZED: That's great! You should be scared! Life is scary if you're doing it right.

STAR: That's where we're different, ladyfriend. I'm not so much a reader.

@SSHOLE: Too busy having sex.

STAR: Not anymore. You not see my last post?

BRENDA: Don't have to be in love to have sex!

ZED: Star, we need to talk. You were supposed to complete your Assignment.

STAR: It sort of stopped being relevant.

ZED: That's not how it works. Assignments are relevant no matter what.

STAR: I'm not proposing to some guy I don't love.

ZED: But you DID love him. You probably still would if you'd followed what we said.

AGNES: It's not fair if we're not all doing it.

This happens sometimes. A thread will start off as mine or Zed's or Elfboy's or whatever, but it will shift and turn into another conversation entirely, before it circles back around to the relevant secret or Assignment. So at first I'm only skimming the comments, but when I realize what a tense, massive conversation it is, I go back and read more carefully.

It's the least interesting part of the whole conversation, except that it's everything.

Star doesn't like reading.

And whoever made notes in *The Secret Garden* loved reading.

BITTY: You don't like reading, Star?

STAR: God, I haven't actually read a book since, like, elementary school. CliffsNotes, girl.

It shouldn't be a big thing. I never knew for sure that Star was my note taker, I only ever hoped. And assumed.

ZED: We can't all slack on our Assignments. It's not fair to the group.

@SSHOLE: Agree. I told off my principal in front of the entire school. I'm suspended for three weeks. I can't be out here alone.

STAR: But dude, what did you get out of that, you know?

@SSHOLE: Respect.

AGNES: He doesn't know yet. He doesn't know how it will all play out. None of us do. But his principal was a jerk. And @sshole got to speak the truth. It's like, opening doors and letting the good stuff come in, you know?

BITTY: I need to hear something good before I do this.

STAR: I don't think you should do it.

ROXIE: Me! You guys said I should crash that audition, and I did, and I have an actual professional paid gig now. Like, I'm an actress. A real one.

There's a chorus of support for Roxie, and I relax enough to eat half of a raspberry ricotta scone Paul likes and Cate hates. It's not so busy at Tea Cozy right now, and Paul keeps looking over here, so I don't have much time. I've got on cords and a turtleneck sweater of Paul's. I could not look like less of a slut, so I'm ready, I guess, to do this. I pretend to be typing something very official and school-like, but Paul's not an idiot, so I have to scan through the rest of the conversation quickly so I can log off. He's ringing up the last three people in line and raising his eyebrows at me.

ZED: I'll give you one last try, Star. You do it in the next three days, and you get a free pass. Since you're such a longtime member.

STAR: We BROKE UP. Like, we aren't even together. Much less getting engaged.

ZED: Just to see what will happen.

STAR: That's not okay!!!

ZED: Because you trust us. Because you believe in what we can do together. Because life's really hard and we're figuring it out as a team.

AGNES: Bitty and I are a team, both doing our Assignments today. Feels better knowing we both are taking risks. Like we're holding hands or something. Cyber hand holding.

STAR: You don't have to do it. You too, Bitty. You don't have to do it.

There's more to read, but Paul reaches over me and closes my laptop. My heart jumps, and it's amazing that I can get so sucked in by LBC that I forget where I am and who's there and what I'm supposed to be doing.

"It's a school day," he says.

"Yes," I say, and give him a shared Paul and Tabby smile, but he's not buying it.

"You have any idea how much trouble I'm in with Cate? And now you want to get me in even more trouble? What's going on with you? Get to school." Paul has new wrinkles around his mouth and eyes and streaking across his forehead. He's older than I thought he was, older than he used to be. He's not joking.

"You're really getting yourself . . . together," I say. He's retying his apron and getting ready to bake another round of scones, and I know he wants me to be on my way, but I want to stare at him, this man who used to be a friend and is now my dad.

"You didn't give me much choice," he says, and I try to place what the smell is, coming off him, that's replaced the skunky-sweet smell of weed. It's chocolate and flour and coffee on his breath, and nothing else. Soap, maybe. "I believe that is what they call reaching your own personal rock bottom."

"Plus the baby," I say.

"I think we did pretty well with you," Paul says. "You like the right books. And the right bands. And you don't play sports. And you don't spend too much time on your hair or anything. I'd call it a win."

Paul packs my stuff up for me. I guess he can tell I'm sort of paralyzed. He offers to drive me to school, but I can get myself there. I can do what I need to do. I have to. Because my last Assignment made Paul get his act together. It's working. LBC is working.

AGNES: Assignment completed.

I want to read more—I missed her secret and Assignment yesterday in the buzz and fury of my own life—but I'm already shaky behind the wheel today, shaky in my whole life today, so I decide to not look at my phone and drive at the same time.

Twenty-Three.

I have the Ziploc of weed in my backpack and my hurt from how Jemma has been treating me and Jemma's locker combination. I have Life by Committee on my phone, in my pocket, and unlike the rest of the kids at Circle Community living their boring drone lives, I have purpose.

And, like, justice.

And for a few glorious moments my head is held high and my shoulders are back and I think I am doing something dangerous and earned and powerful that will change the entire structure of the world.

Dictators must feel this way. And scientists maybe. The super-smart ones. And gods, I guess too. I seriously doubt people feel this way from yoga or self-help books or meditation or even love. Because love didn't end up making me feel powerful at all. I felt small in its shadow. It was bigger than me.

Yes. Yes, this is much better than love.

The feeling vanishes the instant I walk into the lobby.

Artsy photographs are hanging in the hallway that leads from the front door of the school to the assembly hall. They are oversize and framed in gold, making the whole thing look like a New York City gallery instead of a lame private school started by a bunch of tree-hugging vegans.

Which means upon first glance I'm loving it.

Upon first glance I'm thinking: *Sweet. Maybe Circle Community isn't totally lame. Maybe I'll make it through the next year here.*

Then I see a nipple.

It is that nipple that forces everything to click into place.

Two nipples, actually, and small breasts, but all so perky and smooth it does look, legitimately, like art for even an instant longer. Sexy art, art that shouldn't be hanging in a high school, but art nonetheless. That's the first picture or two.

But the third one has a face, and a body, and a nipple, and some gauzy skirt that is all too familiar. And Sasha's honey hair and long lashes on top. Sasha, in the nude, biting her lip. Sasha, half covering her breasts with crossed arms that still show basically everything. Sasha crawling toward the camera like Victoria's Secret models do in commercials for the newest lacy, structured, push-up bra. Except there's no lace, no structure, no push. Just the expanse of her body and the total joy she seems to have at exposing it.

And the fairy wings.

Holy. Shit.

I sit on the floor. Collapse onto it, practically. Cross my legs. Put my head in my hands.

And I'd scream at the pictures if I could, I'd deface them, I'd draw mustaches on them. But the more pressing issue right now, the much, much, bigger problem, is that I have clearly been an idiot.

Didn't I see Sasha taking these photographs of herself late at night?

Didn't I squirm with discomfort at her poem?

Doesn't this seem like something no normal person would choose to do to herself?

Didn't Agnes say we BOTH had big, scary Assignments today?

NO, my mind yells at my body. *NO. AGNES LIVES IN FLORIDA OR SOMETHING.*

My phone's low on batteries, so I practically sprint to the computer lab and hold my head in my hands while I wait for LBC to load. I don't care who sees. I don't care about anything right now except learning that Agnes and Sasha Cotton are not the same person, because they *can't* be the same person, because the world is not that tiny and I am not that stupid.

I hit the mouse a million times—I'm shaking so hard that I keep clicking the wrong links. But when I'm on Agnes's page, staring at her sad-girl avatar and the hundreds and hundreds of posts she's written over the last year, I start to see it all.

Agnes, talking about suicide and falling in love, and jealousy and sexuality.

Agnes, testing the boundaries of herself, her family, her boyfriend, her schoolmates.

Agnes, writing a poem about sex and printing it in her school's literary journal. An Assignment, of course, from before I joined.

Agnes, doing a nude photo shoot a few weeks ago, admitting it to her LBC friends last night, and then being assigned the task of hanging the photos, in frames, in the school's lobby.

> **Secret:** My BF thought the naked pics were weird. I freaked him out. Big-time.
> — Agnes
> **ASSIGNMENT:** Get a second opinion. Hang them up in school.

It's right there. It's been there all along.

Now that I see it, it's impossible to unsee. I can hear her breathy, uncertain voice speaking the words on her page. It's all there in the dense writing of her storytelling and the Sylvia Plath worldview. I review every interaction we've had online, and bile rises from my spinning stomach to my squeezing-tight chest to my now dry, jaw-dropped mouth. She's been advising me on *Joe*. She's been supporting me and telling me I should go for it and reading along as I kiss him.

I swallow down the vomit that is insisting it come out. I'm sitting, but I couldn't get up if you paid me. Everything from my knees down has gone numb, and everything from my knees up is trembling.

I put my head between my legs, the way that I've seen people do on TV and movies but that I've never actually witnessed in real life. I'm not sure what exactly it's supposed to do, but it gives me vertigo, a blood rush to the head, and makes me heave. Nothing comes out, but I cover my mouth with my hands anyway.

And then I step out of the glass cave of the computer lab and into the buzzing, laughing, high-five-giving world in the hallway. I stagger my way through to find Elise, who is bright red and watery-eyed next to Heather. Both girls look at the photos with something way too close to awe.

"I need to talk," I say, slipping my hand into Elise's. She cringes a little and pulls away. Heather clears her throat, and I know they've been talking about me.

"Tab. It's not all about you, you know?" She's looking at the photographs. More and more students and teachers gather around them, but I don't see Joe or Sasha.

"There's, like, a whole reason she did this," I say. I'm begging Elise with my eyes to be my best friend again, if even for just a few minutes.

"I know there is. You. Going after her boyfriend. Making her feel like she had to do something insane to keep him."

Heather clears her throat again. Elise shakes her head, and I try to unhear those words. The things Jemma and Alison and Mrs. Drake and Luke think about me—those are the same things Elise thinks about me. It's all over her face: disappointment, disgust, distance.

"How did I—" I try.

"You pushed her. Excuse us, Heather." Elise takes my elbow and moves me away from the photographs and Heather. We're just a few feet away, so Sasha's big eyes and smooth skin are still haunting the whole conversation. "Did you sleep with him? With Joe? You did, right? I mean, you must have. And she knows. Or suspects. And is trying to compete. Why couldn't you just let her have him, you know?

You could be with some other hockey-playing guy."

"I'm not—"

"What if a college hears about her doing this? What if she gets kicked out? I mean, look at those douches, staring at these pictures like it's porn. She's going to have to live with that. That's who she is now. Because of you."

I glance to Elise's left and catch sight of Luke feeling up the photograph. He cackles while pretending to grab her breasts, his grubby fingers circling the nipples. Elise is wrong about a lot of things, but she's right about something: Sasha shouldn't have to see this.

"Maybe it's a good thing," I say, but the words are weak and small and sound ridiculous when I can hear the boys in the background talking about how her boobs are too small and her stomach too round. It's hard to see how this could be a good thing.

"I literally have no idea what you're talking about anymore," Elise says. "I don't recognize you or understand anything you're saying or doing at this point."

"I mean, we don't know what the future holds, and maybe this somehow will turn out to be a good thing? Or, like, her life will change and shift because she did something scary and strange and special?"

Something happens while I watch Elise's face respond to my words. Zed's words. The words I've been relying on the last few weeks.

They sound all wrong.

I grip my backpack. The Ziploc full of Paul's weed is in there, begging me to bring it to Mrs. Drake, or plant it in Jemma's locker, or do something shocking and daring and LBC-worthy. My mind is in some strange tug-of-war with itself, on one side thinking maybe LBC is a terrible idea, and that Zed is a dangerous dude or at the very least a total stranger, but on the other side still needing to believe in something bigger than my own pathetic life.

Elise's face tells me I should be afraid of what LBC has done to me. She looks not only disappointed or angry or annoyed. She looks scared. Scared of the person I'm becoming, and scared of the possible reasons I have become this person instead of the one she loved looking at books with.

"I have to go," I say, and fly out the door, hoping maybe I'll run into Sasha Cotton, but her car is already gone, so I hop into my own car and drive away.

Twenty-Four.

I drive in circles for an hour before ending up back at Tea Cozy.

My mind's not working that fast, and I couldn't think of what to do or how to understand what's happening until I remembered how it all began: with Paul. With *The Secret Garden*.

"Tabitha! I told you to go to school!" Paul says. He and Cate are at the counter with coffee and cookies and no customers. "I told her to go to school," he says to Cate. They are sitting close enough that their knees touch, and I'm happy to see that, but I want him to see that I am sweating and crying and fighting back more dry heaves, so obviously school is so not the point.

"Where did you get my book?" I say, and I'm out of breath even though I haven't been running or anything. I didn't know I could get out of breath from living life and nothing else.

"You need water," Cate says, running behind the counter to pour me a huge glass.

"I need to know where you got that book," I say again, and I rummage through my backpack, because I can't keep talking and explaining—I need to get answers. I throw my copy of *The Secret Garden* at him, and he blushes the second he sees it.

"Oh shit, Tab," he says.

"Language!" Cate says, and I want to strangle her because she can't change everything about who our family is. She hands me the water and I gulp it down and Paul gives a sheepish smile because he doesn't really know how one tiny lie can change everything.

"I was such a di—a jerk. I was a jerk. I forgot to get you a book in New York. It was too short a trip. And you had been so sad and I wanted to give you a lift, you know? So I found that at Recycled Books in town, and it seemed like something you'd love and that you'd love it even more if it was from New York. . . ." He shakes his head, and I well up with tears. A million or so of them.

"I just . . . I thought that book was from far away, you know? And I thought the person who wrote in it was some mysterious person who lived in, like, a loft in the Village and had all this special New York wisdom, you know?" I'm not ready to tell him the whole story, and I'm too breathless with tears and fear and the rush of knowledge and understanding to get more out anyway.

"Hey, maybe it still was! New Yorkers love Recycled Books! And Vermont in general, right? Who knows, right? Where that book came from?" Paul grabs my hands and squeezes and Cate nods along, partly agreeing with him and partly, I think, pleased with the man he is becoming.

"I have to go," I say, wiping tears and blowing my nose and

scrambling to get my stuff back into my bag. My fingers brush against the bag of weed and I have a grip of feeling in my chest. I guess, somehow, I still haven't totally decided whether I will go through with the Assignment.

I can't. I know I can't.

Except: If I leave LBC, I will be really, truly alone. No Elise. No Joe. No Jemma. No Life by Committee. I can't quite stomach it yet.

"You're going back to school, right?" Paul says.

"Yeah, yeah," I say, but I'm lying, and as soon as I get in my car, I speed in the opposite direction. To the house with the purple door. Sasha Cotton's house.

Sasha's car isn't here, there's no sign of Sasha anywhere, so I wait in the driveway. She has to come home eventually.

An hour passes, two, but I don't even think about giving up. I wait it out, and I can't feel time passing at all, to be honest. I turn up the music in my car and thank the universe that my phone is out of batteries so I can't spend the afternoon looking up everything Agnes/Sasha has been saying and posting over the last year that she's been on the site. I can untangle the whole mess later.

I do sort of halfway consider smoking the weed in my backpack. But that's not me, and I know that now.

I know that Zed is counting down the last few hours on my Assignment, and that it's probably strange that I have suddenly vanished. I make my mind veer away from that too, though. I focus on the mountains. I haven't done that since I found LBC, and I know it doesn't work as well, it's not really a solution to all the problems in my life right now, but they're there and they're majestic and snow covered and will exist regardless of what happens in the next few hours.

By the time Sasha's car turns into her driveway, my countdown is over and Zed must be sending out smoke signals, trying to figure out what happened to me. Sasha drives a mint-green super-old convertible that her mother drove around for years before Sasha got it. It's been a staple in town for as long as I can remember, and it's either totally lame or completely sexy, depending on whether I am feeling annoyed with or jealous of Sasha Cotton at any given moment.

I get out of my car while she parks hers. She's all streaky-faced and messy-haired, and I hate her for being such a sexy, sad person. She sighs as she slams her car door, and she tucks her hair behind her ears as she walks toward me.

I had hours to think about what to say, but I didn't actually make a decision. Every configuration of the sentence "I know all your secrets" sounds ridiculous and soap-opera-y and lame. But I have to say something, because Sasha Cotton doesn't ask any questions. She shifts one hip to the side and lets her hair fall back over her eyes and waits for me to speak.

"You're Agnes," I say, looking at the mountains so I don't have to look at her face. "I'm Bitty."

There's a long pause and I shift my eyes from the mountains to Sasha's face, but there's nothing written there. She's a blank stare, a total and complete lack of understanding.

"I didn't know it was you," I say, and hand over her copy of *The*

Secret Garden. There's a shudder of recognition as she flips through the pages.

"This is mine," she says. I wonder if Sasha Cotton smokes. If that's why her voice always sounds like it's telling a secret.

"My dad got it at Recycled Books," I say, matching the quietness of her words, the emotionless tone.

"These notes were only for me. I never would have brought it in there. These are my private—this is like reading my diary. I don't understand. . . ." Her voice drifts away at the end of the sentence, and she seems to remember something. "The yard sale," she says, shaking her head to herself. And though it's not meant for me, I remember the yard sale too. I thought about it the night Sasha took the crazy pictures. All the strange and wonderful things the Cottons were getting rid of. Including, probably, some of their books.

Sasha Cotton starts to shake. It is a small tremble in her fingers at first, but it moves through her whole body, her thighs especially, which shake so hard they can't hold her up anymore and she has to lean against her car.

Of course, she looks like an old-school, tragic movie star, leaning against her retro convertible and having a panic attack.

"You're Bitty," she says. She flips through *The Secret Garden* some more, and when she reaches the page with the website, she shakes her head some more and says, "Shit." I didn't know Sasha Cotton knew how to swear.

"Yeah."

"So then who—"

Sasha Cotton is not stupid. She doesn't ask the whole question. She swallows and throws the book on the ground with a forceful swing of her arm, and I wonder if Sasha Cotton's father played catch with her on the front lawn like Paul did with me, because she kind of has an arm.

"No," she says. And again, "No!"

"I didn't know," I say, "if that helps."

"I'm calling Joe," she says. It is the last thing I thought she'd say. I don't know why I didn't think about Joe. I thought about what I did with Joe. I thought about how much I loved Joe, or maybe didn't love him but needed him to be someone I could love. I thought about Sasha being devastated over Joe. But I didn't consider that Sasha would tell Joe anything. I didn't picture Joe coming over here and getting involved.

"It's over with me and Joe now. I mean, you know that. You can see it on the site. It's been over for, like, a day. Which, I know, is nothing. But it's over. He loves you. Please don't . . . Let's work this out between us." I pick up the book and brush off the dirt and give it back to her, like the world's worst peace offering.

"I told you to go for it," Sasha Cotton whispers. Her voice breaks and she cries in that perfect Sasha Cotton way: all tears and no sobs and no snot and no hiccuping. "I told you to kiss my boyfriend. I can't—" She turns away from me, and I think that's what I would do in her situation, too.

She hugs herself and hugs the book to her chest, too.

I don't feel bad for Sasha Cotton. Not exactly. It's more like I realize, really realize, that she wrote those notes. The ones that changed my life. That of all the people in the world, she is maybe the one who gets me best. She's the one who made me feel not alone.

Two weeks ago I would have said Sasha Cotton was my nemesis, more so than Jemma or Alison or Luke or anyone else at Circle Community who I sort of can't stand. But today, right now, in her driveway with a mess of secrets and resentments between us, I think Sasha Cotton is maybe my best friend.

"What should we do?" I say. I guess I'm thinking she'll feel the same way, when she has a chance to catch her breath. That she'll see the connection, she'll realize how much I loved her notes in the book and how we are the only two people in this little corner of the world who know about LBC and the strange possibilities life has.

"What do you mean? We ask Zed," she says. She turns back to face me, and her face is red and wet but the tears have stopped pouring out and she looks sure.

AGNES: I want to tell Bitty's secrets.

ZED: She didn't follow the rules. She didn't complete her Assignment.

AGNES: Is that a yes?

ZED: You need a secret to be given an Assignment.

Secret: I hate Bitty and I hate myself and I still somehow love Joe.

—Agnes

ASSIGNMENT: Tell everyone everything.

Twenty-Five.

Sasha Cotton doesn't want me on her porch. She doesn't want to watch me watching her as she watches Life by Committee decide our fate. But I'm not getting in my car and driving away. I can't.

"It makes sense, you know?" I say. The sun is setting and it's sort of beautiful, the way it makes the sky and trees and ground flush a reflective pink. And I actually think Sasha would like it too. That she and I share an appreciation for nature and unstoppable love and excellent books and long pauses and deep thoughts.

"What makes sense? Nothing makes sense," Sasha Cotton says. She is wiping away tears that won't stop coming out. Her hair has the perfect wave-to-curl-to-frizz ratio, and she looks like a painting of a girl in France in, like, the 1800s or something. Her sadness is rooted in history and seriousness, while the rest of us are products of, like, reality TV and *Us Weekly* and that trend where you wear feathers in your hair so everyone knows you're unique.

Sasha Cotton will never have to wear feathers in her hair. Everyone knows she is special already.

Joe knows she is special.

"It makes sense that we both . . . that we loved the same person. That we joined the same group. I mean, your book. Your notes in the book. They were . . . I've never had that much in common with anyone, ever." I almost touch her shoulder, but I decide not to.

"What do you mean you loved him?" She is literally leaking. The girl has sprung a leak. The tears will not stop coming.

"I mean, I thought I did. Or whatever. I got swept up. You saw. On LBC. You read what I wrote, so you know."

"You don't even know him. I've been with him for over a year. We tell secrets on the phone all night long. We talk about going to the same college. He gave me a promise ring. He made me lasagna. He warmed up bread and put garlic on it, and he comes over whenever I'm really upset. He sings along with my favorite songs to cheer me up. He has a terrible voice, did you know that?"

"I didn't know that," I say. I didn't know anything, I guess. I didn't know Joe.

"You should go," she says.

"Are you going to do it?" I say. I can't take my eyes off her computer screen.

"It's an Assignment," Sasha Cotton says, before getting up and going back inside her house.

* * *

I stay out there for a while. Long enough that Sasha could call the police. It's not like the police in town are real anyway. Our D.A.R.E. officer, Officer Mayo, would show up like he did when I crashed my car into a tree when I lost control of it on the ice that day. We chatted about how much I'd grown up, and he told Paul and Cate what a good kid I was.

I'm not afraid of Officer Mayo. I'm afraid of Zed and the secrets Sasha knows and loneliness.

I am really, really afraid of how alone I am.

When I finally get home, I sign on to LBC. Agnes's secret and Assignment load immediately, and I consider writing a pleading message to Zed, asking him to retract Sasha's Assignment.

STAR: This needs to stop.

ZED: Things have a way of working out.

STAR: I'm leaving.

ZED: You're not safe, without us.

STAR: Did you know about Agnes and Bitty?

ZED: No. But I've never seen something so beautiful.

ROXIE: How'd the rest of us find our way here?

ZED: Don't. It's anonymous.

@SSHOLE: Did other people find the website in a book? Or online? On another website?

ZED: Those aren't the questions that matter.

I wonder if no one's ever asked before. I wonder if that's even possible, but I know that it is, because it had never occurred to me to ask. When you are involved in something kind of magical, you don't necessarily want to know how the magic works. You don't want to prove it wrong.

ELFBOY: Our secrets really aren't safe, huh?

ZED: We hold one another accountable. This is something unexpected and perfect. This is why we do what we do. It's in the rules. You knew.

My image of Zed shifts. Like he was this beautiful silhouette of a person. Long lines. Floppy hair. The outline of a cool, holy, unreachable being who knows things. Except now, he's not behind the veil anymore. He's a whole person. Not an outline. Not a shadow. He's a sad guy who is desperate for us to stay. He maybe doesn't have friends. He loves someone who doesn't love him. I flip through his secrets over the last few years since the site began, and they are all about unrequited feelings, and not wanting to weigh more than 150 pounds, and how sure he is that he can remain in control.

He never says whether he's completed his Assignments. I hadn't noticed. I assumed that he was being one of us.

I close my eyes, and I can't get the new Zed out of my head. Too skinny, ribs poking out under an ugly, worn-through, colorless T-shirt. A dirty smell of someone who spends too much time on the computer and not enough time in the shower. Crumbs in his lap. Crumbs of bran and kale and celery and other sad, calorieless foods. A lamp that barely works. A pile of laundry and a pile of dishes and an inability to take care of either.

"Tabby?" Cate and Paul come into Cate's office, holding hands. "What's going on?"

I shake my head. Cate touches her belly with my sister inside, and Paul follows suit.

"We're going to be okay," she says. "Sometimes things get worse before they get better. Sometimes you have to do really hard things, really terrible things, to come out on the other side." I guess she's talking about leaving Paul for a few days, or maybe she's talking about Paul giving me drugs and being a totally terrible father for a second there. Or maybe she's talking in general, about the nosedive my life has taken.

But she sounds like Zed.

"The only way through is . . . through," Cate says. She wrinkles her nose and furrows her brow. "That's not quite the saying," she says. "But you get the point."

"The only way through is through," I repeat.

BITTY: They're not your secrets to tell.

Twenty-Six.

The next morning:

Cate's prepregnancy, post-thirtieth-birthday gold dress.

A rhinestone headband.

A list of all my secrets, as many as Cate and Paul and I could think up.

Caramel-colored cowboy boots.

Hair out in beachy waves.

Purple eye shadow. No eyeliner.

I am ready to go. Paul and Cate said it was okay. That the only way through is through.

Headmaster Brownser has on his tweed jacket and a tired expression, like he is obviously going to retire before most of us graduate and his making-a-difference days are more or less over.

It's a Thursday assembly, a long one, but just as planned, his guest (Cate's friend who was scheduled to give us a lecture on organic farming) has canceled last minute and he's left with an hour to fill. He stands at the mic with a thermos of green tea (we know because he smells like it) and asks if anyone has any announcements.

I let the hockey team remind everyone to come to their game, and the charity club remind everyone that today is the last day to bring any mitten donations.

"I have something," I call out when they've finished. When I raise my hand, my beaded bracelets clatter together and meet around my elbow. Sasha Cotton turns around in her seat, and Joe's hand slips from her shoulder to his own waist.

"Yes?" Headmaster Brownser says, shielding his eyes to see who is speaking out from the crowd.

"Can I come up?" I say.

Shit. I wasn't supposed to ask. When I planned this with Cate and Paul, they reminded me not to ask for permission. "If you don't ask for permission, no one can turn you down," Paul said, and Cate nodded vigorously. She is really into Paul's new therapist, who supplies him with excellent insights like that one.

"That's not usually—"

"I'm coming up!" I say, and I pump my arm in a horrible awkward way that would bother me if I weren't going up there to completely destroy what is left of my reputation.

The aisle up to the stage is long and slippery, and cowboy boots don't have any traction, so I keep almost slipping and then barely catching myself. But I get up there, and Headmaster Brownser is so old or so confused that he just steps aside and gives me the stage, clearing his throat and nodding his head first.

I've been on the stage only a few times, during misguided attempts at musical theater and band, neither of which went anywhere. But the lights are even more blinding than I remember, and that's actually okay, since it blocks out most of the faces in the crowd. The whole school—three hundred kids—is out there, but I can only see the first few rows and hear their breathing and shifting and sighing.

"Hi," I say. I smile. It hurts and the rest of me is trembling and nothing about that smile could have looked believable as an expression of friendliness or joy or warmth. "I have some things to say. Because I got myself into a pickle, and, um, I have to do this because I'm, like, in charge of my own destiny and stuff." Headmaster Brownser, standing off to the side with his head cocked, nods, but I don't know if anyone else does. I just used the word *pickle* in front of my entire school, so I'm hating myself a little. "Like *The Odyssey*?" I try. Headmaster Brownser really likes *The Odyssey*. And I feel like we talked about destiny and fate when we studied it, so I'm hoping that's relevant.

Deep breath.

I could leave the stage right now. No one's holding me hostage in the bright lights. I could leave the stage and let Sasha Cotton do what she's going to do, and go crying to Zed after. I could let everyone else make these decisions for me. It would be easier. Cate and Paul say the last two years of high school go pretty fast anyway, and that in college no one will care.

I could power through another two years and let it all pass me by.

But I won't. Because I don't trust Zed anymore, but he's right, that you only live once.

Someone in the back of the auditorium blows their nose. Then the whispering starts. First soft explosions of voices from identifiable areas in the audience, and then a more general mumble that turns to white noise. I am the person standing between them and the rest of their lives.

"I kissed Joe Donavetti," I say.

It's not graceful. My voice cracks like I'm a twelve-year-old boy, and a drop of sweat falls from my chin to the mic, making a terrible *plop* that echoes in the silence. I exhale hard and try to gain control over my shaking muscles. The ones in my thighs are especially bad, trembling with such intensity I can barely stand. I am not hiding it well, that much is for sure. When I look down to gather the courage to keep going, I get a glimpse of what they are seeing: earthquakes erupting in my legs and causing aftershock tremors all the way up my torso. These are no small shakes; I am swaying from the intensity.

"Uh, Tabitha, I think maybe—" Headmaster Brownser breaks in after way too much time has passed. I shake my head and wave him away with my hand.

"I have to do this," I say. "I kissed Joe. A bunch of times. Knowing he was with Sasha. So, yeah, some of you were sort of right. Not that I'm slutty, or whatever. But about some of who I am. Some of the things I do. They're not great."

Mrs. Drake clears her throat from across the room, and I'm not sure if it's directed at me or at the now-paralyzed headmaster. "And! My dad is a huge stoner. Smokes a ton of pot. He's trying to stop, but it might not work. He smokes at work. At Tea Cozy. He's high when he's making your coffee," I say.

More teachers are moving in on me, but they're coming at me slow, the way you see in the movies when there's a kidnapper with a gun and everyone's being careful not to upset the crazy person. Mrs. Drake leads the crowd with her long, awkward, slow strides and a fake-sympathetic look on her face.

"Jemma and Alison hate me now, but I still miss them. I miss Jemma. Even knowing what she thinks of me, I still wish she'd be my friend. I want her to like me. So, Jemma, you won. I'm hurt. I'm not okay with it." I clear my throat, because now that I've cleared the way with the big LBC secrets, now that I'm somehow free, I want to finish the job. "I hate my unborn sister," I say. "Or I'm jealous of her. But you know, working on it."

Headmaster Brownser isn't letting anyone get close to me onstage. Sort of like I'm a sleepwalker who it would be dangerous to wake up. And I guess that's right. It would be dangerous to stop me now, in the middle of this dream.

"Um, I am falling for Jemma Benson's brother. I'm a virgin. I know you all think I'm a slut. I consider dressing differently, but then I don't. I hate-love my boobs. I was in love with Joe for no reason at all other than it felt really, really fucking good to be in love with someone. I was a bitch to my only friend. I read other people's margin notes in used books. I trusted a total stranger with my life. I'm not sure yet if I regret it. I do terrible and weird things and I'm scared I'm the only one. But maybe, I don't know, maybe someone else is screwed up, like me. Maybe."

Then I remember to breathe. On instinct, my hand rushes to the place below my bra and between my ribs where I have been holding all these unsaid things. I want to put them back in, because when I can't hear my own words thundering in my head and when I'm no longer lost in the adrenaline of secret spilling, I'm *here*. I'm some exposed girl in a weird gold dress who talks too fast and says too much and who no one really likes but now everyone *really* knows.

There are giggles and whispers and uncomfortable coughing and the same squeaking of chairs that haunts every single Thursday assembly. I take a step back, like somehow getting away from the edge of the stage will help anything. And just as Mrs. Drake reaches the ramp to finally get onto the stage and, presumably, carry me off in a straitjacket, Headmaster Brownser at long last *does* something.

"Hey," he says. I think it's to me, so I turn my face toward where he's standing and start to apologize, but he's looking at Mrs. Drake and her slow-walking cronies. "Hey. It's okay. That's okay. Let her breathe." Mrs. Drake pouts and her eyebrows dance all over her face in confusion, but she freezes just as she's ordered. "Very brave," Headmaster Brownser says, so quiet it could just be for me, but the auditorium has fallen into utter silence, so I'm pretty sure everyone can hear his pronouncement. It feels that final, like if our wise old headmaster with his half-bald head and his sagging wrinkles and still-bright blue eyes says I am brave, then he must be right, even if right now it feels wrong.

I try it on for size: I am brave.

"Quite the speech, Tabitha," he says, and puts a slender but strong hand on my shoulder. "Thank you for that. I think we all needed that." He and I stand there, then. Together in front of everyone.

Doesn't he know I said the words fuck *and* slut *and* screw *in front of everyone?*

"I once gave a student a bad grade because his father was a jerk," Headmaster Brownser says. He looks embarrassed for about a second, but then he chuckles. Chuckles so hard he has to cover his mouth with his hand to regain control. "Never said that out loud," he muses. "Thought it. Never said it. Thought saying it would make it *more* true. Make it worse than it was. But I did it either way, right?" I'm the only one onstage with him, so I guess he's sort of talking to me. I nod and muster up a smile.

It is the single weirdest moment of my life. And I have had some weird moments in the last few weeks.

"Well, come on," he says. This time not to me; this time to the whole school. "Who else?"

Then he nods to me and gestures for me to get off the stage. I don't feel ready to join everyone else, but he's practically escorting me, so I take careful steps down the ramp and climb back into my seat. By the time I've gotten myself settled, there is someone else on stage: a senior guy with clear-framed glasses and clear braces. The kind of guy who could not be trying any harder to fit in.

"That was really . . . cool," he says. He has a voice so high, I'm sure when he answers the phone people think he's a woman. "Uh, I don't have anything huge. But I shop at the Salvation Army. With my mom. Not, like, by choice. So yeah. People made fun of me for that before and I denied it and whatever, but it's totally true. So, there ya go." He's beaming. I wonder if I looked that red and sweaty and happy up there. He's too awkward to get offstage gracefully, and he manages to step on his own feet. I do a big inward groan and think this is reflecting poorly on me too. I probably looked just that awkward. He makes eye contact with me on his way back to his seat. Waves, like I'm an inspiring celebrity, and gives me a thumbs-up sign.

It's nice, I know it is, but the worst part of me hates him for it. My ears ring with embarrassment. I'm so busy looking at the floor and feeling bad for myself and the guy with clear orthodontics that I jump in my seat when I hear the next voice: Jemma.

"I'm not very nice," she says. "Sometimes I'm a bitch. Like, I sort of know I'm doing it, and then I get home and feel stupid, but then I just do it again. Or I justify it, you know? But sometimes it's hard to really convince yourself that what you did, you know, isn't so bad." Jemma practically sprints offstage, but it's just as well because without my really noticing it, a dozen or so people have gathered on the ramp leading up to the stage. There's officially a line to get up there, to have all that heat on you, and to own up to everything you hate about yourself or secretly love about yourself but know to hide.

A freshman admits to an eating disorder.

A sophomore says her mom left her dad two weeks ago, but neither of them have told anyone—even the rest of the family—yet.

Two seniors apologize for hacking into another boy's email.

A junior says he cries in the bathroom like a girl. I mean, he actually admits this. To a school of three hundred people.

Headmaster Brownser stays right there on the side of the stage, some pillar of strength, and nods along with the sharing. He makes no move to put a stop to it. The line on the ramp gets even longer: twenty people are in line, then thirty.

"I knew about a friend's dad hitting her, and I didn't do anything," a girl says, in tears. Headmaster Brownser nods, and when the crying girl doesn't calm down, he rubs her back until she can breathe enough to muster a smile and a big, healthy exhale.

Mrs. Drake gets onstage.

"I am not always the best at my job," she mumbles, and then shakes her head and leaves the stage. She doesn't look at me, but she stays in the assembly hall, and whenever someone says something emotional, she checks in with them on their way offstage. All of them. The nice girls. The bad girls. The jocks. The stoners. She looks each of them in the eye when they get offstage.

People keep smiling at me on their way up the ramp, but I am so heart-poundingly stupefied by the response to my outpouring of secrets that I don't smile back. I can't get my head around the way one action done for a totally selfish reason has caused something so large and generous and profound.

Sasha Cotton doesn't move from her seat in front of me. But she does keep looking back at me, and not with hatred. Not with spite or malice or, I think, further plans to destroy me. Her face is wet with tears, no surprise there, but this time they are for a *reason*, they are from real live empathy, and not her own dark place.

Joe is gone.

I lean forward.

"You okay?" I whisper. Normally people would be craning their necks to see a Sasha-Tabitha showdown, but three hundred sets of eyes are glued to the stage. Thursday assembly has never been this captivating. Years of rape-prevention improv shows and organic farming experts and tired local folk bands have programmed us to tune out Thursday assemblies, and I think we are all stunned to be sitting in this room that is suddenly charged with actual feeling instead of just drowning in rhetoric or pretension.

"Yeah," Sasha says. She wipes her face with her long sleeves. Little pieces of fluffy angora cling to her face after. The downside of beautiful lavender expensive fluffy wool sweaters, right?

"Sorry I did that. It wasn't to, like, make it worse for you—" I start, but Sasha cuts me off with an adamant head shake.

"Did you tell Zed you were doing that?" she says. She looks so scared for a girl who once had everything I wanted.

"I recorded it," I say. I click onto LBC and post the recording. It's quick and painless. It's a kind of magic, getting my life back so quickly. Sasha closes her eyes for a few moments longer than a blink. "You could go up and talk, too," I say. I can't read if she's mad or sad or relieved or what. She shakes her head and gives me a half smile that could mean anything. Turns out, I don't know that much about Sasha Cotton at all.

I like her more than I did even five minutes earlier, and certainly a hell of a lot more than I did two months ago. For everyone else in here, the brave thing is to get up there and cry and expose something soft and vulnerable and hidden. But for Sasha Cotton the bravest thing to do is to sit right where she is, and not be the crying, fragile, perfect disaster that she's always been.

Ninety minutes pass, but Headmaster Brownser doesn't make a move to get us herded into class.

Two hours pass.

Two and a half.

I can't count the number of people who have spoken or the number of people waiting to speak. Once in a while someone says something so powerful we all start applauding, sometimes even standing up and cheering. When a senior boy talks about drunk driving and running over a cat and never telling anyone and worrying about it for a year and a half, we applaud. Solemnly, of course. When a really pretty freshman girl admits to having considered suicide, we applaud the fact that she didn't do it. When a cute dork from the junior class tells a crazy popular girl from his grade that he is totally in love with her, we applaud, even though we know she probably doesn't love him back.

"This won't be a shock," Elise says, when she has made it to the front of the line. I try to make eye contact with her now, but I'm sure she can't see me. Or that's what I tell myself. "But I did everything I could to be like everyone else. And I just couldn't hack it. I've been avoiding saying these words for five years, because the second I say them in front of anyone but my . . . um . . . my best friend, Tabby, they'll become unchangeably real. And I know some of you will make fun of me. I know even after today some of you will say totally horrible things or ask me to make out with your girlfriend or call me a dyke, or whatever. But I might as well say it since I think you know anyway, and since this is probably the only moment I'll ever have to come forward with this much . . . uh . . . power. So. Thanks Tabby, for, you know, creating the moment. The moment when I can just fucking say it. I LIKE GIRLS. I have a girlfriend. An awesome one. Okay, everyone? I'm gay."

People clap. People stand up. So many people that Elise has to bow her head and smile and then wave at us all to sit down.

I clap the hardest. I stand the longest.

Three hours have passed since I first got onstage. I've cried so much my eyes hurt, and if I look around, every single other person in the auditorium looks the way I feel. The whole assembly has taken on this weirdly casual air: people aren't returning to their seats—they are sitting on the floor, sitting on one another's laps, crowding in the aisles to be as close as possible to their best friends.

When a techie chick is onstage, Elise asks the girl next to me to let her switch seats, and the exchange is all smiles and gracious politeness. We are survivors of an attack or a natural disaster or a great tragedy. We are in it together, all of a sudden. And it's the sort of wonderful, warm thing that you just know won't last, but you somehow convince yourself to appreciate anyway.

Elise gives me an awkward sideways hug in our seats.

"I'm sorry," I say.

"I'm sorry this hug is so awkward," she says. "I'll give you a real one later."

And then we're okay again. We're Elise and Tabitha.

"This is like margin notes times a million," Elise says when the techie talks about how black nail polish doesn't make her goth. "This is like if we had a copy of the Bible and the entire school had marked it up with their own thoughts on everything important, you know?"

I mean, that's why I'm friends with Elise, right? And it's why she'll get into Harvard. She can take the biggest, craziest day our school has ever experienced and break it down into one perfect sentence.

"It's exactly like that," I say.

Twenty-Seven.

It's one in the afternoon when assembly is over. Five hours have passed, and Headmaster Brownser let every last person talk. Teachers, administrators, and more students than I could count got up onstage to speak.

"I don't think we need to go to classes today," Headmaster Brownser says when the last kid has spoken and we all have grumbling stomachs and dried-out eyes. He doesn't dismiss us right away, after declaring the school day officially over. I think he must be deeply tempted to put a cap on the whole day, to give a profound speech and wrap it all up. But there's no way to contextualize that many stories and epiphanies and secrets.

He shrugs. And that shrug says it all.

We don't go straight home. A lot of the underclassmen have working parents who can't pick them up until later anyway, and there's no bus to Circle Community, and those of us with driver's licenses are too worn out to consider driving anywhere.

"I'll make us sandwiches," Elise says when I collapse onto one of the atrium benches. "You nap or whatever. I'll be right back." The deli meat bar is one of the only not-disgusting options at the cafeteria, so I nod and close my eyes. Normally, I'd watch myself. Wouldn't want to drool or talk in my sleep or be caught quite so exposed. But today pretty much anything is cool, so I curl into a ball, just like I would do in my bed at home, and get ready to take a power nap.

I'm practically asleep when I feel someone hovering over me. I know who it is before opening my eyes. I can smell his berry ChapStick and his Old Spice deodorant.

Joe.

"That was some performance," he says. He's looking at me like he's never seen me before, like everything from my eye color to the shape of my hips is a mystery.

"I wish you'd gotten up there," I say. I fidget and stretch like I'm just waking up from the world's longest nap. I rub imaginary sleep from my eyes. I find his gaze so he knows I mean it.

"Why?"

"Would have liked to know what you have to say." I'm still in the gold dress, and he's in pen-stained khakis and a white shirt that hasn't been bleached enough, so it has dingy stains around the collar and sleeves. I run a hand through my hair and hope it looks as messy-sexy-voluminous as it feels.

I hate that I still care if he thinks my hair is sexy.

"I already told you all my secrets," Joe says. It's a quiet voice, one

I haven't heard lately. It's the voice I imagined when we chatted online late at night. It's the voice I heard in my ear, the one that kept me falling for him. The little part of my heart he still occupies lights up, then dims again. Someday soon, it won't flash for him at all.

I expect him to yell at me. The whole hallway is expecting him to yell at me. There's a stream of students pacing the hallways: making plans to head home, hugging one another, hunting for their backpacks in the pile near my bench, walking to the cafeteria so they can enjoy crappy food while they wait for their rides to come. The movement hasn't stopped, but it's slowed while Joe and I talk. Now that my dirty laundry is aired, the whole school knows what might happen.

Joe doesn't yell.

Elise emerges with sandwiches in hand but keeps her distance. Even she is afraid of the explosion.

Joe's eyelashes are so long, I wonder if they've grown over time, a version of Pinocchio's nose. He bats them, and his brown eyes go a little watery and he steps in closer to me. Just that one step brings in another wave of smells. I shut my eyes against the force. When I open them again, his face is close to mine.

"You shouldn't have told everyone everything. But. I'll tell you all my secrets," he says. Softer. Lower. Closer to my ear.

It feels good, that whisper. I feel it on my spine, his words like a feather sliding up and down the places on my back that tickle. I shimmy against it, a spasm in my shoulders so intense we both laugh. I almost want to kiss him. I think of the silvery font of my Assignment to Kiss Him Again, and wonder what would have happened if that was always my Assignment, if I'd been told to kiss him again and again and again.

I could do it right now. He'd give in, I think. He'd let me pull his face to mine.

But the second his face turns away from my ear, the impulse goes with it. My spine stops tickling and itching with want. My shoulders stop shaking. My heart stops flickering for him.

"You never told me secrets. You only ever told me crap," I say. I whisper, too. I keep it low. I bat my eyelashes. His face falls, and he knows, he *knows* it's true.

It feels fucking good.

Twenty-Eight.

I try to stop myself, but when I climb into my car and ready myself to go to the Cozy, I sign into LBC.

Except I can't sign into LBC.

The site won't load. My password doesn't work. I've been blocked.

Sasha Cotton knocks on my car window and holds her phone up. Her screen is like mine. Blocked. I roll down my window and Sasha Cotton is crying, but the tears look to be a different size and shape than her usual ones.

"They're gone," she says. "We're out."

"We're out," I repeat, and although I suppose I knew that would happen, I thought I'd have the option of logging back on, if I needed it. I don't cry, but I could, if I wasn't swallowing so hard.

"What am I gonna do?" Sasha says. And she's really asking me, not rhetorically. Her eyes are big, and she grips the window frame and bites her lip waiting for my answer.

"I have no idea," I say. I'd like to tell her to ditch Joe. I'd like to tell her to stop crying and to confront her mom and to become friends with me and Elise and to not take weird photos in front of her house, and to toughen up because life's really hard and you can't go around sighing and weeping all the time, even if you're Sasha Cotton.

But I don't tell her any of that.

"I think we could be friends," I say. "If you ever want to talk. Or hang out at the bookstore. Or whatever." It's probably the biggest thing I've done this whole time. I pat her hand, the one on my car, and give a shrug and a smile like Headmaster Brownser did.

"I'm not sure I like you yet," she says, but I have a feeling she will, sometime. The girl from the margin notes would like me.

I drive away.

Straight ahead are the mountains. I thought they never changed, that they were the most predictable, solid, unchangeable things ever. But a little bit of snow has melted, even in one of the coldest months in Vermont. Cate and Paul love that those mountains are so dependable, but I have never been so happy to see the unlikely green patches near the white, snowy tops.

Little pockets of surprise. Unpredictable and hopeful. Acting of their own accord. Not answering to anyone.

Not a Secret:

Devon kissed me.

I assigned it to myself to kiss him again. And again.

And again.

Acknowledgments

An extra-large thank-you to Patricia McCormick, a wonderful advisor, mentor, and inspiration. Your encouragement, insight, availability, and kindness gave me the courage to write the first draft of this book and to keep working on it through creative and personal ups and downs. I am insanely lucky I got a chance to work with you and learn from someone I admire so deeply.

To Victoria Marini, spectacular agent and friend. You quell anxieties and hold my hand through disappointments and celebrations. You make both me and my work stronger. I'm so happy we get to do this together.

To my editor, Anica Rissi. Thank you for believing in this book and making it real. Thank you for pushing me to be the best writer I can be. Thank you for teaching me so much about craft and story and the magical other things that make manuscripts into books. You're incredible.

Thank you, Katherine Tegen, Alexandra Arnold, and the rest of the team at Katherine Tegen Books. I'm astounded by the work and love you put into *LBC*.

Special thank-yous to very early readers of *LBC*: Brandy Colbert, Alison Cherry, Caela Carter, Sona Chairapotra, Amy Ewing, Mary Thompson. You shaped so much of this book and helped me see the light at the end of the tunnel. More thank-yous to other readers along the way, who pushed me and selflessly gave time and energy into this project: Alyson Gerber, Dhonielle Clayton, Lenea Grace, Taylor Jenkins Reid, Sarah Weeks, Jess Verdi, Riddhi Parekh, and the New School Writing for Children Class of 2012.

Thank you to my entire family for always supporting me, and especially Mom, Dad, and Andy for a lifetime of encouragement and book loving.

Thank you to Frank Scallon for listening, cheering, reading, and being all-around awesome.

As always, thank you to my incredible friends who build me up with love and fun and long, long talks when I need them. Special shout-outs to Anna Bridgforth, Julia Furlan, and Kea Gilbert. who are leaned on extra hard when things are tough.

And for all varieties of help along the way: Kalah McCaffery, Liesa Abrams, Bethany Buck, Red Horse Café, Victoria Marano, David Levithan, the Lucky 13's, Ian and Nivia Dougherty, Mrs. Scallon, Jennifer Haydu, Ellie Haydu, Judy Ross, BookCourt.

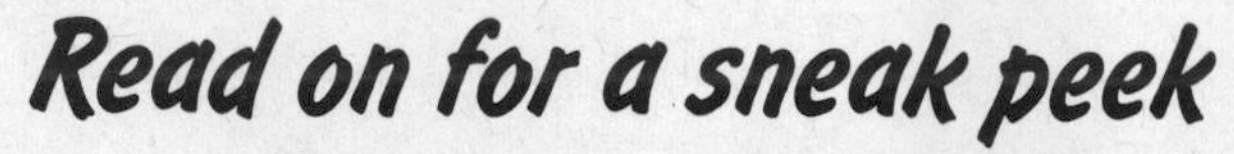

at Corey Ann Haydu's latest, *Making Pretty*. . . .

An intoxicating new friendship, an all-consuming romance, and an unexpected family announcement send Montana spinning into the most important summer of her life.

one

I should not be going to a bar.

Karissa and I have matching Elmo T-shirts, but hers is cut to show a lot of skin and mine is layered over a ripped long-sleeved black shirt and under a polka-dot cardigan I stole from my dad's third wife, Natasha.

"Act cool, Montana," Karissa says. "Act twenty-one."

I take my hair down from its ponytail and cock my head to the side and try to look bored.

"Does this look twenty-one?" I ask. We're across the street from Karissa's favorite bar, Dirty Versailles. It's on the Lower East Side of Manhattan and allegedly lives up to its name. Dive meets fancy French palace. It is the opposite of surprising that Karissa likes it.

"You'll need this," she says, handing me a lit cigarette. She lights a new one for herself. "You smoke, right?"

"Yes, ma'am," I say. I like to call Karissa "ma'am" because she's twenty-three and she hates it.

I take a drag on the cig. My best friend, Roxanne, started smoking at college this year so I started too, wanting to be up to speed when she got home for the summer. I don't like the taste but I like how much my older sister, Arizona, hates it and how much my dad would hate it if he were home enough to know.

I like how it compresses the time and space between Roxanne and me. With each dirty drag I can almost pretend I spent the year upstate at Bard splitting cigarettes with Roxanne and her Argentinian roommate, or in Maine with Arizona, making out with boys in white baseball caps.

Karissa moves us across the street so that we're smoking right in front of the bar, where the bouncer can see us.

"Look edgy," she says. "Look sexy. Look like you don't give a crap and could go anywhere but have chosen to grace this bar with your presence."

I'm not convinced I can pull that off, but I don't want this night with Karissa to end. She has on silver leggings and cowboy boots that she spray-painted neon blue, and her hair is so long and wild she could be a mermaid or a lioness. I'm a little bit in love with her, in the way I used to be in love with my cool teenage babysitters when I was like ten years old.

I blow my smoke up instead of out. I thank myself for wearing skinny jeans instead of the ugly shorts Roxanne and Arizona hate. It's impossible not to wonder if I should have done some sort of makeup situation.

Karissa stamps out her cig, so I do the same.

"Pretty K!" the bouncer says when she touches his arm and smiles.

"Hey, buddy," she says. He's a little bit in love with her too. Everyone is. The boys and men in our acting class. Strangers walking from an Italian dinner to a crappy sports bar. The short dude in the sketchy bodega who sold her the cigarettes.

"Come on in," the bouncer says.

"This is Montana," Karissa says, putting an arm around me and kissing my cheek. "She cool?"

The bouncer looks me up and down. It seems like A Moment. I've been asking myself this very same question all year long. Am I cool?

I've had a lot of time to mull it over, in the absence of my sister and my best friend. It's the kind of question I've been working out, listening to stories of dorm parties and gender studies classes and roommates with dreadlocks and how quiet and sweet and full life outside the city can be.

I haven't come up with an answer, and the bouncer looks unconvinced.

"She young?" he says.

"Younger than me!" Karissa says. "But old enough."

"Fine, fine, get her in there," the bouncer says. "But I can't promise she'll fit in."

"Isn't the point to not fit in?" Karissa says. Every word out of her mouth is perfect. Wry and flirty and smart and funny and killer.

Goddamn it I want to be her. But I'll settle for having her take me under her wing for now.

The bar is exactly what it promised to be. Everything is painted gold but also chipping. Chandeliers with fake crystals hang from the ceilings. Half the lightbulbs are out.

It's funny how something sad is automatically more beautiful than something happy.

It applies to people too. Karissa is the sad kind of pretty. Like a very wise Tinker Bell. Tinker Bell's sad too. All wrapped in unrequited love and unbelievability and misery. Karissa, Tinker Bell, and this bar are all lovely for the same reasons.

"Tinker Bell is sort of a tragic literary figure, right?" I say. It seems smart and interesting in my head, like a brilliant thesis I've come up with that Karissa could get behind. Something that will astound and impress her. Make it clear I'm worth the trouble of sneaking into a bar.

"Huh. Maybe," she says. "But I'm an Ophelia girl personally. Crazy and gorgeous and loved and ill-fated. Not that I'm gorgeous. I'm like the opposite of gorgeous." Karissa makes a nervous gesture with her hand running through her hair, and she is completely gorgeous. "But I'm a little crazy, like all the best people are."

She looks at me like I'm supposed to say something, and I want to say something even though I have nothing to say.

"They so are," I say. "I'm, like, bonkers." It's a word Roxanne uses all the time so I am a total fraud, but it works. Karissa beams.

"And Ophelia's about a million times better than Juliet, you know? Juliet had a stupidity to her. Ophelia is all tragedy, all the time," she says. I nod and wonder at talking about Ophelia on a Thursday night at a downtown bar next to a guy with a beard and a green drink and a neon-yellow bow tie.

"Ophelia commits to the tragedy of life," I say, playing with the gold tassel on my bar stool. "She knows how it is."

"Yes!" Karissa says, before turning to the bartender and ordering a bottle of red. He gives us goblets and some kind of French wine and fills everything to the tippy top because he's so distracted by Karissa. It doesn't matter that her teeth are crooked and her chin is a little small and she's even flatter than me. It doesn't matter that she's freckled and that her hair is light brown and not honey blond or platinum blond or champagne blond.

She is charged. And beautiful. And telling me to drink faster, harder, more enthusiastically.

"Let's be drunk," she says. "Let's be drunk best friends who rule the world."

"Best friends?" I say. The music is loud and I wonder if I've misheard her. I've been aching to have a best friend again. Even though Roxanne has been back from college for a few weeks, it hasn't felt the way it did last year or the ten years before that. She talks about people whose names I've never heard. People who have names I didn't even know were names. People who go only by their last names. People who go by shortened versions of their last names: Hertz and Scal and Jav and Gerb. It's hard to keep up.

Arizona gets back tonight. We haven't spoken in over a month, which seems impossible for someone I used to co-parent a stuffed elephant with. She won't even be living at home over the summer. Dad's letting her split a summer sublet with one of her new Colby friends. I hate that the word *sister* has this shifting, changeable definition that doesn't mean two people who share a room and a brain and a speech pattern and a body type anymore.

I'm over it. Over them. Over the things I knew and did and thought. I'm with Karissa now.

"I think we could be best friends, don't you?" Karissa says. She slams down her goblet and fills it up with more wine. Her teeth are insta-purple. "If I find you a cute college guy to hook up with, would you ditch your other best friends and become mine?"

"I'd definitely consider it," I say, but really I'm looking everywhere for the guy I see sometimes in the park. I'm pretty sure we have developed a whole relationship based on continuous, awkward eye contact over the last two months.

"It's rare to have a real connection with someone," Karissa says. She leans in close to me. She smells like baby powder deodorant, and I know from experience, even though I can't hear them now, that her cheap metal earrings are making tiny clanging noises. "You're in high school, so maybe you don't know this, but you'll mostly hate people when you're in your twenties, and you'll be wondering why everyone's trying to be so boring. They're all scared."

I don't tell her that I'm scared.

I do tell her that I've seen a lot of women on a quest to be boring.

My dad's a plastic surgeon. A fancy one who specializes in marrying women, changing everything about them on his operating table, and divorcing them when they're as close to perfect as he can get them.

That's not what's written on his business card or anything. But that's how it goes with Dr. Sean Varren.

“There’s a guy for you,” Karissa says, pointing across the bar to a dude in a plaid button-up whose mohawk is so tall it almost touches one of the low-hanging chandeliers.

“I think he’s for you,” I say. He’s handsome in the same unknowing, wild, fantastic way that Karissa is beautiful. He doesn’t look kissable because he doesn’t look knowable.

“For you!” she says. “Be brave. Live big.” She shakes her mane and the light catches the glittery blush she wears. Her eye shadow is ironic blue, and it matches not only the boots but also a thin headband she’s strapped across her forehead.

I pull my Elmo shirt down so that it covers my stomach. I wave at Mohawk Man. He waves back but doesn’t come over. We pound the rest of the bottle of wine. It’s a brand-new feeling—I’m used to chugging beer or taking shots of cheap liquor, but I’m not used to wine at all, in any context. It hits all slow and sleepy, and I like that it tastes purple, royal, sweet.

Roxanne favors Malibu rum and kegs of light beer.

If Karissa’s my new best friend, everything we do will be different and new and better.

She orders another bottle.

I’ve made it. I’m here. I’m hers.

When we are drunker and it’s later, we end up in a booth in the back. The guy with the mohawk bought us some beers and talked about art for a while, but he must have felt like a third wheel, because Karissa and I have this secret-language way of talking. It doesn’t matter that we've only known each other for six months and that there's no real reason for us to be friends now that acting class is over. It doesn't matter that I'm seventeen and she's twenty-three. We're connected. We fit. We're mismatched and cozy in the back booth. We make sense in a weird and wonderful way. Like math except sexy and cool.

I'm getting texts from Arizona asking where I am, saying she got home and ordered us a pizza, saying I was supposed to be there to welcome her home after her post-freshman-year European backpacking trip. She could have returned to New York when her semester ended three weeks ago. She chose even less time with me. She keeps choosing less time with me, over and over.

I don't reply to the texts.

I can't stop swinging my hair around like Karissa does. She makes it look so good, and I'm convinced I could be a little like her, if I tried harder. Arizona texts again, a bunch of question marks instead of words, so I start to feel bad. Punctuation marks make me feel more than words, sometimes.

"I think I need to get home," I say. "My sister's waiting for me. I told her I'd hang out even if she got home late. Start our summer together off right or something. Pizza. Bonding. All that."

"Your sister's back," Karissa says. She doesn't make a move to pay the bill or slide out of the booth. "You must be so happy."

"Mmmm. I miss the way things were with her," I say, and it's the truest thing I've said all night and maybe all month. Karissa hits the bottom of her umpteenth glass of wine. She shakes her head like she's trying to clear it. Wipes her mouth and teeters on the edge of weepiness.

"I need to tell you something about me," Karissa says.

"Anything," I say.

"I'm sort of messed up, okay? Like . . . okay. Okay. This is such a weird thing to announce, but if we're going to be friends, real ones, it's like, we have to know the big things, right? So we need to get all the big things out there, as, like, foundation." Karissa pushes her hair behind her ear in this ballerina way and I am certain she will be famous someday, even if it is simply for that one gesture.

"Let's do it," I say, leaning forward. I wonder if people are listening in on us. I would.

"My whole family is dead. Car accident four years ago. You talking about your sister made my heart—I don't know. I feel like I can't even have a normal conversation if you don't know that about me. Like, you won't understand anything I say if you don't know that, right?"

"Right," I say. Her eyes fill up and mine do too, a mirror image of her. She is Ophelia.

I feel desperately sad for her and a little bit sad for myself that she didn't tell me before. That I've known her all this time without really knowing her. "Are you . . . how are you? About it?" Drunkenness is a blessing right now, because everything I say sounds smooth and deep. I can look right into her green eyes and not blink or blush or get nervous.

"I'm a mess," she says. "I'm not like anyone else." She's whispering, and little pieces of crystal on the chandeliers above chime whenever the air conditioner clicks onto a higher level.

"That's . . . wow. Wow. I'm sorry. I don't know what to say. It's incredible you, like, get up and walk around every day. Seriously."

Karissa sighs and licks her lips that must taste like wine and lipstick, and she brushes her hair aside again and again.

"I can tell you have something dark in there too," she says. "Something that happened. Or something missing. Or something you want." Even through the beginnings of tears, she sees me. It's a little scary, to be seen.

"All three," I say, thinking of my mother who left us and my father who keeps marrying new women and the emptiness of the house without Arizona and the way three stepmothers in ten years feels less like a surplus of stepmoms and more like a deficit of mothers.

I say some drunk version of this, wondering at the way the words come out wrong and lopsided and unclear, like I can't recite my own biography.

"It's stupid, compared to what you've been through," I say. But Karissa holds my hand across the table. Kisses it. There's a reason books are written about girls who've lost everything.

"Girls without mothers are, like, strong and weak at the same time," Karissa says. "We're all powerful, you know? Like, we have a special secret power and secret pain and they're both more, like, vast than anyone knows."

If anyone else classified me as a girl without a mother, I'd hate them, but with Karissa it seems like a point of pride. Like something

I'm supposed to celebrate with her. Like she's inviting me into a club that I'm not totally qualified for.

Arizona would hate it. She's always saying we have each other and Dad and we don't need anyone else, as if we're made to need less than most people.

"We're going to have champagne to close this night out," Karissa says when I can only manage weepiness and compliments as a reply. She makes the bartender come to us, leaving his post at the bar to bring champagne right to the table, and I know he sees in her what I see. What we all see.

"To everything we don't have," she says, her voice hitching and settling in the single sentence.

We clink and drink, but Karissa stops me before my second sip.

There are enormous, dark portraits of former French kings on the walls, powdered wigs and all. They're in oversize gold frames and decorated with neon graffiti.

"We'll have everything, someday," Karissa says, so sure it sounds like fact. I wonder what it's like to have hope after you've lost everyone that you love. What kind of strength it must take for her to utter that sentence.

"I've never been this drunk," I say, which has nothing to do with anything except it's getting hard to see or think from behind this haze.

"You're freaking adorable," Karissa says. "You remind me of my little sister. She died in the crash too." It aches, hearing her say the words so plainly. Something so large and awful should only be talked about with flowery language and metaphors. Her saying it in such a basic way twists me up inside.

"Oh my God, Karissa, I'm so sorry. I'm so, so sorry," I say. I've never before been this sad about someone else's life.

"We so get each other," she says, her voice all thick and slurry too. "You and me against everything that has sucked in our lives. Two sad girls together. Can we toast to two sad girls?"

I grin. I feel as light and bubbly as the champagne, next to Karissa.

Don't miss these titles by
COREY ANN HAYDU
Secret: I kissed someone else's boyfriend.
Assignment: Do it again.
LIFE by COMMITTEE
COREY ANN HAYDU
Making Pretty
COREY ANN HAYDU
KT KATHERINE TEGEN BOOKS
An Imprint of HarperCollinsPublishers
www.epicreads.com